Death of a Crabby Cook

Penny Pike

FIRST IN A NEW SERIES!

$7.99 U.S.
$9.99 CAN.

PARTY-

"[Presley Parker is] an appealing heroine whose event skills include utilizing party favors in self-defense in [this] fun, fast-paced new series guaranteed to please."

—Carolyn Hart, Agatha, Anthony, and Macavity award–winning author of *Death Comes Silently*

"A party you don't want to miss."

—Denise Swanson, national bestselling author of *Little Shop of Homicide*

"Penny Warner dishes up a rare treat, sparkling with wicked and witty San Francisco characters, plus some real tips on hosting a killer party."

—Rhys Bowen, award-winning author of the Royal Spyness and Molly Murphy mysteries

"There's a cozy little party going on between these covers."

—Elaine Viets, author of the Dead-End Job mysteries

"Fast, fun, and fizzy as a champagne cocktail! The winning and witty Presley Parker can plan a perfect party—but after her A-list event becomes an invitation to murder, her next plan must be to save her own life."

—Hank Phillippi Ryan, Agatha Award–winning author of *Drive Time*

continued . . .

"The book dishes up a banquet of mayhem."

—*Oakland Tribune* (CA)

"With a promising progression of peculiar plots and a plethora of party-planning pointers, *How to Host a Killer Party* looks to be a pleasant prospect for cozy mystery lovers." —Fresh Fiction

"Warner keeps the reader guessing." —Gumshoe

"Delightful [and] filled with suspense, mystery, and romance." —Reader to Reader Reviews

"Grab this book. . . . It will leave you in stitches."

—The Romance Readers Connection

"Frantic pace, interesting characters."

—*Publishers Weekly*

"I highly recommend this book to all mystery readers, cozy or not. This is a party that you don't want to miss."

—Once Upon a Romance

"Presley is a creative, energetic young woman with a wry sense of humor." —The Mystery Reader

ALSO BY PENNY PIKE
(Writing as Penny Warner)

The Party-Planning Mystery Series

How to Host a Killer Party

How to Crash a Killer Bash

How to Survive a Killer Séance

How to Party with a Killer Vampire

How to Dine on Killer Wine

Death of a Crabby Cook

A FOOD FESTIVAL MYSTERY

Penny Pike

OBSIDIAN
Published by the Penguin Group
Penguin Group (USA) LLC, 375 Hudson Street,
New York, New York 10014

USA | Canada | UK | Ireland | Australia | New Zealand | India | South Africa | China
penguin.com
A Penguin Random House Company

First published by Obsidian, an imprint of New American Library,
a division of Penguin Group (USA) LLC

First Printing, August 2014

ISBN 978-0-451-46781-2

Printed in the United States of America
10 9 8 7 6 5 4 3 2 1

To my gourmet husband, Tom,
who enjoyed helping me with the research

Acknowledgments

Many thanks to my fellow writers Colleen Casey, Janet Finsilver, Staci McLaughlin, Ann Parker, and Carole Price. Thanks to the wonderful food truckers who gave me their delicious recipes and secrets! And a special thanks to my wonderful agent, Andrea Hurst; to expert reader Martha Schoemaker; and to my incredible editor, Sandra Harding.

Cupcakes are dead. Long live cream puffs!

—Darcy Burnett, *San Francisco Chronicle* restaurant critic

Chapter 1

Life sucked.

Forget counting calories. I needed this cream puff.

It would have been the perfect spring day in San Francisco—no fog, sunshine, with a light, salty breeze coming off the bay—if it weren't for the news I'd just received from my editor at the *San Francisco Chronicle*.

"Darcy, I'm afraid we have to let you go," Patrick Craig had told me moments after I'd arrived at my soon-to-be-former desk. "As you know, times are tough in the newspaper business."

As a parting gift, he'd promised to give me some freelance assignments from time to time, the first being a review of the San Francisco Crab and Seafood Festival, which was being held for the next two days at Fort Mason. My assignment: write up a critique of the festival and an article about the Oyster Shuck-and-Suck Contest. I hated oysters. The slimy things made me gag. But as a now-unemployed restaurant critic, what choice did I have? If I didn't take this gig, I'd soon be living on Top Ramen.

I sat on a bench near the daily food truck gathering at Fort Mason, trying to figure out tomorrow's story angle as I watched the prelunch crowd gather. Hungry gourmands were queuing up at the dozen colorful food trucks that were parked each day in the prime spots. The names were almost as entertaining as the decorated trucks themselves. Road Grill, a bright red truck with giant grill marks painted across the front, served "exotic meats" and was by far the biggest crowd-pleaser with the longest line. The Yankee Doodle Noodle Truck, yellow, with images of noodles the size of octopus tentacles, had its fair share of fans, as did Kama Sushi, blue and covered with tropical fish, and the Coffee Witch, featuring a sexy cartoon witch stirring a cauldron of steaming brew. No food truck stop was complete without a bacon truck—this one called itself Porky's.

But my favorite was a truck called Dream Puff, featuring a giant chocolate-laden cream puff painted on a vanilla background. The cream puffs, everything from strawberry mocha to pralines and cream to lemon meringue, were to die for—not to mention the "Dream Puff Guy" who served them.

But it was the Big Yellow School Bus, a former school bus converted into a food truck, that got most of my business on my lunch breaks. I was a frequent diner there, mainly because it was owned and operated by my eccentric aunt Abby, and she gave me free food.

Currently soothing the news of my job loss with a Caramel Espresso Dream Puff, I was interrupted by the sound of shouting coming from the middle of the circular food truck court. I recognized the fortysomething, balding man as Oliver Jameson, the owner and chef at Bones 'n' Brew, a brick-and-mortar restaurant across from Fort Mason. The seasoned place had once been a popular dining spot in the city, but business had fallen off over the past couple of years, and the quality had gone downhill too. I'd written a review last year about how the restaurant hadn't changed much since Jameson's father, Nigel, ran the place thirty years ago. In his many letters to the newspaper's editor, Oliver Jameson had blamed the "inundation of rat-infested roach coaches that had set up shop across the street from my distinguished dining establishment" for his business losses. But as a restaurant critic—or former restaurant critic—I had a hunch it was because Jameson hadn't updated his menu or decor in decades.

"Get outta here, you old bag, or I'll call the police!" Jameson yelled at the petite sixtysomething woman opposite him. The big balding man gestured threateningly at her with a meat tenderizer as he bellowed, "Take your botulism-riddled bus and go park it in the Tenderloin where it belongs!"

As for the "old bag" in question, well, that would be my aunt Abigail Warner. After retiring from her job as a high school cafeteria cook last year, she'd bought an old school bus and converted it into a portable eatery featuring her specialty—classic American comfort foods with a gourmet twist. I was a big fan of her Crabby Cheerleader Mac and Cheese, filled with local crabmeat.

"It's a free country, you hash-slinging fry cook," my aunt yelled back at the towering man. "You're losing business because your fat-saturated menu is out-of-date, and your fried food is overpriced. Don't blame me for your bleeding cash problems."

Aunt Abby waved a knife at him. In her small hand it looked like a deadly Samurai sword.

"And if you plant one more dead rat anywhere *near* my truck, I'll take my Ginsu knife to your dangling—"

"Aunt Abby!" I yelped, rising from the bench. I hurried over to the battle site, hoping to run interference before my aunt was arrested for assault, battery, or improper language in public.

Aunt Abby lowered her menacing weapon when she saw me approach. I knew she was feisty—she had to be in order to survive serving "meat surprise" to a bunch of surly teenagers for all those years—but I didn't know she had a murderous streak. Still, I didn't blame her. Ever since she'd started her food truck business six months ago, she'd encountered nothing but problems, everything from permit red tape to parking tickets to jealously competitive restaurant owners.

"Come on, Aunt Abby," I said, prying the knife from her tight grip. The growing number of gawkers slowly went back to their handheld meals as I dragged my aunt to her neon yellow bus a few feet away. *Nothing like a little drama to whip up an appetite,* I thought.

Among the creatively decorated circle of trucks, Aunt Abby's bus stood out. Not only was it big and blindingly yellow, but she'd hung schoolroom chalkboard signs on the outside offering her famous fare: Teacher Tuna Casserole, Principal Potpie, Science Experiment Spaghetti, and other old-school comfort foods.

I followed my aunt through the accordion doors and up the steps, listening to her curse under her breath—words she'd no doubt learned from her high school students. "Dillon!" I called out to her six-foot, twenty-five-year-old son, who was working the service window. "Keep an eye on your mom, will you?"

"I don't need to be watched," Aunt Abby snapped, scowling as she retied her food-smeared apron in a complicated double fold. "What I need is rat removal—from Bones 'n' Brew."

"What happened?" I asked.

She took a loaf of bread and began slicing it with the knife she'd been waving.

"I don't want to talk about it," she said.

I shot Dillon a look and mouthed, "Watch her!" Then I stepped out of the bus in search of Oliver Jameson to see if I could find out what all the fuss was about. Unfortunately, he'd disappeared, no doubt back to his restaurant across the street. I thought about going after him but didn't have the energy. What I needed was another sugar boost to help my job-loss morale, so I wandered over to the Dream Puff truck for another medicinal cream puff, this time cappuccino cream.

Jake Miller, the Dream Puff Guy, as I called him, was just about as delicious-looking as his cream puffs. I couldn't help but notice him when he stepped out of the truck to refill the napkin dispenser or the sprinkle shakers in his formfitting blue jeans and muscle-hugging white T-shirt. I'd heard from my aunt that he'd once been a successful attorney, but for some reason he'd given up the Italian suits and lawsuits to whip up heaven in a puff pastry. Luckily for me.

Unfortunately, I'd gained five pounds just trying to get to know him.

When I reached the window, I saw the small sign: BE BACK IN 5 MINUTES. Bummer. The cream puff—and eye candy—would have to wait.

Glancing around at the circle of wagons, including the

latest ones that had set up temporary shop—the India Jones truck (Masala Nachos), the Conehead truck (Garlic Ice Cream), the Humpty Dumpling truck (Great Balls of Fire!)—I suddenly realized an idea was staring me in the mouth. Now that I'd been laid off, I could write that cookbook I'd always wanted to pen.

Granted, I wasn't much of a cook, but I *was* a total foodie and had tasted thousands of gourmet meals and written hundreds of restaurant reviews for the paper. As a reporter, I knew a hot trend when I saw one. Nothing was hotter than the food truck/food festival phenom currently sweeping the country. All I had to do was go to a bunch of food festivals, interview the food truck chefs, gather some recipes, and type them up in a breezy style, and I'd find myself on one of those cooking shows hawking my bestselling book!

I saw only one stumbling block. How was I supposed to support myself until the book royalties poured in? Not even a dreamy cream puff could fix that.

"Darcy!" Aunt Abby called from the service window of her bus.

I headed over, hoping to substitute one of Aunt Abby's freshly baked chocolate-pecan-caramel bars—aka Bus Driver Brownies—for the cream puff. But as soon as I stepped inside, she handed me an order.

"Dillon had to go do something, and I need a BLT, stat," she commanded, meaning I was to make one of her most popular menu items *right this minute*! In spite of my lack of culinary skills, I figured I could manage a sandwich assembly. Heck, I could even do a microwave reheat in an emergency. But that was about it.

"He left you during lunch rush?" I asked as I dutifully

washed my hands, then slipped on a fresh cafeteria-lady apron. I struggled with the fancy double fold, gave up, and simply tied it around my waist. "What was so important he had to run off?"

Aunt Abby shrugged and tossed me a bag of multigrain bread. "He said it was something urgent. I swear, that boy will be the death of me. Good thing I caught you on your lunch hour. When do you have to get back to the paper?"

"I'm in no hurry," I said, not ready to tell her the truth. But the fact that Dillon had just left her on her own really bothered me. Ever since he'd dropped out of college to "find himself," he'd been living at home and working part-time at his mother's food truck. When he wasn't at the truck, he was holed up in his bedroom, playing on his computers. It seemed as if sudden disappearances were becoming typical of the boomerang computer whiz. What could be so important that he had to leave in the middle of the lunch rush? An urgent update on his Facebook page? A lifesaving tweet? I almost said something snarky but stopped myself. After all, he was Aunt Abby's son—my cousin—and if it weren't for my aunt, I'd probably be homeless.

I opened the bread package and removed two soft slices; they smelled both sweet and savory. As I assembled the sandwich—thick, apple-smoked bacon, vine-ripened tomato slices, leafy green lettuce, ripe avocado, and aioli spread on multigrain bread—I half listened to my aunt complain about the war between the food truckers and the brick-and-mortar chefs. She'd had more than one run-in with Oliver Jameson, as had several other truckers at Fort Mason. But in the past year, Aunt

Abby had also butted heads with the health department, the chamber of commerce, and what she called the "parking enforcement goons." My aunt wasn't the easiest person to get along with, but I admired her sassy attitude and endless energy. I think it's what kept her going after her husband, Edward, died last year.

As long as I didn't have to work with her for longer than a few hours. Then I'd be a nut case.

I wrapped the sandwich in butcher paper and handed it to my aunt. She shot me a look, rewrapped it, then called a name out the window and passed the sandwich to a guy talking on his cell phone. "Here," she said, handing me three more orders. "You make them; I'll wrap them."

Two hours later the line finally thinned out. "Thanks for your help," Aunt Abby said. "I don't know where Dillon's got to, but you saved me." She glanced at her Minnie Mouse watch. "Uh-oh. I hope I didn't make you late for work. You'd better get back to the newspaper before you lose your job."

I started to tell her what had happened—that I was now on a permanent "lunch break" from the paper—but I decided to wait until a more convenient time. Like never.

I sighed. "Okay, well, I guess I'll see you at home."

Aunt Abby frowned at me suspiciously, as if I'd just eaten all of her prized brownies. "Everything all right?" she asked, her pencil-thin eyebrow arched in question.

I nodded and stepped out of the bus. Okay, so I'd explain everything tonight, after I'd had a glass of wine. Or two. I knew I'd feel better after eating the chocolatey brownie I'd just tucked into my purse. Free food was one of the perks of being related to Aunt Abby. Through the open window of the bus, I heard her break into a rousing rendition of Disneyland's "It's a Small World." The earworm would no doubt haunt me the rest of the day.

I stopped by the Coffee Witch and grabbed a Love Potion Number 9—a latte made with a melted 3 Musketeers bar—then enjoyed my sugary treats as I drove "home": that being my aunt's thirty-five-foot Airstream currently parked in the side yard of her Russian Hill home. It was the perfect location, close to the Marina District, Ghirardelli Square, and Fisherman's Wharf. In desperate need of shelter after my breakup with Tool-Head Trevor, a reporter at the *Chron*, I'd moved into her rig "temporarily." That was six months ago. Now, with no more money coming in, my plans to eventually move out would have to be put on hold.

My widowed aunt had lived in her small Victorian home for most of her adult life, ever since she'd inherited it from her parents. Today the house would be worth a fortune, but she had no intention of selling it. Although she was my mother's sister, I'd hardly known her when I'd asked to rent the RV. She was considered the black sheep of the family, but no one had ever told me why. As I'd gotten to know her better, I found her charming, clever, and creative—and so different from my discerning mother and hippie father. My parents had divorced soon after I went away to the University of Oregon to study journalism, claiming they each wanted "new beginnings." My dad moved to New Mexico to live in the desert and smoke dope, while my mom headed for New York in pursuit of culture and romance.

And Aunt Abby was supposed to be the crazy one?

I parked my recently purchased convertible VW Bug in her driveway and headed around to the side yard, where she kept the Airstream. A Disneyana fanatic, Aunt Abby had decorated the interior of the rig with friends of Walt. I wiped my feet on the Grumpy doormat, checked the Cheshire Cat clock on the wall inside, and dropped my purse on the sofa bed, which was covered with a Minnie Mouse throw.

Still depressed from the job news, I changed out of my black slacks and red blouse into khaki pants and an ironic "Life Is Good" T-shirt and lay down on the Tinker Bell comforter in the bedroom for a quick nap. As I dozed off, I hoped to dream up some ideas for extra cash until my fab book deal came through. With pending unemployment benefits meager and short-lived—and car payments coming due—I had a feeling food truck leftovers would be my staple for the next few months.

The theme song from "It's a Small World" woke me from my nightmare—something about eating a poisoned apple. Probably heartburn from overdosing on sweets and coffees. I knew the call was from Aunt Abby. Dillon had programmed personalized ringtones to alert me to some of my callers' identities. That way I could ignore my ex-boyfriend, who hadn't given up on getting back together. His tune was appropriately "Creep" by Radiohead. I fumbled for the phone, saw Aunt Abby's dimpled, smiling face on the small screen, and answered the call.

"Come in the house," she commanded. "I want you to taste something."

I checked the Cheshire Cat clock on the wall: four

p.m. I'd slept for more than two hours! Craving another brownie, I fluffed my bed hair, then stepped out of the Airstream and walked across the patio to the back of the house. I entered the dining area through the sliding glass door and called out to her.

"I'm in the kitchen," she yelled back. Passing through her cozy family room, I headed for her favorite place in the house and found her busily rolling small balls of dough in her hands. Basil, Aunt Abby's long-haired Doxie, wagged her tail at my aunt's Crocs-covered feet, no doubt hoping for a dropped morsel.

"I saw your car. You got off work early?" Aunt Abby asked. She'd changed out of her cafeteria-lady apron, khaki pants, and white T-shirt into a pink athletic suit that clashed with her curly red hair but matched her pink lipstick perfectly. The ensemble was covered by a "Cereal Killer"–emblazoned apron.

I nodded and glanced around for something to eat.

"Everything all right?" As a former cafeteria worker—she preferred the term "food service chef," *never* "lunch lady"—she often bragged she could make sloppy joes for five hundred. Only problem was, she had trouble cooking for fewer than that. At the moment, it looked like she was preparing enough dough balls to feed the San Francisco Giants and all of their fans. I leaned over and inhaled a whiff of her current experiment.

"What is that—a cheesy cake pop?" I asked. I spotted a rigid foam block filled with round balls held aloft by lollipop sticks. Before she could stop me, I popped one into my mouth.

It took only one bite to realize this was not the cake pop I'd been expecting.

"Blech!" I said, spitting the contents of my mouth into the sink. "What *was* that?"

"A Crab Pop," she said, grinning at my reaction. "My specialty for tomorrow's festival. They're tiny cheese biscuits filled with crab and dipped in white cheddar cheese."

"Good grief!" I fanned my mouth as if it were on fire. "I need an antidote!"

"For goodness' sakes, Darcy, it's not that bad. I thought you liked crab."

"I do, but not as a surprise when I'm expecting something sweet!"

"Have a brownie. They're over there." She nodded toward a foil-covered plate on the counter.

I picked up a square and stuffed it in my mouth as if it were chocolate crack. "That's more like it," I said as soon as I'd swallowed the delicious, chewy mass.

"So, now, tell me," Aunt Abby said as she continued inserting lollipop sticks into the newly formed balls. I tried not to watch. "Why were you home early? Rough day of restaurant reviews?"

I decided to get it over with and tell her the truth. "You could say that. The *Chron* laid me off today. I've been reduced to a stringer." Another wave of anxiety swept over me as the reality of the statement set in.

Aunt Abby stopped what she was doing and looked at me sympathetically. "Oh, Darcy. I'm so sorry." An instant later she perked up again. "But you know what they say: 'When your soufflé falls, turn it into a pancake.' "

My aunt was full of these crazy food sayings. Maybe that was one of the things that had driven my family members crazy.

Without missing a beat, she continued. "So why don't you come work for me part-time? The food truck business is getting busier every day, what with all the local festivals popping up. There's practically one every weekend." She counted them off. "The Ghirardelli Chocolate Festival is right around the corner. Then the Gilroy Garlic Festival, the Santa Cruz Fungus Festival, Isleton's Spam Festival, Oakdale's Testicle Festival—there must be over two dozen of these fests every year. And I could really use the help. Especially since Dillon has been leaving me in the lurch so often. I'll definitely need you tomorrow at the Crab and Seafood Festival. They're expecting a hundred thousand hungry people at the two-day event."

"As long as you're not serving any oysters," I said.

"Oysters are actually good for you," Aunt Abby said, shaking her head at my resistance to all things mollusk related. "They're full of zinc, iron, calcium, vitamins. They boost your energy. And your sex drive." She raised an eyebrow at me.

That's all I needed, a boost to my sex drive, after being boyfriendless for months.

"Just the thought of eating something that slimy is disgusting."

"You don't have to eat them raw," Aunt Abby said, shaking her head. "You can eat them smoked, boiled, baked, fried, steamed, or stewed."

"No, thanks. I will not eat them baked or fried. I will not eat them stewed or dried. I do not like oysters or clams. I do not like them, Sam-I-Am."

"Chicken," my aunt said.

"I'll eat chicken," I replied, "but I refuse to swallow anything from the mollusk family. Besides, I heard oysters can contain bacteria." I pulled out my cell phone and asked Siri to call up "death by oysters," then read aloud an excerpt from the site. "*'In the past two years, thirty-six people have died after consuming oysters.'* "

"You're talking about Gulf Coast oysters that get warm and spoil quickly," Aunt Abby said. "We don't have that problem here in the cold San Francisco Bay. But don't worry. I'm not making anything with oysters. Just crab."

"You know I'm not much of a cook, Aunt Abby," I said. "Besides, I'm planning to write a cookbook using recipes from food trucks and festivals. That should keep me busy for a while."

Aunt Abby raised that damn questioning eyebrow again. It was her signature look. "Darcy, you just admitted you don't cook and you're planning to write a cookbook?"

"I'll admit the art of cooking eludes me. Eating, on the other hand, is one of my passions." It was true. I read food magazines and cookbooks as if they were romance novels. "And writing a book filled with popular food festival recipes doesn't take any culinary talent."

"Maybe not, but what are you going to do for money until your book is published?"

I slumped down onto a kitchen stool, feeling the lump of chocolate in my stomach turn to raw dough. She was right. I needed money. Now. I shrugged. "Work for you, I guess."

"Work for who?" rumbled a low voice from behind me.

I turned around to see Aunt Abby's son, Dillon, looming in the doorway. He towered over his five-foot-two mother. He was dressed in a threadbare "Zombies Ate My Sister" T-shirt and ridiculous Captain America flannel pajama bottoms. His curly dark red hair was in desperate need of a comb and some gel and scissors, and the two-day growth of stubble on his face looked more like an oversight than a fashion statement. He pulled a box of Trix from a cabinet and poured some directly into his mouth, dropping several colorful balls on the tile floor. They were quickly lapped up by Basil, who always acted as if he were starved.

"I asked Darcy to help us out in the food truck," Aunt Abby said.

"Wait. *What?*" Dillon said, his open mouth full of fruity colors.

I didn't relish the idea of working with a slacker like Dillon either, but I didn't see much choice.

"Well, you keep disappearing," Aunt Abby said to Dillon. "And with Darcy's help, maybe we can get ourselves on that TV show *The Great Food Truck Race* and win fifty thousand dollars." Her bright eyes twinkled.

Yeah, right.

"Seriously," she continued, after seeing my disbelieving reaction. "My business is booming, thanks to all the work Dillon has done promoting us on Twitter and Facebook and those other sites. Right, son?"

"Yeah, but—" Dillon began, but before he could finish, the doorbell rang.

"I'll get it," Dillon said; then he lumbered out of the kitchen for the front door, still holding the cereal box.

Seconds later, he yelled out, "Mooooom!"

"I'm coming!" she yelled back. "That boy. Can't he even sign for a delivery?" She wiped her hands on a towel, untied her apron, primped her curly hair, checked her lipstick in the microwave oven reflection, and headed for the door.

Moments later Aunt Abby returned to the kitchen. Her Betty Boop smile drooped, the color had left her Kewpie-doll face, and even her pink lipstick seemed to have faded. Dillon appeared behind her, frowning.

"Aunt Abby?" I asked. "What's wrong?"

"That was the police," Aunt Abby said, sounding dazed and staring at her clasped hands.

"The police?" I repeated. "What did they want?"

She shook her head. "I'm not sure. They want me to come down to the station with them."

I felt the hairs on the back of my neck stand up. "Why?"

Aunt Abby looked up at me but her eyes were unfocused. "Oliver Jameson is dead."

Chapter 2

"What?!" I blurted when I heard the news.

Aunt Abby shook her head woefully, her perky curls barely bouncing. "I don't know why they want to talk to me, but there are two cops waiting outside to take me to the station."

I flashed back tp the scene I'd witnessed earlier—and the knife my aunt had been wielding in her hand.

Uh-oh.

"Mom?" Dillon said, staring at his mother.

Aunt Abby shifted her glance out the kitchen window. "Oh, I . . . may have said something to Oliver Jameson that could be taken as a threat."

"Like what?" Dillon asked, his mouth hanging open.

She shook her head. "I don't know. Something about a knife . . ."

She'd been so furious with the chef from Bones 'n' Brew that she'd actually threatened him with that ginormous kitchen knife.

"Mo-om!" Dillon whined, his face looking whiter than his usual indoor pallor. "A knife? Seriously? You didn't hurt him . . . did you?"

"Of course she didn't!" I answered for her.

Another impatient rap at the door interrupted me from defending her further.

Aunt Abby shook her head. "I told the two officers to give me a few minutes so I could change clothes. I can't wear this loungewear to the police station. And my hair's a mess. I need to freshen up."

I could tell she was trying to keep her tone light, but her voice cracked, giving away the stress that lay beneath the surface.

"I'll need my purse . . . and a sweater . . . maybe a bottle of water . . . and a snack. . . ."

My aunt was rambling. She was probably in shock. I wrapped an arm around her.

"Don't worry, Aunt Abby. Dillon and I will go with you."

"Darcy, they're not going to let us ride in the cop car with her," Dillon said, the voice of doom.

"We'll take my car and follow her," I said, then asked Aunt Abby, "Did the police say when Jameson was killed?" I wondered if she had an alibi for the murder. Hopefully she was in her School Bus serving comfort food to the city's starving citizens.

"I don't know. . . . He must have been killed sometime after I . . ." She hesitated.

"After that fight you had with him?" I said, finishing her thought. "But I took you back to your bus and you stayed there the rest of the day, right?" I turned to Dillon for confirmation, hoping he'd shown up after I left.

Dillon shot a look at his mother that told me all was not well in food truck land.

"Dillon! You *did* come back, didn't you?"

He nodded, but there was something he wasn't telling me. And then it dawned on me.

"No!" I said, glancing back and forth between Aunt Abby and Dillon. "Aunt Abby! Tell me you didn't leave the bus after Dillon returned." I could feel the adrenaline rushing through my body and grew more alarmed.

Aunt Abby pressed her lips together, then shrugged. "After Dillon came back, the lunch crowd had died down, so I told him to hold the fort while I . . . did a few errands."

"What errands?" I heard myself sounding more and more like a police interrogator. Why didn't I just throw in *"Do you have an alibi for the time of the murder?"*

"Just stuff I had to take care of," she said simply.

"Mo-o-om?" Dillon said. His concern for his mother was evident in his rising voice and furrowed brow. "You went over there and saw him again, didn't you!"

"No! . . . I mean, well, not exactly. . . ." Aunt Abby looked away.

"Who? What are you talking about?" I asked, confused.

"What do you mean, 'not exactly'?" Dillon continued, ignoring me.

"Well, I might have gone to the restaurant, just for a minute. . . ." Aunt Abby said.

The restaurant? Uh-oh. "You went to Bones 'n' Brew?" Had my aunt gone over there to confront Oliver Jameson again? Not good. "Why? What were you thinking?"

"I was . . . looking for something," she said evasively.

"What could you possibly have wanted from Bones 'n' Brew?" I asked.

"Something," Aunt Abby said. "Anything to shut him

up and get him to leave me alone. I was tired of him hassling the food truckers, especially me. I figured if I could find something to hold over his head, maybe I could get him to back off."

I dropped my head in my hands, stunned at this possibly incriminating news.

Dillon frowned. "Like what?"

"Like some health or safety violation . . . or rat poop. Bones 'n' Brew has been around practically since the 1906 earthquake. It's got to be riddled with violations. I figured Jameson was probably paying some government official to look the other way so he could stay in business all these years. I thought he might even have hired someone to help him pester the food trucks. So I went to his place to look for something I could take to the authorities."

I shook my head at how naive she'd been. The police could arrest her for any number of reasons—illegal trespassing, corporate spying, theft. Who knew what the SFPD would throw at her?

In addition to possibly murder.

A question flashed through my mind: Where had Oliver Jameson been killed?

This time there was a pounding, not a knocking, on the door. A voice called out, "Mrs. Warner?"

"I'll be right there," she called back in a singsongy voice. "I'd better get my things."

We followed her into the bedroom, where she picked out a pair of yellow slacks and a ruffly yellow blouse covered in a floral print. Completely inappropriate for a visit to the San Francisco Police Station.

"Did you see him?" I asked my aunt as she stepped into her bathroom to change.

"Who?" she called out.

"Oliver Jameson!" Dillon and I said together.

"Oh no. He wasn't around. At least, not at first. That's why I went when I did. I saw him leave, so I sneaked in the back door, through the kitchen."

Great. There would be witnesses in the kitchen who could confirm she'd been on the premises.

Aunt Abby appeared in the bathroom doorway, dressed, her hair fluffed, her lipstick fresh.

"Did you steal anything?" Dillon asked.

"No! Of course not!" She picked out a sweater from her closet.

"Did you touch anything?" I asked.

"I don't think so. . . . Maybe . . ."

"Mom, think! Did you go anywhere else besides the kitchen?" Dillon demanded.

"Just his office . . ." Aunt Abby headed down the hall.

I rolled my eyes and pictured my aunt in an orange jumpsuit. No doubt it would clash with her red hair. I steadied my panicked voice. When we reached the foyer, I whispered, "What did you do in his office, Aunt Abby?" I didn't want the cops on the other side of the door to hear.

She shrugged again. "I just looked through a few of his desk drawers and some of the papers on the desk, that sort of thing. I didn't steal anything, honestly."

Stealing something was the least of my worries. Her fresh fingerprints would be all over Oliver Jameson's office.

"So did you find anything?" Dillon asked.

Aunt Abby grinned. The sparkle returned to her eyes. "Well, as a matter of fact, I found a folder hidden under his leather ink blotter, but I didn't get a chance to look inside because I heard a commotion coming from the hallway, so I hightailed it outta there."

"Did anyone see you?" Dillon asked.

"I went through the office window. It opens onto the back alley."

I tried to shake away a vision of my aunt Abby crawling through a window like a common burglar.

"That's it?" I asked.

"I think so," she said.

"Mrs. Warner," a megaphoned voice announced on the other side of the front door.

Aunt Abby unlocked the door and swung it open. She smiled sweetly at the two uniformed officers.

"Dillon and I will follow you to the station," I said to her.

She turned to me and whispered, "You'll take care of Basil if anything happens?"

"You'll be fine," I said, trying to reassure her. "You'll be seeing Basil in just a little while."

She blinked a couple of times, then headed out the door.

I eyed Dillon's sleepwear and he got the message. He ran to his room to change.

I stood watching as the two officers escorted my aunt to their waiting car. At least they hadn't handcuffed her. I thought about calling a lawyer, then told myself the police would quickly realize my aunt couldn't have committed any real crime—like murder—and would let her get back to preparing for tomorrow's Crab and Seafood Festival.

Now who was the naive one?

* * *

The San Francisco Police Department is located in one of the seamier parts of the city. Luckily the area is crawling with cops, so I didn't feel particularly threatened by the alcoholic, homeless, and mentally deranged characters passing by. Since cutbacks had closed many of the rehabilitation centers, homeless shelters, and mental hospitals, the streets and parks seemed to be the only places left for those who weren't in the mainstream. Once again I felt lucky to live in Aunt Abby's RV, or I might have found myself in a similar situation.

Dillon and I pulled up behind the police car and waited for Aunt Abby to get out of the backseat. In her yellow outfit, right down to the matching Crocs, she stood out among the people who frequented the police station. With her eyebrows neatly redrawn, her eyelids coated with a shiny yellow shadow, and her lips painted bright red, she was more suited to a clown party than a police visit.

To my surprise, Dillon had managed to find a pair of semiclean jeans, ripped only at the knees, an old, once-white T-shirt that read "Occupy Wall Street," and rubber flip-flops. It was actually an improvement on his usual fashion statements. His dark curly hair sprung out from his head and hung over his eyebrows, obscuring his dark green eyes.

As for me, I'd changed into something simple, subtle, and professionally casual—black jeans and a tan shirt. Someone had to look normal in this family.

We were escorted through the metal detector, which we passed with flying colors, after dropping off our cell phones, loose coins, and other metal accessories.

So far, so good.

Next we were shown into a waiting room, while the uniformed officer who had driven Abby asked the desk sergeant to call someone named Detective Wellesley Shelton.

"Know any good lawyers?" Dillon whispered to me. Without his cell phone to hold, he kneaded his fingers and fidgeted nervously. I rarely saw him without some kind of electronic gizmo, even when he was eating.

I glanced at Aunt Abby. Dillon's question was valid. Aunt Abby was about to be questioned in a murder investigation, and as far as I knew, she didn't have an alibi or an attorney.

The only lawyer I knew was an old guy who had handled my parents' divorce. Before I could come up with other possibilities, a tall, stocky man in a dark suit opened the door. He was African American, around fifty or sixty, I guessed, judging by his curly salt-and-pepper hair and graying mustache. He wore glasses, an SFPD lapel pin, and several gold rings on his fingers, except on the ring finger of his left hand. For some reason, I just notice these things.

"Ms. Warner?" he said in a smooth, low voice.

We all stood up from the bench where we'd been asked to wait. The detective looked at my aunt, flanked by her makeshift bodyguards.

I reached out a hand and took the lead. "I'm Darcy, Abby's niece. This is Dillon, her son. We're here for support."

He hesitated, looked us up and down, then shook my hand and said, "Fine by me. Ms. Warner?" He reached over for her hand; she smiled at the imposing detective and daintily shook his hand. "I'm Detective Shelton. Will you follow me, please?"

The detective held open a door to let us pass, then led the way to an office at the end of the hall. Three desks filled the small room, all empty. I noted the time on the wall clock—it was after five p.m. No doubt the other officers were done for the day. It looked like lucky Detective Shelton was in for some overtime.

"Have a seat." He gestured for my aunt to sit in the sturdy wooden chair opposite his desk. Dillon and I scavenged a couple of folding chairs that leaned against a wall.

"Thanks for coming, Ms. Warner," he continued. "As the officers told you, the owner of a restaurant across the street from the food trucks at Fort Mason was murdered this afternoon. A witness mentioned you had an encounter with the deceased chef earlier today, and I wondered if you might have seen or heard something that would help us. If you don't mind, I'd like to ask you a few questions."

From his soothing tone, I felt like we were meeting with a family counselor rather than a police officer. His Barry White voice was gentle and relaxed, and it was obvious he was trying to put my aunt at ease. My first thought was that it was some kind of police trick. Where were the tough interrogators I'd seen on *Criminal Minds* and *NCIS*, or even that chick on *The Mentalist*?

"So, Ms. Warner—"

"Please, call me Abby," my aunt said sweetly, batting her heavily mascaraed eyelashes. "Everybody does. Being called Ms. Warner reminds me of my high school cafeteria days, and believe me, I'd like to forget about those years." She flashed him a toothy, candy apple red smile. The woman couldn't help herself!

"All right, then. Abby." He flipped open a notebook and held a pen at the ready. "How well did you know Oliver Jameson, the owner of Bones 'n' Brew?"

"Not that well," Abby said, sounding sincere as she shook her headful of curls. "I mean, we were both in the food service business, but he owned that aging dive across the street and I operate a nice clean food truck, a school bus, actually. Converted. I call it the Big Yellow School Bus—a kind of play on words. The name Bones 'n' Brew is just crass, don't you think?"

My aunt was rambling again. I had to stop her before she incriminated herself and was led off to jail in chains.

"Officer," I said, interrupting her, "what my aunt wants to tell you is that a lot of the food truck owners have had encounters with this guy because he objected to them being so close to his restaurant. I understand he wasn't the most pleasant man to deal with. I have a feeling he'd made a number of enemies, no doubt some in his own kitchen. . . ."

Detective Shelton held up a hand to stop my own rambling. "Well, Ms. . . ."

"Darcy."

"Well, Darcy, my job is to collect information. We don't operate on feelings here at SFPD. According to a number of witnesses, your aunt was seen having a heated argument with the victim shortly before he died, and"—he checked his notes—"wielding a knife—"

Aunt Abby leaned forward and slammed her hand on the detective's desk. "That jerk put a rat under my stove!"

The room was silent at my aunt's sudden outburst. Realizing she'd overreacted, she sat back and folded her hands in her lap as if she were in church.

Well, great, I thought, cringing. She'd just given herself a motive for killing Oliver Jameson: revenge. And now it appeared she couldn't control her temper. All we needed was the weapon—the knife she'd been waving at him earlier—and she'd be wearing orange pajamas for the rest of her life.

"Ms. Warner . . ."

"Abby," she said, her tone soft again, her sweet smile back on her face.

"Abby," the detective said, enunciating her name. "Where were you between the hours of one and four this afternoon?"

"Wait a minute!" Dillon said, finally coming to life. "I thought you just wanted to ask her some routine questions about this guy. You don't think she had anything to do with this, do you?"

"Oh, I couldn't kill anyone, Detective," Aunt Abby added. "Not even someone I hated as much as Oliver Jameson. I mean, look at me. I couldn't hurt a fly. I don't even like killing rats."

My petite aunt was hardly the physical type to commit murder. Then again, we still didn't know how Oliver Jameson had died.

"What was the cause of death?" I asked.

"That's privileged information," he said to me, then returned his dark brown eyes to Aunt Abby. "So where were you this afternoon, Ms. Warner, if you don't mind my asking?"

Aunt Abby turned crimson. Her eyelashes fluttered

like trapped butterflies trying to escape, and she squirmed in her chair. Glancing at Dillon and then at me, she cleared her throat and faced her inquisitor.

"I . . . took a walk after the lunch rush. I had some errands to run."

"Can you give me a list of those errands and where you went exactly?"

She shrugged. "Sure, but if you're looking for an alibi, I don't think anyone saw me."

Detective Shelton frowned. "Did you happen to stop by Bones 'n' Brew during your errand run?"

Aunt Abby looked him right in the eyes, smiled confidently, and said, "Absolutely not!"

I shot a look at Aunt Abby. She'd just lied to the detective! When she didn't meet my eyes, I turned to the detective, the hairs on the back of my neck tingling. "Can you at least tell us where the body was found?"

He hesitated, then said, "In his office."

Oh God.

I wondered how soon they'd find my aunt Abby's fingerprints all over the proverbial cookie jar.

Chapter 3

Aunt Abby swooned in her chair. "Is it hot in here?" she asked, snatching one of the detective's papers from his desk and fanning herself with it. He shot her a disbelieving look about her previous statement, but she seemed oblivious to it.

"Are we done, Detective?" Dillon wrapped an arm around his rosy-cheeked mother. "She's had a long and tiring day and needs to rest. I'd like to get her home, if that's okay."

I studied the detective, wondering if my aunt's sudden hot flash was a clear sign of guilt to the investigator. But instead of slapping handcuffs on her, he rose and said, "Of course. If we have more questions, we'll be in touch. Thanks for coming down."

Like she had a choice, I thought.

Dillon and I helped Aunt Abby up as if she'd suddenly become an invalid. She gave the detective a tremulous smile and returned the paper to the desk, then headed out, flanked by the two of us. Dillon held her arm, while I placed a comforting hand on her back.

What an act.

When we reached the door, the detective called out, Columbo-style, "Just one more thing . . ."

We froze, then turned around.

"You aren't planning to leave town, are you?"

Aunt Abby shook her head. "No, Detective." Under her breath she mumbled, "Where would I go? Has he forgotten I've got the Crab and Seafood Festival tomorrow?"

"And if you remember anything else, give me a call," he added.

After I helped Aunt Abby into the tiny backseat of my car, we drove home in silence, each of us lost in his or her own thoughts. I didn't know what she and Dillon were thinking, but my mind was spinning like a Cuisinart, dicing and chopping various murder scenarios. Who killed Oliver Jameson? A disgruntled diner? One of his kitchen staff? A random crazy person? Just about anyone could have done it. Even, I supposed, a food truck chef.

Like Aunt Abby?

No way! She wouldn't even drop a live lobster into a pot of boiling water, let alone kill a human being. That much I knew. But someone obviously had. And I had a feeling that if I didn't try to find out who it was, Aunt Abby could soon find herself in her own pot of hot water. Especially when the detective discovered my aunt's fingerprints at the restaurant and realized she'd been in the dead man's office and lied about it.

When I wrote a review for the *Chronicle*, I always interviewed the primary source—the owner—and worked my way from there—to the chef, the waitstaff, and the customers. I planned to tackle Aunt Abby's problem in a similar manner. While the main source, at this point, was deceased, I could at least try to find out more about him from the people who knew him. Then maybe I'd have a list of possible suspects to check out.

Hopefully Detective Shelton would be doing the same thing.

Unfortunately, it appeared he'd already put my aunt on his suspect list.

We arrived at Aunt Abby's home a little after seven. My aunt said she had stuffed bell peppers in the freezer she'd microwave for dinner and set about busying herself with preparing the meal. Dillon went off to his bedroom, no doubt to answer e-mails, update his Facebook page, tweet his latest thoughts, and do a bunch of other Internet-related stuff. Maybe I could ask him to check Craigslist and find me another reporting job—once this murder business was resolved.

I headed for the RV to change into my comfy jeans and a "Bay to Breakers" T-shirt I'd stolen from my ex-boyfriend. After pouring myself a glass of cheap wine, I sat down at my laptop at the tiny kitchen table and Googled "Oliver Jameson Bones 'n' Brew."

Yelp popped up first. I opened the page and began reading the comments by amateur critics.

". . . lousy food, poor service . . ."

". . . This used to be such a great place, but it's really gone downhill. . . ."

". . . Save your money and spend it at one of the yummy food trucks across the street. . . ."

Ouch.

The reviews continued much in this vein, including the one I'd written about the restaurant's decline. Only rarely did I see anything complimentary. I wondered how the restaurant had managed to stay in business all these years with so many negative comments.

Next, I checked for a Facebook or Twitter link to either Oliver or the restaurant, but I found no social media contacts. Maybe the place was too old-school for that kind of networking. Or maybe Jameson didn't feel he needed to get the word out anymore, since the restaurant had been around for so long.

Finally I found a piece another reporter at the *Chron* had done on Bones 'n' Brew a number of years ago. It mentioned that Oliver Jameson had taken over the restaurant from his father, Nigel Jameson, after the older man passed away from a heart attack. A photo of the two men proved the "like father, like son" theory, at least in physical characteristics. Both had male pattern baldness—one advanced, one with trim still around the edges. Both were stocky, as if they'd enjoyed their own cooking a little too much. And both were about the same height. They even wore nearly identical chef's whites with their names embroidered in black. But while Jameson Senior sported a smile, revealing a row of crooked teeth, Junior looked as if he'd just bitten into a lemon.

After a little more research, I found a solid lead, thanks to *Gastronome*, an online magazine that featured stories on various chefs from around the world. According to a recent article, Oliver Jameson's place once had a prestigious reputation, earning two Michelin stars. Since then, the rating had plummeted. The critic, a woman named Paula Bouchard, called him a "second-rate chef" and a "third-rate human being." Jameson shot back at her in a letter to the editor, calling her "Palate-less Paula" and "Big Mac Bouchard."

Harsh. I wondered if there was something else besides food that had caused such venom.

The article noted that Jameson had also had numerous confrontations with his kitchen staff and was known to have fired some of the best sous chefs in the business. At one point, he'd threatened his former pastry chef with a meat skewer and had to be bailed out of jail by his father. Jameson had also been accused of lying to a group of vegetarians for not disclosing that he used chicken stock in his soup, of buying out-of-date ingredients from questionable suppliers, and of using illegal poisons to handle his vermin problem. Within the last seven years, most of his staff had either quit or been fired and had sued him.

Hmm. Not a terribly nice or reputable guy. He apparently had anger-management problems, in addition to being a bully, a liar, a slob, and an arrogant SOB.

That certainly increased the list of possible suspects.

Well, at least Aunt Abby wasn't the only one who'd had run-ins with Oliver Jameson. But how would I narrow the list down? That was the question.

Before I shut off the computer, one more link regarding tomorrow's Crab and Seafood Festival caught my eye. Oliver Jameson's name reared its ugly head once again, this time protesting the event.

"Enough with these pseudo food festivals that are attracting the wrong kind of people to our neighborhoods," Jameson was quoted as saying. *"These greasy-spooners calling themselves chefs could be selling all kinds of crap. Those questionable food trucks are littering our beautiful city. Send them to the zoo to feed the animals and leave this area to those of us who run reputable establishments, like Bones 'n' Brew."*

Again, wow. If Aunt Abby really had put that knife in Oliver Jameson's back, I probably wouldn't have blamed her, nor would a lot of other people.

My cell phone chirped. I checked the text message. Aunt Abby had typed, `Dinner ready.`

`OMW`, I texted back, letting her know I was on my way. Before I turned off my laptop, I did a quick search for food trucks at Fort Mason. Yelp listed a dozen of the ones that claimed semipermanent spaces, like Aunt Abby's Big Yellow School Bus. I recognized all of them and in fact had sampled from most. I did a quick scan of the various reviews.

"The Love Potion Number 9 from the Coffee Witch is incredible!!!" wrote Ann P. from the Mission.

"Loved the Sushi/Salsa Wraps at Kung Fu Tacos! I'll be back!" wrote Janet F. from Pacific Heights.

"Try the Red Velvet Dream Puffs from the Dream Puff truck—they're to die for!!" wrote Colleen C. from Noe Valley.

"I'm totally addicted to the Principal's Potpies at the Big Yellow School Bus!" This one was signed Dillon W. from the Marina.

Dillon W.? Hmm.

The glowing reviews continued until I found myself nearly drooling on my laptop. But it was the last one at the bottom that really caught my attention.

"I was checking out the food truck scene at Fort Mason the other day and overheard some guy complaining there were too many trucks invading the city. Turned out he was the owner of a restaurant across the street. I guess he doesn't appreciate the competition. Doubt his place will

last long with awesome food trucks like this." Signed, Food Truck Fan.

I had a feeling Fan was talking about Oliver Jameson.

I awoke at six thirty the next morning, temporarily forgetting I didn't have a regular job anymore. I made myself a breakfast of yogurt, strawberries, toast, and one of those flavored, one-cup coffees, which would keep me going until I could get to the Coffee Witch. After I showered, I dressed in my uniform—khaki pants and a plain red top. I slipped on my red laceless Converse All Stars, said good-bye to the Disney gang, and headed over to Aunt Abby's to help her prepare for today's Crab and Seafood Festival.

While I'd never worked at a food festival before, I'd certainly gone to many of them in my capacity as a food critic. It was one of the better perks of the job. I loved the Gilroy Garlic Festival and the Ghirardelli Chocolate Festival, but the Crab and Seafood Festival was one of the best, in spite of my distaste for mollusks. The event was held at various spots along the marina, including Fort Mason, with views of the Golden Gate Bridge, the boats at the yacht club, and the expansive, grassy lawns. Various musicians played throughout the day, everything from indie pop to alt-rock, from blues to zydeco, adding to the celebratory atmosphere. You couldn't help but hoist a few Guinness stouts to wash down all the fish fare. One of my favorite events was the Shuck-and-Suck Competition, where oyster lovers raced to see how many of those slimy things they could eat in a timed period. And although the festival wasn't cheap, the proceeds benefited the Leukemia and Lymphoma Society, so it was all for a good cause. Of course, being press, I always got in free.

I checked the time on my cell phone. Aunt Abby said we had to be at the School Bus by nine to prepare. The gates opened at eleven. This year the event was expected to draw more than a hundred thousand people. I couldn't imagine serving such a crowd!

"Aunt Abby?" I called out after letting myself in the open back door.

"She's not here!" Dillon yelled from the recesses of the house.

Surprised he was up so early, I followed his voice to his room, hoping he was decent. I peered in from the doorway. His bedroom was essentially unchanged since high school. The ragged Harry Potter comforter lay in a crumpled heap at the foot of the unmade bed. Clothes were strewn about the room as if the place had been burglarized. Piles of comic books, graphic novels, and computer magazines towered in uneven piles on every flat surface. A souped-up PC that Dillon had assembled from custom components sat on a desk, his gateway to the virtual gaming world. He also had one other desktop computer, three monitors, a laptop, two printers, and a couple of tablets. The only noise in the room came from the cooling fans that kept the big computers from overheating.

But it was his pet white rat, Ratty, that kept me from actually entering his room. It didn't matter that the creepy thing was in a cage.

Dillon lay in his bed working on his laptop. A coffee cup that read "I Escaped from Alcatraz" sat overturned on the small table beside him, empty and dried up. He still wore his SpongeBob Squarepants pajama bottoms and a stretched-out Angry Birds T-shirt. His feet were bare and his toenails needed clipping. The room smelled of old food mixed with dirty socks and a hint of pot.

"Where is she?" I asked from the doorway. If the rat didn't get me, I had a feeling hantavirus or some other hazmat disease would.

"Said she was going to work," he said without looking up.

I checked the time on my cell phone: seven. "Already?"

He gave a one-shoulder shrug.

Huh. Apparently she'd left early for her "busterant," as she liked to call it, no doubt anxious to get ready for the onslaught of festival customers. Odd that she hadn't called or texted to hustle me along. I started to leave, sensing I'd better get over there quickly to help out, then had a thought. Maybe Dillon could do some online investigating to help take the heat off his mother.

"Dillon, I did some research on Oliver Jameson last night and turned up some interesting stuff. I thought maybe you could find out more about him."

"Done that," he said, continuing his typing.

"Really?" I blinked, surprised at his sudden display of initiative. "What did you find out?"

Still typing on his laptop, Dillon recited much of the same information I'd located on the Internet the previous night.

"Yeah, I saw all that. Anything else?"

He pulled his fingers from the laptop and met my eyes. "Did you know that Bones 'n' Brew was in Chapter 11?"

"No kidding? How did you find that out?"

"Public record," he said.

"Was the place about to close?"

Dillon shrugged again. "Chapter 11 usually means reorganizing in order to stay afloat. Sometimes it works. Sometimes it doesn't."

I knew that. "Anything else?"

"I'm working on a few leads," he said coyly.

I rolled my eyes. "Well, I need to find out what really happened to Oliver Jameson and I could use your help, since you're an expert in all things electronic."

"Like I said, I'm on it." He returned to his typing. The conversation was over. Dillon wasn't the most social person on the planet. And when he was focused on his computer stuff, he was in another world. A touch of undiagnosed Asperger's? I wondered.

I headed for the kitchen to grab any leftover chocolate goodies for breakfast but found nothing to satisfy my sweet tooth. I hoped the Dream Puff Guy would be opening soon. I needed a shot of sugar to go with my cup of caffeine in order to survive this new job.

I got in my coffee-colored VW Bug and drove to Fort Mason, wondering if I had the stamina to make a hundred thousand BLTs, should the need arise. When I arrived, I drove my small car around to the back entrance, checked in with the security guard, and squeezed in behind Aunt Abby's School Bus. About half a dozen of the food trucks at Fort Mason have semipermanent parking spaces, and Aunt Abby was one of the lucky ones who didn't have to move her bus every day. Instead, she drove her Toyota back and forth and parked behind the bus.

Odd. Her car wasn't there yet. Instead, her reserved space was taken up by the Meat Wagon delivery van. Where was she? Picking up last-minute ingredients for the festival?

I caught a glimpse of the van's driver, a skinny, shaggy-looking guy wearing a Meat Wagon T-shirt, jeans, and ornate black cowboy boots with gold embroidery and silver toe tips, headed for the van. I'd seen him a few times before when I stopped by Aunt Abby's bus in the morning. Tripp was a regular who delivered daily to Chef Boris Obregar's Road Grill truck, parked next door to Aunt Abby's bus. He spotted me, winked, bared a mouthful of crooked teeth, and spat out the toothpick sticking out from his thin lips. With a last leering nod, he jumped into the truck and drove off.

What a creep.

I got out, inhaled the fragrant air—a mixture of the salty San Francisco Bay, exotic foods, and strong coffee—and followed my nose to the Coffee Witch. If I was going to work this eight-hour festival, I'd need more caffeine than the one cup my little coffeemaker provided.

The Coffee Witch, owned and operated by a young woman named Willow something, offered a variety of bewitching concoctions, everything from Simple Spells (vanilla lattes) to Potent Potions (double-shot mochas) to Enchanted Espressos (triple-shot espressos). This morning Willow looked as if she'd had a few too many of her own cauldron-created coffees. She was moving at hyperspeed, serving the other food vendors who needed her magic mixtures to survive the day. Her hair, blond at the tips, black at the roots, and cut in jagged layers, only added to her frenzied appearance. Fast, perky, and full of energy, she was perfect for this job.

"'S'up, Darce?" she said to me when I finally reached the front of the line. "Heard about your downsizing at the paper. Bummer. Your usual?"

Boy, word spread as fast as an outbreak of ptomaine poisoning among these food truck vendors. I had to remind myself not to tell Aunt Abby any of my darkest secrets.

"Hi, Willow. Yeah, I've got to up the amperage today if I'm going to help out my aunt at the festival. How about one of your Voodoo Ventis?"

"Sweet," she said, grabbing a humongous paper cup. "Heard you're writing a book."

Damn Aunt Abby!

"Uh, well, I thought maybe a book filled with recipes from food trucks and food festivals would be something that people might buy. Got a recipe you want to share with me?"

"Totally! How about my Fiendish Frap recipe? That's my bestseller in the afternoon. Secret ingredient: Peppermint Patties."

"Great! I'll come by in the next day or so and follow up. I thought I'd add some background to the recipe, like how you came up with it—stuff like that."

"Sweet." She passed my steaming-hot drink through the window of her renovated postal truck, which now sported her witchy image and logo.

I paid her, sipped my coffee, and glanced around at the eclectic array of food trucks, thinking this cookbook idea was going to be easier than I'd thought. And why not? The food trucks would get their names and photos in the book, which was great publicity. And I'd get yummy recipes and make a ton of money.

"Heard about the murder?" Willow called out to me, leaning from the window after serving another caffeine addict. "Totally freaked me out."

"I know! Weird, huh?" I hoped she didn't know about Aunt Abby's visit to the police station. "Did you happen to see or hear anything yesterday?"

"Besides your aunt taking on the dead guy with a knife?"

Great. If Willow knew, then all the food truckers knew.

I sighed. "Yeah, besides that."

"Nope. Cops came by late yesterday, asking questions. Told them pretty much everyone around here has gotten into it with that jerkwad."

"You too?" I asked.

"A couple of times," she said, then took another order from a customer.

So Willow had been interviewed by the police too? But apparently not down at the station. I wondered if the cops had talked to all the food truck owners about Oliver Jameson's death.

Had they found out anything that could take the focus off my aunt?

Or had they learned something that could make things worse?

After Willow was done with her customer, I asked, "What did Oliver do to you?"

"First he hit on me. I mean, seriously. Like I'd ever go out with a fat, old, bald guy like him. When I told him to go screw himself, he said he had friends at the health department, hinting that he could get them to shut me down. I just laughed at him, told him I had 'friends' there too, you know what I mean?"

"You told the police about that?"

"Sure. Like I said, it seems like all us truckers have had problems with that jerk. But the cops didn't take me to jail, so I figure I'm in the clear. Maybe they already have someone in mind."

Like my aunt Abby, I thought. The coffee in my stomach turned to acid.

"Let me know if you hear anything, will you, Willow?"

"Totally," she said as another customer sidled up.

I watched Willow as she took the order. I hadn't noticed how attractive she was underneath that crazy hair and with all those piercings and tattoos. But apparently guys were always hitting on her—even old fat guys like Oliver Jameson. Maybe they liked the idea of walking on the wild side.

I glanced around at the circle of food trucks, wondering if any of the other truck owners had seen or heard anything yesterday. I made a note to question as many as I could, later, after the festival crowd died down. Right now I wanted to get to Aunt Abby's bus. Surely she was back and needing me to help prepare for the long and busy day.

I walked over to the bus, but when I arrived, I found the door still closed and locked up tight.

Huh.

I checked my cell phone. A quarter to nine.

It was getting late. Where was Aunt Abby?

I felt a sudden tingling at the back of my neck. Was Aunt Abby all right? Had something happened to her?

After all, there was a murderer on the loose.

I started to text her, then glanced over at the Bones 'n' Brew restaurant across the street and felt another chill.

If this was a random killer, maybe none of us was safe.

Chapter 4

Ten o'clock rolled around like the wheels of a bus, with no sign of my aunt. I was really starting to worry. I tried her cell (no answer), called Dillon (no word), and paced around the food trucks to see if any of the chefs had seen my aunt. If she didn't show up soon, I was calling the police.

After checking in at India Jones (sampling some Masala Nachos), then the Humpty Dumpling Truck (resisting the Polish, Swedish, and Chinese dumplings), I was just about to talk to the chef at Porky's, when I heard, "Hey, Darcy!"

I turned to see the Dream Puff Guy waving at me from across the way.

Jake Miller stood outside his cream puff truck, wearing his usual sexy jeans and formfitting white T-shirt. In one hand he held a brick-sized metal box; he waved me over with the other. Maybe he had some news about Aunt Abby, I thought as I waved back and headed for his truck. He knelt down by the front of his truck and slid the box underneath. Then he rose, picked up a small bottle of antibacterial liquid from his outside counter, and squirted a glob into his large hands.

Good thing he was cleaning up. I knew what was in

the box—rat poison. I'd learned from Aunt Abby that rodent infestation is inherent to the restaurant business, but making sure a food truck was free of vermin was a state health-and-safety law. Food trucks were a little easier to keep clean than, say, older restaurants where there are lots of nooks and crannies to hide, but it was still an issue. Aunt Abby did her best to keep the rats and other vermin at bay.

Unfortunately, she explained to me, you can't use snap traps or rodenticides where food is being prepared or served, since the poison might accidentally contaminate the food. She and the other truckers used bait boxes—tamper-resistant stations—like the one I'd just seen Jake tuck under his truck. The idea was to keep the toxins away from the food and kill the rats before they got into the trucks. Apparently Jake Miller dealt with rats the same way.

"Hey!" Jake said, rubbing his hands together.

I blinked. In spite of the fact that I'd been to his truck almost daily since he'd pulled in to Fort Mason a couple of months ago, I had no idea he knew my name. Our conversations had pretty much been: "Piña Colada Dream Puff, please," "Cappuccino Dream Puff, please," and "Key Lime Dream Puff, please." For someone who was used to asking serious questions for news articles, I'd found myself tongue-tied around him.

Maybe it was because he was so hot. And I hadn't been with a guy since Trevor the Tool.

"Hi," I said, then felt my brain turn into a cream puff. "Uh . . . are you ready for the big festival today?"

"Getting there," he said. He grabbed a long rod from the side of his truck, inserted it into a small hole at the top, and twisted it, working his considerable muscles as he opened the awning overhead. When he turned to face me, I saw a little spot of white fluff on his cheek. I was tempted to wipe—or lick—it off, but I held my tongue.

"You helping out Abby again today?" he asked. He returned the long pole to its spot, then began setting out shakers filled with powdered sugar for the cream puffs.

Wow. He knew I'd worked in Aunt Abby's bus yesterday? *And* he knew my name?

"Yes," I said, glancing nervously at my aunt's busterant. There was still no sign of her. "You haven't seen her, have you? I thought she'd be here by now."

Jake squinted in the direction of the bus. The rising sunlight brought out the gold in his thick, sun-bleached brown hair and revealed the tiniest feathery lines near his eyes. I guessed him to be in his early to midthirties.

He shook his head. "No, but I haven't been here too long. By the way, I heard what happened to the chef from Bones 'n' Brew yesterday. Is your aunt all right?"

"Oh yes, she's fine. So, do you know my aunt Abby well?" I said.

Jake grinned, revealing a mouthful of straight, white teeth. "We're kind of like a big family here. Everybody trades food, offers support, shares news. There aren't many secrets in the food truck community. And I'm really fond of your aunt. She reminds me of my mother."

"She's quite a character," I said, wondering if his mother was as quirky as Aunt Abby.

"She mentioned that you live with her." He eyed me, his eyes sparkling. "That must be fun."

Oh God. What else had she told him about me? That I thought he was hot? That I ate so many cream puffs because I had a crush on him? I was sure I was blushing the color of his Red Velvet Dream Puffs.

"Uh, yeah, I'm just staying there temporarily. Until I find a place of my own." *And get a full-time job and a regular paycheck,* I thought.

"So, any dirt on the murder?" he asked.

"What? No. How would I know anything?" I asked testily. I glanced again at the School Bus. Where was Aunt Abby?

"You're a reporter, right? For the *Chronicle*? I thought you might have some dirt on who killed Oliver Jameson."

So he knew I'd worked at the newspaper too. He just didn't know I mostly wrote restaurant reviews. I'd have to duct-tape Aunt Abby's mouth shut in the future.

"Actually, I'm only part-time now," I lied.

He looked surprised. "Really? How come?"

Boy, this guy was direct. "Downsized," I said, shrugging. "The economy. You know."

He nodded sympathetically. "I hear you. Everyone seems to be struggling these days, especially newspapers. It's like they've shrunk to little more than pamphlets. It's a wonder they're still in business."

"Well, I'm writing a cookbook in my spare time," I added quickly, so I didn't sound like a complete loser. "I plan to fill it with recipes from all the popular food trucks and festivals. Maybe you'd like to contribute one of your cream puff recipes, say, your Piña Colada Dream Puff? It's free publicity."

"Sounds good. But I'd have to show you how I make them rather than just hand over the recipe. There's a trick to it." He actually winked at me.

It felt like my face was on fire. The thought of spending

time with Jake Miller inside his cozy cream puff truck, making Piña Colada Dream Puffs together, sounded like a dream come true.

"And you'll have to wait until after the festival," he added. "Then I'll know how well the crowd likes my Crabby Dream Puffs."

Before I could stop myself, I made a face. I thought of cream puffs as sweet desserts, not savory snacks. The thought of biting into a crab-flavored cream puff made me a little seasick.

He laughed at my reaction. "They're pretty good. And they look like little crabs. You'll have to try one."

I changed the subject. "Have you done the Crab and Seafood Festival before?" I asked, knowing he was a recent addition to the Fort Mason food trucks.

"Nope. This will be my first. Last year I was wearing a suit, carrying a briefcase, and banking billable hours as an attorney. I'm looking forward to this. It should be fun."

"You're a lawyer?" I said, knowing full well he was because Aunt Abby had told me when I questioned her about the hot guy in the cream puff truck. A thought came to me. Maybe Jake Miller would come in handy with my aunt's recent legal situation.

"Yep. Up and quit, after deciding to go into business for myself. Crazy, huh?"

"Not at all," I said. *Maybe a little,* I thought. What guy would give up cash-paying clients for cream puffs?

"Well, if you love beer and crab, you'll love the festival," I added. "It won't be long before this whole area is filled with bands, booths, and billions of people."

"Can't wait. I love seafood, especially oysters. How do you like yours? Raw? Barbecued? Deep-fried?"

"I like mine left in the ocean where they belong."

"Really? No oysters for you?"

I shook my head, remembering the handful of people who'd died as a result of eating oysters. Speaking of dying, my thoughts returned to the death of the chef. "Jake, did you happen to know Oliver Jameson?"

Jake shook his head. A lock of his sun-bleached hair fell in his eyes and he combed it back with his fingers. "That detective came around asking questions yesterday afternoon, but I didn't have much to tell him."

"What did he say?"

Jake frowned. "Nothing much. He did mention the argument your aunt had with him, but I told him she was harmless. Plus, we'd all had our run-ins with the guy."

That was a relief. "As a former lawyer, is there any chance you could find out exactly how Jameson was killed?"

"I suppose I could make some calls. I still have a couple of cop friends at SFPD. Why? Are you really that worried about your aunt being a suspect?"

I shrugged, trying to appear casual to hide my true concerns. "A little," I said. "I know she had nothing to do with it, but I'd still like to know what happened." If Jameson was shot or strangled or axed to death, surely that would let Aunt Abby off the hook. She didn't own a gun—as far as I knew. She was too petite to strangle even a chicken. And while she was adept with a food chopper, I doubted she'd had as much experience with an ax as Lizzie Borden.

"Consider it done."

"Thanks." I glanced again at the School Bus, growing more concerned about my aunt's absence with every passing moment. But to my relief and surprise, the bus doors were open and the lights inside were on.

"She's back! Thank God! I have to go. Thanks again, Jake."

"Hold on!" he said as I started to step away. He disappeared into his truck. Seconds later he reached out through the service window. In his hand he held a cream puff covered in a bright orange drizzle, with slivered almonds sticking out of the creamy filling. The two dots of chocolate frosting on the top made the cream puff look like a small crab. Incredible. This guy was an artist when it came to decorating baked goods.

"On the house," he said as I reached for it. "Don't worry. This one is filled with sweet orange cream and topped with a tart orange frosting. No real crabs were harmed in the making or baking of it."

I didn't know which I liked better—the Dream Puff or the man who'd just handed it to me.

"Aunt Abby?" I called, entering the School Bus through the open accordion door.

Aunt Abby had already donned a fresh cafeteria-lady apron and was hurriedly working on what appeared to be crab mac and cheese, guessing from the ingredients on the counter in front of her. She had iPod earbuds in and was singing along to the soundtrack from *Frozen*.

"Where have you been?" I demanded, my hands on my hips. "I've been looking all over for you!"

She pulled out an earbud. "What?"

I repeated the question.

"Oh, I had some errands to run," she said, not meeting my eyes as she picked up a large knife.

I thought about the other "errands" she had run yesterday—when Oliver Jameson was being murdered.

"We have to get ready for the festival opening!" I said, putting on my own apron. "I've been frantic, wondering where you were. What do you need me to do?"

"Crack more crabs," she said, pointing the knife at a bowl filled with crabs.

I eyed the knife, remembering the way she'd waved it at Oliver Jameson the previous day. She seemed to read my mind and lowered her arm, then returned to chopping already-shucked crab.

"When is Dillon getting here?" I asked, pulling on a pair of rubber gloves. "I saw him this morning and it didn't look like he was ever getting out of bed."

"I told him to come around eleven," she answered. "Could you start the water boiling for the noodles?"

Boiling water was right up my alley. I filled the pot from the sink spigot, turned on the burner, and set the pot on top. "Well, don't scare me like that again. When I couldn't find you, I started asking around at the food trucks."

"Oh, is that why I saw you at Jake's truck?" Aunt Abby said, smirking.

"He was one of the people I asked," I said, trying to sound casual.

"Jake . . . Isn't he the one you're hot for?" This time Aunt Abby smiled wickedly as she chopped the crab into pieces.

"I *never* said I was hot for him!" I snapped. "I don't

even *know* him. I may have mentioned he was kind of cute—that's it. But apparently he knows a lot about *me*. What have you been telling him, Aunt Abby?"

She lifted a shoulder. "We're like family here. We talk."

"That's what *he* said. I hope you haven't told him all about my personal life!"

Aunt Abby grinned. "So what did he have to say?"

"Nothing much. We just chatted. He gave me a free cream puff."

"Umm-hmm," Aunt Abby mumbled under her breath.

"What?"

"Nothing. Did he say anything about the murder?" The sound of the big knife chopping crab on the cutting board accented her words. Those might be small hands, but they suddenly looked pretty powerful.

"He said the police talked to him and several of the other food truck chefs to see if they knew anything about Jameson's death." I paused. "They all knew about the argument you had with the chef."

Aunt Abby visibly tensed, but she said nothing and resumed her chopping. Had I hit a nerve?

"You know he's a lawyer, right?" I asked. "He said he has friends at the police department and that he'd try to learn more about Jameson's murder."

Aunt Abby blinked rapidly, the knife still in her now trembling hand. Something was going on in that adorable curly-haired head of hers. I put a hand on her shoulder. "Aunt Abby? What is it?"

"Nothing." She shook her head. "You'll let me know what he finds out?"

I didn't get a chance to reply. The man himself appeared at the School Bus service window. He was frowning.

"Jakey!" Aunt Abby said, sounding more anxious than glad to see him.

Jakey?

She set down the knife and wiped her hands on her apron. "Darcy said you might talk to the cops for me. Did you find out anything?"

He nodded. "May I come in for a minute?"

"Of course." Aunt Abby rinsed her hands in the sink. Jake stepped inside and inhaled. "Smells good in here. What's cooking?" He looked in the pot of boiling water on the stove.

"Water," I said smartly.

"Crab mac and cheese," Aunt Abby added, drying her hands on a towel. "What's up, Dream Puff Boy? If you talked to the cops, then spill it. Don't hold anything back."

I loved it when my aunt talked like a mob moll.

"I just got off the phone with a friend at SFPD." He popped a small piece of crab into his mouth, then licked his lips.

"Wow," I said. "That was fast."

"And?" my aunt said.

My heart suddenly started racing at the news we were about to hear. Or it could have been that lip licking.

"He said they don't know exactly what killed Jameson yet, but there were no signs of struggle or injury on the body. No stab wounds, gashes on the head, things like that."

My heart leapt. No knife wounds. That had to be good news for Aunt Abby.

Jake continued. "They found him in his office, sitting in his chair, slumped over his desk."

I knew about the office, but none of the details. I was impressed with Jake's connections. "Maybe he had a heart attack!" I said, then glanced at Aunt Abby for her reaction. Her eyes were wide. From anticipation? Or fear?

Jake shook his head. "They think it might have been something he ate."

"Like what?" Aunt Abby asked.

"Some kind of soup. They found a bowl of half-eaten soup on his desk."

"So it was accidental food poisoning," I said, relieved.

Jake bit his lip, as if he didn't want to say what he was about to add. "Maybe not so accidental."

"You're telling us the police think Oliver Jameson was deliberately poisoned?" I asked, stunned at this news. I looked at Aunt Abby, but she didn't meet my eyes. Her pink cheeks went as white as her still-clean apron.

"Soup?" she said quietly.

Uh-oh. I felt my stomach lurch, as if I'd just eaten a bowl of poisoned soup myself. Aunt Abby said she had been in that office sometime before Oliver Jameson died.

They say the proof is in the pudding. Or in this case, maybe it was in the soup.

Chapter 5

Aunt Abby and I worked together in silence after Jake left. I didn't know what my aunt was thinking, but I pondered the latest news—Oliver Jameson had been poisoned, seemingly by a bowl of soup, in his own restaurant office.

Was it accidental, as in food poisoning?

Or deliberate, as in someone had murdered him?

The police would no doubt find evidence that my aunt had been sneaking around the place, leaving fingerprints and who knew what else that a forensics team could uncover. I set down the wooden spoon I'd been using to stir the noodles I'd just tossed into the pot of boiling water and turned to my aunt. She was ladling the crab mac and cheese mixture into small disposable cups.

"Aunt Abby, you heard Jake," I said to her, frowning. "The cops are going to dust Jameson's office for fingerprints if they haven't already and they're going to find out you were there. Why did you lie to them? You're bound to be discovered. Isn't obstruction of justice a felony? You could go to jail for that."

My aunt avoided my gaze. "Wouldn't you have done the same thing?"

"No. But then again, I wouldn't have gone snooping

around in the guy's restaurant either. What were you thinking?"

Aunt Abby stopped filling the cups and took a deep breath. "I told you, Darcy. I was looking for something—anything—to keep Oliver Jameson from bothering me and the other food truckers."

I knew what she meant. "You wanted something to blackmail him with, didn't you?"

Aunt Abby tilted her head, almost coquettishly, and finally returned my gaze. "I wouldn't call it 'blackmail,' exactly. More like . . . 'leverage.'"

Shaking my head at her recklessness, I asked, "What did you expect to find? Bad checks? Doctored books? Naughty pictures?"

She shrugged and went back to her ladling.

I pressed on, ignoring the bubbling noodles. "Did you touch anything in the restaurant kitchen on your way to Jameson's office?"

"No," Aunt Abby said, focused on scooping up the mac and cheese mixture. "I mean, I don't think so. Except maybe . . ."

"Except maybe what?" Extracting information from Aunt Abby was like pulling crabmeat out of a tiny claw.

She batted her long lashes. "I may have moved a few of his things around in the kitchen. You know how chefs are about their *mise en place*."

"Their what?"

"*Mise en place*. Their kitchen stuff. Chefs like their utensils and prepped food arranged just so. That way they can access things quickly. Sort of like a doctor and his instruments. Or a reporter and her pencils."

Ha. "So you—what?—messed with his meese-on-whatever?"

"It's pronounced *meeze awn plaas*. It's French, you know."

Frustrated with her answers, I snapped, "I don't care if it's Siberian. You touched his stuff! Your fingerprints will be all over that too! And since you worked for the school district, your prints are on file."

She rolled her eyes as if she didn't really care, but her face flushed cherry red, giving away her anxiety underneath. Maybe she was finally beginning to realize how serious this was.

She sighed. "Darcy, his things are probably covered with lots of other fingerprints besides mine. That doesn't prove anything."

"Yes, it does. It proves you were there when you said you weren't. Those *other* fingerprints no doubt belong to the people who work at the restaurant. You had no reason to be there—and yet, you were sneaking around your competitor's place of business."

"Well, they can't tell *when* the fingerprints were put there, can they?" Aunt Abby argued.

"No, but—" I took a deep breath. I needed to calm down. The timer for the noodles sounded and I poured the contents into a colander that sat in the stainless steel sink. Once the water drained off, I dumped the noodles into a large bowl and stirred in the premeasured cheese and cream, as Aunt Abby had directed. After making sure the pasta was thoroughly coated, I set the spoon down and resumed my inquisition.

"Aunt Abby, you have to call that detective—what

was his name?—and tell him the truth. It will only look worse for you if you don't, because he's going to find out. Remember what happened to Martha Stewart?"

"You mean that time she burned her soufflé on her TV show?"

"No, the time she was convicted of obstruction of justice and went to prison!"

"Darcy, I can't tell him I was lying! I've worked too long and hard making a go of my business and I'm not going to the slammer just because of some small fib about where I was when."

Small fib? I was sure that's what Martha Stewart thought too.

Before I could argue, I felt the equivalent of a 4.5 earthquake rock the bus. A deep voice at the door said, "What's all the commotion?"

Apparently Aunt Abby and I had been shouting loud enough to attract the attention of the chef next door. Chef Boris Obregar stood in the doorway, his round face flushed, his large head topped precariously with a tall white toque. Boris was the owner of the Road Grill food truck, which was parked next to my aunt's bus. Her bus had listed the moment he'd hoisted his sizable weight onto the lower step. This man loved his own cooking.

Boris was loud and crude, and I didn't care for his menu selections. He served what he called "exotic meats," but what I'd call "road kill" food—burgers made from possum, hot dogs from ground snake, and something he called "gator balls," which I only hoped wasn't a literal label. Aunt Abby called him Boris Badcook behind his broad back. No doubt he had his fans, but I had a feeling a lot of the male customers came to get an eyeful of his attractive assistant, Cherry Washington. She tended to offer up a pair of ample boobs when taking customers' orders. With her long mocha legs, short-shorts, low-cut tops, and halo of tight black curls, she could have gotten a job at any Hooters in the state. Why she chose to work with Boris and his freaky food was a mystery to me.

Just the thought of eating wild animals made me almost consider becoming a vegetarian, like Sierra and Vandy, the vegans who ran the Vegematic truck. But Boris's food was wildly popular with a diverse crowd, and the man himself was a jovial guy with permanently rosy cheeks, a cropped white beard, and caterpillar eyebrows. While he reminded me of Santa Claus, his red face wasn't from the cold, and he was jolly. More likely his coloring came from the vodka I'd seen him drinking behind his truck during breaks. He'd even offered me a hit one time when I spotted him having a snort.

"I could hear you two arguing way over to my place," Boris said, a remnant of his Slavic accent punctuating his words. "You want to drive the customers away? Bad enough there's been a murder in the neighborhood."

Odd. We had only just learned that Oliver Jameson's death was a possible homicide. "Why do you think Oliver Jameson was murdered?" I asked.

Boris shrugged his beefy shoulders. "What else could it be? The guy was asking for it. Everybody around here hated him. He hassled Willow, the vegans, Jake, everyone. He used to send me poison-pen letters, threatening to shut me down, just because I serve exotic gourmet fare to my patrons."

Gourmet?

"He threatened you?" Aunt Abby asked, perking up.

"Sure. About half a dozen times," Boris said, wiping his sweating brow with the bottom of his heavily stained apron. Were those dark streaks human blood?

"Where are the letters?" I asked, thinking Aunt Abby was on to something. The police would want to know about this.

"I tore 'em up," he said, gesturing with his hands.

"What? You should have saved them," I said.

"What for? I didn't plan to reread them."

"You could have turned them over to the police," I argued.

"They were poison-pen letters. They weren't signed, 'Love, Oliver.' "

"But the cops might have found fingerprints or something," Aunt Abby added. "And they could have been used as evidence, in case he did something else to you. Something worse."

"Oh, *pah*!" Boris said. "I got my revenge."

That caught my attention.

Boris laughed. "No, I didn't kill him. I ripped up the last note he sent me, went into his kitchen, and threw the pieces all over the food. Ha!"

"What did he do when he found out?" Aunt Abby asked, wide-eyed.

"Nothing. I told the woman chef working there to tell him, 'Nobody messes with Chef Boris.' I'm sure he got the message, because he didn't bother me again."

"What did the letters say?" Aunt Abby asked, her frown deepening.

I turned to her. "Aunt Abby? Did you get letters too?"

"No," she said quickly. "I'm just curious."

Chef Boris lifted his toque, revealing a bald pate, and scratched an itch with a sausage-sized finger. When he was done, he replaced the hat. I hoped he washed his hands frequently.

"Mostly crap like, 'Stop the slop, you pig!' and 'Serving rat soufflé, you rodent?' "

Hmm. Aunt Abby had mentioned she suspected Oliver of planting a rat in her kitchen a week or so ago. Coincidence? Too bad Boris had destroyed possible evidence that Oliver had been threatening him. It might have taken the focus off Aunt Abby.

"I gotta get back to work," Boris said. "Just thought I'd check on you when I heard the shouting, what with this murder and everything. By the way, I'm serving a fried eel omelet today for the festival. Stop by for a sample."

Just the thought of putting a piece of eel—dead or alive, raw or cooked—in my mouth made me want to heave.

As soon as the XXL chef stepped off the bus, the vehicle leveled itself, but a small aftershock followed, causing a teetering spoon at the counter's edge to fall. The spoon hit the floor and slid under the stove. I bent down to retrieve it.

And screamed.

"What's wrong?" Aunt Abby said, startled by my reaction.

I reared back, shaking my hand as if something was stuck to it. "There's a rat under the stove!"

Aunt Abby grimaced. "That rat bastard!" she mumbled, then asked, "It's dead, right?"

"I don't know! I didn't check its pulse!"

"Jameson!" Aunt Abby said, venom in her voice. "I'm sure he planted it there. I don't know how he got in here, but it had to be him. Talk about vermin. He's the epitome of the word. Rodenticide is too good for that rat bastard."

Stunned, I looked at Aunt Abby as if she'd just confessed to murder.

Aunt Abby read my mind, as she often seemed to do. "You can relax, Darcy. I didn't kill Oliver Jameson with rat poison, if that's what you're thinking."

I blinked.

"I didn't kill him with anything!" she added.

"Do you keep rat poison on the bus?" I asked.

"Of course. But I only use it in the bait box."

Hmm. I wondered if the police would look for rat poison in Aunt Abby's bus. "Where do you keep the actual poison?"

She nodded toward a high cupboard door at the far end of the bus. "Check for yourself," she said. "Meanwhile, I'm gonna get rid of the body."

For a moment I thought she meant the body of Oliver Jameson. Then I remembered the rat.

While Aunt Abby slipped on disposable gloves and knelt down on the floor, I pulled the box of rodenticide from the cupboard and read the label.

"Contents: Bromethalin. Warning: Highly toxic. Can cause paralysis, convulsions, and death. . . ."

Death.

"It is illegal and unsafe to use rodenticides in any area where food is being prepared or served unless it's contained in a bait box. . . ."

I wondered if it was illegal to keep the package of pellets in the cupboard.

I read on: *"Use bait stations and traps filled with rodenticide pellets and place them outside the building to prevent vermin from entering. Check with local authorities for correct usage in your area."*

Would the local authorities be knocking on the door any minute?

Aunt Abby stood up, holding the trap by her gloved fingertips. A dead rat the size of a small lobster dangled from it. I turned away, nauseated. "Get that disgusting thing out of here!"

The lifeless pest didn't seem to bother Aunt Abby as much as it did me. Holding the trap at arm's length, she stepped out of the bus and headed for the community Dumpster a few yards away.

How had that rat gotten inside Aunt Abby's bus? Was it dead or alive when it entered? And would the police wonder what other rat my aunt Abby might have disposed of lately?

After we finished preparing the first batch of crab mac and cheese cups—a dish Aunt Abby was calling Crabby Cheerleader Mac and Cheese—she and I worked on the other popular comfort foods that were my aunt's specialties—the Fire Drill (eye-watering chili), the Field Trip (BLT wedge salad), and the Science Experiment Spaghetti. By the time the gates opened at eleven a.m., we were amped and ready to rock. Thoughts of rats, poison, and murder were the furthest things from my mind.

I braced myself as the stream of crab lovers swarmed into the area. The constant rush kept us both hopping, me mostly at the service window, Aunt Abby with the cooking. By two p.m., when the crowd had died down a bit, I was more tired than I'd ever been working at the newspaper. Interviewing people for a story was a piece of cake compared to working in a food truck. The small kitchen was in shambles, I reeked of fish, and my sleek brown hair had been steamed into bushy waves. How my aunt did this every day at age sixty-plus was mind-boggling. I wasn't sure I'd last another hour, let alone a week.

I really needed to write—and sell—my "Food Truck and Festival Cookbook" proposal to a publisher. Fast.

"Take a break," Aunt Abby said after handing a straggling customer the last in a third batch of her Crabby Macs. "You deserve it. You did a great job. I couldn't have done it without you, seeing as how Dillon didn't stick around for very long."

"Yeah, where is he, anyway?"

Aunt Abby shrugged as she donned a fresh apron and tied it around her waist with experienced hands. "I don't know. That boy. He's been acting strange lately."

I wanted to say, *"You mean stranger than usual,"* but I bit my tongue. "Well, thanks for the break. You sure you'll be okay?" I was grateful for a chance to catch my breath—and get a breath of fresh air. I'd been nibbling on mistakes and leftovers throughout the morning and early afternoon, so I wasn't hungry, but I badly needed another jolt of caffeine.

"Go! I'll be fine."

I wandered over to the Coffee Witch, ordered a magical potion called the Alchemy—a double latte with one pump of Belgian chocolate—and sat down on a nearby bench. Sierra Montoya, the thirtysomething woman who co-ran the Vegematic truck, joined me a few minutes later, holding some kind of blended green drink. She looked more like she'd come from the gym than her truck, wearing tight shorts and a tank top on her toned body. Her face was bare of makeup and her short brown hair looked salon cut and easy care.

Aunt Abby had filled me in on most of the food truckers during serving lulls. She said Sierra owned the veggie truck with her partner, Vandy Patel. They'd named their business the Vegematic as a sort of homage to an old *I Love Lucy* episode. Both were avid supporters of PETA and protested regularly at various demonstrations around the city, bringing along signs that said things like MEAT IS MURDER!, CARROTS ARE COOL!, DRINK YOUR VEGETABLES!, and WHO KILLED BAMBI? They'd even set out signs in front of their Vegematic truck, just to irritate Chef Boris. Aunt Abby said the two women had argued frequently with the Road Grill chef, and he'd taken to ruffling their feathers with his own signs, for instance, RABBIT FOOD IS FOR RABBITS, PLANTS HAVE FEELINGS TOO!, and PROUD TO BE A CARNIVOR! (misspelling the word "carnivore"). Unfortunately, their food trucks were parked right next to each other, and Aunt Abby said the heated glares between the two factions could fry an organic egg.

"Hi," Sierra said after a long drag from the straw in her green drink. She glanced at my coffee.

Did she just wince at my less-than-healthy beverage, loaded with fat and sugar? Or was that my imagination?

I smiled and said, "Hey. Busy day, eh?"

She took another sip, then said, "I saw you helping out at Abby's bus."

I nodded. "This food truck business is a lot harder than I expected."

She snickered. "Tell me about it. Luckily it's not this crazy every day. But we need the business. New food trucks seem to be setting up shop all over the city. Competition is getting stiff." She nodded at Chef Boris's Road Grill rig. "If only we could get rid of a few of the less desirable trucks, like that one. His food is disgusting! Alligator, black bear, elk, kangaroo, turtle. Meat like that should be illegal. And *he* should be locked up. Along with that guy from Porky's. What a stupid name."

Uh-oh. I had wanted to sip my coffee quietly, but her mini-rant had piqued my interest. "Selling exotic meats isn't illegal?" I asked, curious.

"Fair game," she said, adding finger quotes to the word "game."

"Wow. Are there any animals that aren't legal to cook and sell, besides horses, dogs, cats?"

"Actually, there's no real ban on dog and cat meat—they're just frowned upon."

Oh my God.

I thought of Aunt Abby's little dog, Basil.

"You can't sell haggis," she continued. "It's made out of sheep's lung. You can eat the stomach, heart, and liver of a sheep, but not the lung. Go figure. Pâté is now illegal. And you need a license to sell fugu."

"Fugu?"

"It's puffer fish—the stuff they use to create zombies, if you believe that sort of thing. Apparently it can paralyze you."

Whoa. I was sorry I asked. Where did she get this morbid information?

"That's what's so crazy about this business," she added. "It's not illegal to cook and eat antelope or buffalo, or even lion meat, but it's just plain wrong, you know? Boris should be strung up by his prairie oysters for crimes against nature."

Prairie oysters? I had a feeling she meant balls.

Sierra stood up and tossed her empty recyclable cup into a "green" bin. "Gotta get back to work and hopefully keep a few more customers from practicing animal cannibalism."

"No crab dishes at the Vegematic truck?"

"Nope. We've got a great Seaweed Stew though. You should try it."

I was beginning to feel guilty for enjoying the occasional burger and hot dog. While I ate my veggies like my mother had always told me, I just couldn't wrap my mouth around tofu wieners, cauliflower burgers, or seaweed stew.

"Sierra?" I called out to her as she started to head back. "I guess you heard about the death of Oliver Jameson. The chef from the restaurant across the street?"

She nodded. "Bones 'n' Brew? Who hasn't? Not sorry to see him gone. He was always hassling us about our vegetarian menu. I'm sure he felt threatened by us—thought we were converting people to vegetarianism and causing him to lose business. I doubt he served a single vegetable beyond decorative parsley."

"Why do you think he felt threatened by you?"

"One morning our signs had all been torn down. I immediately thought it was Meathead Man—Boris—but the next time it happened, I'm pretty sure I saw someone in chef's whites running toward Bones 'n' Brew. I swear, if I'd caught him, I would have beat the crap out of him."

"Sierra!" a voice called from across the food truck area.

We both looked in the direction of the Vegematic. Sierra's partner, Vandy, stood outside, hands on her hips, scowling at us. From a distance she looked like Sierra's sister. Both had warm latte skin and dark hair and eyes. But Vandy wore her hair long, and makeup enhanced her dark eyes. When I thought they were related, I was surprised to learn they were a couple. I smiled and waved at Vandy; she didn't smile or wave back. Either the sun was in her eyes, or she was dissing me on purpose. *But why?* I wondered.

As I watched Sierra walk back to her truck, I didn't doubt she could beat the crap out of Oliver Jameson or anyone else. Those muscles in her biceps and triceps hadn't come from eating her veggies. She'd been working out and was probably strong enough to strangle an ox. Not that she would, of course, being a vegetarian.

Then again, you didn't need muscles to poison someone. Boris and Sierra, and perhaps scowling Vandy, all had a reason to dislike Oliver Jameson. Enough to kill him?

Chapter 6

Unrest among the food truck community? I wondered as I headed back to Aunt Abby's Big Yellow School Bus. Were there too many trucks invading the city, as Sierra had said, providing a glut for gluttons? Or was it just competitive jealousy—too many cooks spoiling the profit margin? All I knew was, things were heating up now that murder had been added to the menu.

One thing was clear: Oliver Jameson had more enemies than just Aunt Abby. Boris, the weird-meat guy, had had run-ins with him. So had Sierra and Vandy, the vegetarians. Willow the Coffee Witch didn't care for him either, even though he had frequented her truck for his morning jolt. I wondered if Jameson's coffee had tasted a little bitter of late, perhaps with a hint of almond?

All this speculating was getting me nowhere. None of these people seemed like killers. But the cops still had Aunt Abby on their list of suspects, thanks to that public fight she'd had with the Bones 'n' Brew chef. Jeez, she'd even brandished a knife at him, in front of witnesses, no less. Now that Oliver Jameson was dead, the cops seemed to be taking her threats seriously. Were there other suspects on Detective Shelton's list besides my aunt?

Boris, Sierra and Vandy, and Willow might have had strong enough reasons to murder Chef Jameson. But it could have been another one of the several food truck owners parked at Fort Mason. Then again, someone close to Jameson could have done it—a disgruntled employee? A jilted fiancée? A former friend? A secret stalker turned killer?

Or was it just a random intruder?

It couldn't be random though. Not if Jameson was really poisoned. That took planning, not to mention opportunity.

My generic list was beginning to look endless. I had to go about this in a systematic way, much like I did when reporting a story for the newspaper. The "five *W*s"—and "sometimes *H*"—almost guaranteed a complete news report. Maybe that would work for me now.

I made a list of questions based on the five *W*s and filled in what I already knew:

Who is the story about? Chef Oliver Jameson
What happened? He died, poisoned from eating soup (accidental food poisoning or deliberate murder?)
When did the event take place? Yesterday, between lunch and dinner
Where did it take place? In his office at the Bones 'n' Brew restaurant
Why did it happen? Good question . . .

I added an *H*.

How did it happen? Did an unknown subject enter the restaurant, poison the soup, and give it to Oliver

Jameson? Or did the killer leave it there for Jameson to find . . . ?

Underneath the list, I jotted down the names of possible suspects that came to mind: Boris, Sierra, Vandy, and Willow. Reluctantly I included Aunt Abby's name, but only because the police had her on their list, and I didn't want to forget how serious things were.

Anyone else? Dillon crossed my mind.

Maybe he'd killed Oliver Jameson to protect his mother? He didn't have anyone to verify his alibi for the time of the murder. Nah. Neither Dillon nor Aunt Abby had it in them to kill someone. If I was going to include him, I might as well add Dream Puff Guy as well. And that was just silly. Wasn't it? To my knowledge, Jake Miller didn't have any beef with the Bones 'n' Brew chef. But at this point, I didn't know that much about Jake, just like I didn't know much about Willow, Boris, Sierra, and Vandy. Perhaps the more I dug into Oliver Jameson's life, the longer my suspect list would grow.

So how was I supposed to find out more about Oliver Jameson?

A thought popped up like a piece of hot toast from the toaster. I could use my recipe research for my "Food Truck and Festival Cookbook" as a red herring, so to speak. Or was it a MacGuffin?

It didn't matter. Under the guise of collecting recipes for the book, I could interview all the local food truck vendors and find out who else might have had a reason to kill the chef. As a bonus, I'd be gathering recipes for my book, killing two birds with one stone. A bad analogy, I realized, but apt.

Under normal circumstances, interviewing the food truckers would be easy, but with Jameson dead, they might not be cooperative. And how would I worm my way into the Bones 'n' Brew restaurant to question Jameson's employees? My cookbook was focused on food festivals and trucks, not competing restaurants.

So far, only a handful of people knew I'd been downsized at the newspaper. Maybe I could pose as a *Chronicle* reporter who was assigned to write a proper obituary for a "beloved" local chef. I still had my press pass, my credentials, business cards, trusty notebook, and fake Montblanc pen. I was sure whoever was in charge at the restaurant now would welcome a heartwarming story—and some good publicity. All I had to do was figure out how to spin murder in a positive way.

"So when's quitting time, Auntie?" I said around seven, exhausted from the first day of my food service career. In the late afternoon, the Crab and Seafood Festival crowds had surged again relentlessly, and lines for all the vendors had snaked across one another in the congested courtyard. I was surprised that so many people attended, what with the hefty admission charge, parking problems, and crowds, but attendees seemed to really enjoy the food, beer, music, and crabby specialties.

Now that the fog had rolled in and the masses had ebbed, many of the trucks were beginning to close down. Some had even run out of food, unprepared for the sheer number of people. A few of the attendees turned, shall we say, crabby when they learned their favorite vendors were closing. The most vocal were those who'd had too much beer and not enough solid food.

But overall, the day had been a great success for Aunt Abby's crab experiments—her Crabby Cheerleader Mac and Cheese, Crab Pops, and Crabtown Fry (bacon, eggs, and crab substituting for oysters, named after a dish famous during the California gold rush). She'd managed to keep her seemingly endless line of hungry folks sated. After all, she'd been a pro at feeding large groups during her high school cafeteria days, and she'd planned well. All we had left to do at the end of the day was clean up the mess and count the money. I'd never seen her cash register so full of dough.

"Let me do those pots," I said to my aunt. "I'm sure you've got a million other things to do."

"Are you sure?" she asked. "I don't want you to burn out on your first day. You might not come back tomorrow."

I assured her I would return, but secretly I worried that if I didn't sell this cookbook, I might never get out of the bustaurant business. I took over the dishwashing, leaving my aunt to prepare for the next day's menu.

I hadn't realized how much went into running a mobile business—and in such tight quarters. I didn't know how she did it, up nearly every day at the crack of dawn, ordering and collecting the food from the local bakery, deli, and farmers' markets, before pulling up behind her bus and transferring everything to her tiny portable kitchen. Then, after turning on the generator and propane tanks, she went to work pounding prime meats, mixing fragrant sauces, slicing fresh bread, and generally whipping up her brand of comfort specialties to serve throughout the day—often two to three hundred orders or more in the space of four to six hours.

When it was time to close up shop, she spent the rest of the day cleaning utensils, pots, and surfaces, tossing out garbage, and saving leftovers for the homeless shelters, before heading home to experiment with new recipes. No wonder she had a line of faithful customers when she opened her service window around eleven every morning. She was devoted to serving good-quality food and she worked hard to provide it. Her energy seemed boundless.

Me? I was ready to collapse after only one day.

"So are you really coming back tomorrow?" Aunt Abby asked as I dropped my spattered apron into the soiled linen basket.

"Unless I die of exhaustion," I said. "We could have used more help this afternoon. Where did Dillon disappear to? He was only here an hour or so." Aunt Abby's son had come in just in time to help with the lunch rush, then vanished for the rest of the event. What was up with him?

Aunt Abby shrugged. "He said he had something important to do and that you could handle his usual job. I think he might have been a little jealous."

"Jealous?" I rolled my eyes. "I doubt that." Most likely he'd returned to his bedroom, changed into his pajamas, and spent the rest of the day playing games on his computer.

I gave my aunt a hug and headed for my car, which was squeezed in behind the bus next to Aunt Abby's Toyota. I couldn't wait to get home to the RV and take a shower and a nap.

Two hours later, after I'd washed off the grease, fish smell, and sweat, put on the Minnie Mouse pajamas

Aunt Abby had bought me, and had a nap, I made myself a cup of herbal tea and headed for my laptop to plan interview questions for my murder suspects. As soon as I opened my computer, I had a thought. Something had been nagging at the back of my mind throughout my shower—something I'd read in one of the Internet articles when I'd done a search for Oliver Jameson. I keyed in the words "Bones 'n' Brew."

There it was—a link to a story headed CANNIBALIZING FOOD TRUCKS. Essentially, the article had confirmed all the complaints among many brick-and-mortar restaurants regarding the increasing number of food trucks in the city. It was nothing new, I thought, but this time, instead of skimming the article, I read it carefully.

> *"We've had nothing but trouble since the food trucks began occupying the Fort Mason area," said Oliver Jameson, chef and owner of Bones 'n' Brew, a city landmark for more than fifty years. "It seems like anyone who can boil macaroni, burn road kill, or blend a carrot can simply pull over and start serving food. It took my family years to build up this restaurant, and now all these squatters are trying to lure customers to their overpriced, subpar food. That's why I'm working on a petition to have them all removed."*

I glanced at the date on the article—it had appeared less than a week ago. I guessed the examples he'd cited were references to Aunt Abby's mac and cheese, Boris's meats, and the vegetarians' fare.

"He's overreacting," said Sierra Montoya, co-owner and chef at the Vegematic food truck. "Most of us offer foods you don't normally find at the local restaurants. And since when has free enterprise been a problem in the United States? I say, if you can't take the heat, get out of the kitchen business."

Jameson says he plans to pursue a lawsuit against the food trucks and has repeatedly called the health department to look into these "roach coaches," questioning their cleanliness and safety.

"When you cook for large numbers of people," Jameson said, "you have to make sure everything is sanitary or you're apt to poison your customers. I've seen rats the size of cats running around those trucks at night. The owners don't seem to understand the need for pest control. I suspect one of the truck owners—I won't name names—catches those rodents and cooks them up in his 'gourmet' kitchen, then calls them 'exotic' meat. Disgusting!"

Rats the size of cats? My stomach lurched at the thought of Chef Boris grilling up freshly caught rodent meat. Surely he didn't! Aunt Abby claimed Oliver Jameson had planted rats in her kitchen to get her in trouble with the health department. I'd seen one with my own eyes, trapped under her stove. Had Jameson put it there? If so, how had he gotten inside?

I smelled a rat. A two-legged rat.

I returned to the article.

Chef Boris Obregar from the Road Grill truck argued that the rats were already in the area because of the restaurants. "We're all careful about having a clean kitchen and a healthy environment for our customers," he said. "Keeping vermin away is everyone's responsibility, including Oliver Jameson's."

My head was spinning like a rat on a hamster wheel. Both sides were accusing each other of causing the infestation problem. But that didn't seem to be a strong enough reason to murder Oliver Jameson. I read the last line of the article:

"Everyone just needs to calm down," said Jake Miller, owner of the popular Dream Puffs truck. "Eat a cream puff."

I smiled at the words, which reminded me of my own mantra: "Stay calm, and eat a cream puff." If more people did that, we'd probably have a lot fewer murders. But it didn't change the fact that Oliver Jameson was dead. Poisoned like a rat. As unpleasant as he was, he didn't deserve to die so horribly.

I had an idea and checked the Cheshire Cat clock on the RV wall: nine thirty p.m. Maybe it wasn't too late. I hastily changed out of my pj's and into my khaki pants, a long-sleeved black sweater, and my ballet flats. Grabbing my red leather purse and black leather jacket, I got in my car and drove over to the Bones 'n' Brew restaurant to see if I could get a little taste of Oliver Jameson's world.

The crime scene tape had been removed from the front entrance of the brick Bones 'n' Brew building, but a sign on the door read CLOSED. I wasn't surprised. Not only was it late at night, but I figured most of Oliver Jameson's staff were either mourning his death—or celebrating the time off. I wondered when—and if—the restaurant would reopen for business. Nevertheless, I hoped I'd find someone inside, dealing with the daily demands of managing a large restaurant, even one that was temporarily closed.

The front door was locked, so I walked around to the back staff entrance, knocked on the door, then tried the knob. It opened. I let myself in thinking anyone could walk in here—even a murderer.

The kitchen was empty—and a complete mess. Dishes, pots, pans, and utensils appeared to have been left wherever they'd been when news of Jameson's death was announced. Half-cooked food was dumped in the large sinks or garbage pails, remnants clung to the pans and bowls, and sauces had puddled and gelatinized on the counters. The stench was overwhelming, and I was tempted to plug my nose at the cooking carnage.

"Can I help you?" came a voice behind me.

Startled, I whirled around to see a thirtysomething woman wearing an apron over her sleeveless T-shirt and jeans, and a pair of rubber gloves on her hands. She sported chin-length brown hair, unstyled, no makeup, and about twenty extra pounds on her frame.

"Oh! Sorry!" I said, startled, my heart beating out of my chest. "I'm Darcy Burnett. I write for the *Chronicle*. I was wondering—"

"Get out of here!" the woman said fiercely. I noticed a spray bottle of cleaner in her hand and a long scrub brush in the other. Both could be used as weapons, if necessary. I didn't plan to make it necessary.

"No, wait! You don't understand," I said, holding up a notepad in self-defense. "I'm planning to write a commemorative obituary about Mr. Jameson. I just wanted to interview someone from the restaurant to make sure I got everything right. A lot of people will miss him and I thought a story about him and Bones 'n' Brew would be of interest to those who enjoyed his food."

The woman frowned, then lowered the spray bottle. "You could have called," she said. "It's awfully late."

"I know, but I'm on deadline," I lied.

"You want to write an obit about Ollie?"

"Yes," I said, digging in my purse for my credentials. "Are you from the janitorial service?"

She smiled, relaxing the frown in her forehead, and sat down on a nearby stool. "No, actually, I'm a chef here. My name's Livvy, short for Olivia." She set down her supplies, then removed her gloves and placed them on the counter.

Oliver and Olivia? No wonder she called herself Livvy. "Oh, great! Then you worked with Mr. Jameson. Could I ask you some questions about him? For my article?"

"You mean worked *for* him. Nobody works—worked—*with* Ollie. Not even his sister."

"He had a sister?" This was a surprise to me. I hadn't seen a sister mentioned in any of the Internet articles, only his father.

"You're looking at her."

Wow. I hadn't seen that one coming. The two were

physically similar—both around six feet tall and several pounds overweight—except Livvy wasn't bald.

"Oh. Uh, did the two of you own the restaurant together?"

"In theory." She pursed her lips before continuing. "Our father turned the business over to Ollie. Gave him a fifty-one percent share because he was male, and me forty-nine because, well, I'm not." She rolled her eyes. "Ollie's more the front man. He handled the business end. I oversee everything and do some of the cooking. But maybe you shouldn't put that in the obit."

"Sure. Like I said, I'm here to do a commemorative story on him and the restaurant. Bones 'n' Brew is one of the great ones, and we've lost too many other iconic San Francisco restaurants—Caribbean Zone, Cadillac Bar, Ernie's, Yamato, Mildred Pierce, the Castle, Old Spaghetti Factory. I'm hoping my story will help keep the restaurant alive—if you plan to stay open."

I could tell she believed me by the way she visibly relaxed. In fact, she looked downright tired, and I felt for her. Losing her brother must have been quite a shock and a big loss. And now the responsibility of cleaning up this mess and getting the business back on track—it was a lot to handle.

I reached over and placed my hand on hers. No wedding ring.

"Maybe this isn't a good time to talk," I said gently. "I didn't realize Oliver Jameson was your brother. In all my research on the Internet, I never saw your name mentioned."

"That's the way he preferred it," she said. "He wanted me behind the scenes, which was fine with me. Ollie was the one who liked the attention. Unfortunately, it was his dramatic personality that made the news more than the restaurant."

I thought of all the comments he'd made about the food trucks on the Internet. "Any idea who might have killed him?" I asked softly. "Off the record, of course."

"Too many to choose from," she said, sighing. "He was always arguing with someone—the staff, the suppliers, the local government, the competition, even me."

"The food truck owners too?" I added.

"Oh yes. Ollie thought the evil trucks were going to put us out of business. What he didn't realize was we were putting ourselves out of business by clinging to the old menu and the old ways. I kept trying to get him to update the recipes for today's customers. You know, less fat and salt, more herbs from my garden, stuff like that. I'm a student of the Magical Kitchen."

"Magical Kitchen?" I repeated, frowning. I'd never heard of such a thing.

She nodded. "Cooking, to me and many others, is actually magic. It's alchemy. The stove is like a sacred altar, the equivalent of medieval hearth fires." She glanced at a small figurine that hung from the ceiling and hovered over the sink. A witch on a broom, much like the one tattooed on her arm.

Sounds like a bunch of mumbo jumbo to me, I thought as I smiled at the ugly crone who oversaw the kitchen. "Is that a lucky charm?"

"It's a kitchen witch. Ollie thought it was silly, of course, but it was supposed to bring us good luck. Chefs are full of superstitions, you know. Toss salt over your shoulder if you spill it. Tape a penny to a knife for good luck. Although . . ." She drifted off, then said, "Apparently not even feng shui was enough to protect Ollie. Or my dad."

I didn't know what to say. I knew their father had died, but had it been under unusual circumstances?

She caught my look and continued. "Dad died last year. Complications from Alzheimer's. He handed over the reins to Ollie a few years before that, when he started to forget things."

"Sad," I said.

She nodded, then stood up from her stool. "Well, I better get back to cleaning up this mess."

Was I getting the brush-off? I couldn't let this opportunity slip by. "I only have a couple more questions. What was it like working for your brother?"

She laughed. "Pretty much impossible. I mostly ignored him and did my own thing. Kept asking for new recipes. Tried to change some of the decor. Everything I did seemed to irritate him though."

"The police said he died from eating poisoned soup. Any idea how that could have happened?"

"Crab bisque, to be exact." She closed her eyes for a moment, as if trying to escape the thought. "You know, the irony is that was one of the new recipes I wanted to add to the menu. I was hoping he'd try a sample. . . ."

She drifted off again, then suddenly jerked back to the present and looked at me, her eyes narrowed. "Listen, like I told the police, I have no idea how the bisque may have ended up with poison in it. I certainly didn't kill my brother. I loved him. He's the only family I have left. Was, that is. And what a horrible way to die."

"Could someone have tampered with the soup?" I asked.

She grimaced as if she'd just tasted something bad. "Could have been anyone. He never kept his office locked."

Nor the back door, I thought.

I wondered if she might have had a reason to kill her brother. Sibling murders certainly weren't unknown. But before I could ask her another question, she said, "Look, I'd be happy to talk to you about Ollie's *legacy*, but this isn't a good time." She larded the word "legacy."

"How about tomorrow?" I asked.

Livvy shrugged. "Maybe . . . after I've had a chance to clean up the place."

I noticed that areas of the kitchen had a powdery white residue. Had the cops dusted the kitchen and office for prints? "Did the police find anything?"

Livvy shrugged.

I wondered if the police had found evidence of Aunt Abby's snooping yet.

My phone suddenly played "It's a Small World," Aunt Abby's ringtone. I said, "Excuse me," to Livvy, then turned away and answered the call.

"Aunt Abby?"

"Darcy?" Her voice sounded tremulous.

I should have told her I was going out. She probably came over to the RV and found me gone. Now I'd upset her. "I'm fine, Aunt Abby. I just had a few errands—"

She cut me off. "Darce, the police jus' called. They wanna talk to me again. They have more questions."

"Now?" I asked, noting the time on the kitchen clock.

"Yeah . . ."

Aunt Abby sounded strange. This couldn't be good.

Did the cops have something more on her that related to Oliver Jameson's death?

Oh God. It had to be her fingerprints.

Chapter 7

"I'll be right there," I said, trying to reassure her. "Where's Dillon?"

"I dunno," Aunt Abby said, slurring her words. "I can't get a hold of 'im and he hasn't returned my calls. I'm worried about 'im. He's disappeared again."

Again? What was up with him?

"He's not in his room playing computer games?" I asked. One day he was going to vanish into virtual space.

"No, I checked."

"All right. Sit tight. I'll be right home."

"Acshully, I'm not at home. I'm still at the School Busch."

Did she just say "School Busch"? I checked my watch. "You're still there? I thought you were pretty much done when I left."

Silence.

Something was wrong.

"Aunt Abby? Are you all right?"

More silence, then, "Sorry, Darshy. I thought I heard something outside."

Aunt Abby sounded really weird. "Is there someone there?"

No response. "Aunt Abby! Are you alone? Are any of the other food truck people there?"

A long moment passed, then: "The other trucks look dark."

"Listen to me, Aunt Abby. I'm right across the street at Bones 'n' Brew. I want you to lock the door and don't open it or leave the bus until I get there, you hear?"

Nothing.

"Aunt Abby!?"

"Hurry, Darshy. . . ."

I hung up, alarmed at the way my aunt had sounded. The fact that she was alone, in her bus, with no one around, added speed to my step.

I was about to dash for the back door when I realized I'd almost forgotten about Livvy. She must have seen the look on my face and heard the urgency in my voice. "Is anything wrong?"

"Uh, no. But I have to run. I'll come by tomorrow, okay?"

She waved her hand around at the messy kitchen. "I'll be here, cleaning up all this crap."

I picked up my purse and ran across the semidark street to Aunt Abby's Big Yellow School Bus. The food truck area was completely dark, except for a glow from the School Bus windows. What had caused her to sound so odd? Had she seen a prowler?

A prowler who could also be a killer?

I approached the bus, glancing around for any sign of danger, then knocked on the door and called her name loudly. "Aunt Abby, it's me, Darcy!"

Seconds later the accordion doors opened. Aunt Abby stood at the top of the steps, her usually perfect hair disheveled, her eyes unfocused.

I started to enter the bus when I heard footsteps behind me. Without checking to see where they came from, I bounded inside and shoved the doors closed and locked them, my heart in my throat.

"Darcy?" a muffled voice outside called my name.

I peered out of a glass pane and saw a shadowy figure heading toward the bus.

A man in a black leather jacket stepped out from the shadows. He was carrying something long and thin and heavy looking in his right hand, but I couldn't quite make it out in the darkness. Then I saw the man's face.

"Jake!" I said breathlessly. I unlocked the doors and pulled the handle to open them.

"Sorry if I startled you. What are you two doing here so late?" he asked.

"Thank God!" I said, ignoring his question. "Come in! I think Aunt Abby needs help."

Jake stepped up into the bus, still holding what looked like some kind of heavy stick. He set the object on the stainless steel counter, pulled a paper towel from the holder, and wiped his hands.

"Gearshift broke," he said offhandedly, tossing the paper towel away. "So what's wrong with your aunt?"

I glanced over at her. She sat on a stool, looking dazed and mumbling under her breath. I lowered my voice, hoping she didn't hear me. "I'm not sure," I whispered to him. "She called me a few minutes ago and said she thought she heard a noise outside, but she sounded really strange. I thought maybe someone had been prowling around."

"I haven't seen anyone," Jake said.

"That's not all," I added. "The police called her. They want to see her again."

Aunt Abby picked up a coffee mug sitting nearby and took a long sip, then licked her lips.

"Let me have a look at her," Jake said. He approached her slowly. "Abby? Are you all right?" He spoke to her as if she were a child.

She nodded, sending her messy curls dancing. "I'm . . . fine."

Jake reached over and gently took the mug from my aunt's manicured hand. The words "The Coffee Witch" were printed on the side of the cup. Apparently Aunt Abby had stolen one of Willow's personalized ceramic mugs. Great. Now the SFPD could add "thief" to her rapidly expanding rap sheet.

Jake sniffed the contents of the mug, then set it down and eyed her, crossing his arms and causing his biceps to double in size. Apparently when he wasn't baking cream puffs, the guy worked out.

"Abby," he said.

"What?" Aunt Abby said, not meeting his eyes.

I glanced at the mug, sniffed it, then leaned in and took a good whiff of my aunt.

Her eyes met mine. "What? Why're you both starin' at me?" She reached for the mug and took another hit before Jake could stop her. After swallowing the mouthful, she blinked several times as if to clear her vision.

Her eyes were red spiderwebs, and her breath reeked! That wasn't coffee.

My aunt Abby was drunk.

My mouth dropped open as I turned to Jake.

"She's been drinking!" I whispered to him, not wanting Aunt Abby to overhear me, but she seemed too out of it to notice or care.

Jake grabbed a paper cup from the counter and filled it with water from the sink.

"Hey, Abby!" he said loudly, as if she were hard of hearing. He handed her the cup. "How about some water? You look a little tired. This should help."

"How is she going to face the cops like this?" I whispered. "She needs coffee!" I peered out the window but knew before I checked that the Coffee Witch was closed for the night.

"No worries," Jake said. "She's probably dehydrated. Water flushes out the alcohol and should sober her up pretty fast. Does she have any energy drinks? They usually have double the amount of caffeine as coffee. That might help her concentrate until her system is clear."

I thought about her upcoming interrogation with the police. Were they already on their way? "How long will that take?"

"Depending on how much she's had, probably an hour or so. But we don't know how long she's been drinking. Meanwhile we can keep her alert with the energy drink. Give her some crackers or a piece of bread."

"To absorb the alcohol?"

"No, that's an old wives' tale, but it'll slow the absorption process while the alcohol metabolizes. Hopefully it'll keep her from appearing intoxicated."

"How do you know all this?" I asked, surprised at his knowledge of alcohol effects.

"I handled a couple of DUI cases for my dad when I was an attorney. He was an alcoholic," he said matter-of-factly.

I could relate. I wanted to add that my dad was a pothead, but that wasn't something I shared easily like Jake had just done. I hoped addicted fathers weren't the only things we had in common.

"Yuck!" Aunt Abby said, pulling the proffered cup of water from her lips as if it were poison. "Tastes awful! Where's my coffee mug?"

"I don't know," I said, pretending to glance around. But I did know. The moment Jake brought her water, I had dumped out the remaining contents and placed the mug in the sink.

I pulled out an energy drink from the fridge. "Drink this, Aunt Abby. You can't let the police see you like . . . this."

"Like what? I'm perf'ly fine," she said, rising from her stool. After a brief sway, she sat down again.

"Aunt Abby," I said, trying to sound stern like my mother used to. "It's an energy drink. You need it."

She accepted the can reluctantly and took a swallow, then made a face. "Now I'm gonna hafta pee every half hour instead'a every hour like normal. Thanks a lot."

I turned to Jake. "Any chance you could stay here until the cops come? We could use a good lawyer."

Jake glanced away. "Uh . . ."

"Please? I have a feeling she's going to need more help than I can give her."

Jake ran his fingers through his sun-bleached hair. "First of all, I don't practice law anymore, remember? And secondly, I don't know what I can do to help."

I grasped his arm. "I'm sure you know a lot more about her rights than I do. I'm not asking you to represent her or anything, just help me protect her while they question her." I could hear the pleading in my voice and didn't like it.

Jake pursed his lips and nodded. "Okay, just give me a minute to lock up my truck and I'll be right back. But like I said, I don't know how much help I'll be."

I released his arm. "Thank you! I owe you one."

"I plan to collect." He smiled before leaving.

My imagination ran wild and I blushed. What exactly did he have in mind? Unfortunately, I didn't have time to fantasize at the moment.

"We'd better get goin'," Aunt Abby said. She stood up.

"Where?" I asked. "I thought the cops were coming here."

"No, I said I'd meet 'em at my housh."

"Oh, well, you're in no condition to drive, so I'll take you home. Get your stuff and we'll go when Jake comes back."

When Jake returned from his truck, we helped Aunt Abby off the bus, locked it up, and headed for my car, parked across the street in the Bones 'n' Brew parking lot.

"What's your car doing here?" Jake asked.

"Uh, I stopped by the restaurant to see if anyone knew anything about Oliver Jameson's death."

"Find out anything?" Jake asked.

I shook my head. I didn't plan to share my discoveries with anyone. At least, not yet.

I unlocked my car.

"Whoa," Jake said, looking over my tiny Bug. "I'm not sure I'll fit." He opened the door and held the seat forward for Aunt Abby to climb in back. At over six feet, Jake couldn't possibly fit in that small space, and even the front was a bit of a squeeze.

I pushed the ignition button, flipped on the blinker, then pulled into traffic.

"Don't drive so fast!" Aunt Abby called from the back. "You're making me carsick!"

Great. That's all I needed. Trying to push the vision of a vomiting aunt out of my mind, I turned to Jake. "Any idea what the police want with her this time? Could they arrest her?"

"No idea," Jake said, "but I doubt it. These days the police are really cautious about arresting someone unless they have enough solid evidence for the district attorney to pursue the case. They may read her her rights, but she won't have to answer any questions if she doesn't want to."

"Won't that make her look guilty?"

"It's her right—and the cops expect it. She can stop whenever she wants, but overall it's in her best interest to tell them what she knows and to be honest."

I glanced at my aunt in the rearview mirror, hoping it wasn't too late for honesty. After all, she'd lied about being in the restaurant yesterday afternoon—around the time that Jameson was killed. "Drink your Red Bull, Aunt Abby," I directed her. I watched her grimace as she reluctantly took another sip.

"If I drink any more, I'm gonna pee my pants," she snapped. At least she wasn't slurring her words so much anymore. Or threatening to throw up.

"Darcy," Jake said quietly. "Do you know if the police have something specific on your aunt?"

"Uh . . . no," I said as I turned onto Aunt Abby's street. Best not to tell him about her fingerprints unless I had to.

"Are you sure? Maybe they know something more about that fight she had with him before he died?" he asked.

"It wasn't a fight!" Aunt Abby interjected from the backseat before I could answer. Apparently she could hear us fine in spite of our whispering. "That rat threatened me! I was just defending myself!"

"Calm down, Aunt Abby." I glanced at her in the mirror. "Drink your Red Bull."

No one spoke as I pulled into Aunt Abby's driveway. I punched the ignition key, killing the engine.

Jake turned to me. "Unless they found some hard evidence that puts her at the scene or a witness, they really don't have a case. She might have had a motive, but it sounds like several other people did too."

Fingerprints? "Oh boy," I mumbled.

"What?" Jake asked.

It was time to confess. "Okay, well . . . there might have been fingerprints. . . ."

"What?" Jake said.

"I only touched a few things," Aunt Abby called from the back.

Jake turned around and frowned at her. "Like what?"

I saw my aunt shrug in the mirror. "Like I told Darcy, just some stuff on his desk when I went looking for something I could use against him to get him to shut up."

"In the legal profession, that would be called blackmail," Jake said somberly. "Did you touch anything else besides the stuff on his desk?"

"I don't know. His chair, maybe. I don't remember."

"Did you go anywhere else in the restaurant, touch anything else?" Jake asked.

Aunt Abby said nothing.

"Think, Abby," Jake insisted. No longer in his Dream Puff Guy persona, he now sounded like a real attorney.

Aunt Abby remained silent.

"Abby?" Jake prompted her.

"I guess I might have rearranged some things in the kitchen. Like his *mise en place*."

Jake looked at me for a translation.

"His prep stuff for cooking," I said. Then I remembered something Oliver's sister Livvy had said. She'd mentioned that she was the one who oversaw things and did some of the cooking. Was it her stuff that Aunt Abby had fooled with? And did that matter?

Jake shook his head at this latest confession. His frown deepened when he looked at me.

Aunt Abby leaned forward, her head between ours. "So should I pack a bag?"

Before we opened the door to the police, I gave Aunt Abby a handful of mints to cover her boozy breath and seated her in a kitchen chair, hoping she'd appear normal. Basil sat in her lap, and she petted him vigorously, as if giving him a dry shampoo. Jake sat next to her, no doubt planning to catch her if she happened to fall over.

"Hello, Detective," I said to Detective Shelton as he stood on the porch. "Thanks for coming." I glanced behind him to see if there were other officers with him but under the streetlight, I saw no one else in the parked white car.

"It's just me," the detective said. "May I?" he gestured toward the inside of the house. I opened the door wider to allow him entry.

"Of course!" I said. "Aunt Abby's in the kitchen. She's always cooking up something," I added with a nervous laugh. He followed me through the foyer to the kitchen.

I took a seat opposite Aunt Abby and indicated a chair at the head of the table for him. The detective eyed Jake suspiciously before sitting down. I wondered if Jake looked familiar to the cop.

"This is Jake Miller," I said, introducing him. "He's a close family friend." It was a small lie.

I turned to Jake and smiled. I was glad he was there. If only he'd brought a cream puff—I could really have used one at the moment. And maybe a sip or two from Aunt Abby's stolen coffee mug.

"Thanks for meeting with me again, Ms. Warner," the detective said after settling into his seat and pulling out his notebook and pen. "I just have a few more questions."

Basil growled at him. Aunt Abby resumed her shampooing. "Certainly, Detective." She batted her eyelashes flirtatiously. No doubt her libido had been loosened by the remaining alcohol still circulating through her body, but at least she wasn't slurring her words. "What would you like to know?"

He got right to the point. "Were you in Oliver Jameson's restaurant yesterday?"

Her hand froze on the dog.

Uh-oh, here it comes.

I shot a look at Jake and shifted in my seat.

"Yesterday?" she asked, as if trying to remember.

"Yesterday," the detective repeated.

"I may have been. It's not like I never went inside Bones 'n' Brew from time to time. Of course, the food was pig swill. I wouldn't be caught dead *eating* there."

Did she have to use that turn of phrase?

He drew in a patient breath. "And what about yesterday?"

Jake interrupted. "Aunt Abby, you don't have to answer any questions without an attorney present."

"You *are* an attorney, Jake," she blurted. "Besides, I have nothing to hide."

The detective stared at Jake. "Are you her legal counsel?"

"No, sir," Jake said, shaking his head and holding his hands up. "I'm just here as a family friend. I don't practice law anymore."

Detective Shelton nodded. "So you *were* an attorney, but now you're not."

Jake nodded but said nothing.

"I see," Detective Shelton said.

Really? What was that supposed to mean?

He turned to Aunt Abby. "Well, Ms. Warner, your 'family friend' here is correct. You do have the right to an attorney." I didn't like the way he emphasized the words "family friend." His sarcasm was clearly evident.

"I don't need a lawyer!" Aunt Abby exclaimed. "I'm innocent!"

The detective cocked his jaw. "Then let me ask you again: Did you go to the Bones 'n' Brew restaurant yesterday, the day of Oliver Jameson's death?"

She rolled her eyes upward, as if thinking. "Yesterday . . . yesterday . . . It was such a hectic day. Yes, I believe I did."

The detective raised an eyebrow, then made a note. "Why did you go there?"

Aunt Abby sighed. "I, uh, wanted to tell that jerk to stop bothering me. But he wasn't there."

"By jerk you mean Oliver Jameson," the detective said, jotting down another note.

"Yes," Aunt Abby said.

"How long were you there?" Detective Shelton asked.

Aunt Abby shrugged. "Only a few minutes. I looked around a bit. I thought maybe I could find something that proved he'd left a rat in my bus—or anything that would get him to leave me alone."

I put a hand on Aunt Abby's wrist, trying to stop her from talking too much.

"Why do you think he left a rat in your bus, Ms. Warner?"

"Isn't it obvious? He was trying to run all us food truckers out of business!"

She grasped the dog's fur. I squeezed her arm in an attempt to calm her.

The detective sat back and steepled his hands. "Ms. Warner, the crime scene techs found your fingerprints in Jameson's office—on his desk, his chair, his drawers—all around where the body was found. I'm going to ask you again, what were you really doing there?" He sounded less patient than when he'd first begun his questions.

"I told you. Snooping."

The detective jotted her comment on the pad in front of him. "And what did you find while you were *snooping*?"

"Nothing, unfortunately."

The detective took a deep breath and let it out slowly. The tension in the room was so thick, I could have cut it with a dull spatula.

"Ms. Warner, the techs also found your prints in the restaurant kitchen," he continued.

She shrugged. "I told you, I may have touched a few things in there too, but I didn't poison his soup, if that's what you're implying. What about his employees? I'll bet it was one of them, fed up with his bullying. Why don't you ask them?"

"We have. But none of their fingerprints were found on the soup bowl in his office."

"I never touched any soup bowl!" Aunt Abby said, nearly rising out of her seat. Basil yipped and she eased back down.

Was that a smirk I saw on the detective's face? "No, the bowl was wiped clean."

Aunt Abby looked visibly relieved at his words. But I knew it was a trick question.

"However, we're still looking for the container of bromethalin," the detective continued.

He watched her carefully, raising an eyebrow.

My heart skipped a beat.

Aunt Abby suddenly looked lost, as if she'd taken a detour on a strange road and had no idea where she was.

Jake rose. "I think we're done here, Detective. If you're going to charge her with something, do it. Otherwise, I'm going to ask you to leave now."

I could feel my toes go numb. Was this a good idea—challenging the detective like that? It felt as if Jake was practically begging the detective to take my aunt into custody.

The cop's phone rang.

I glared at Jake as Detective Shelton took the call. What had Jake been thinking?

"Shelton," the detective said, then paused and looked down at his notepad.

I watched the cop's face, wishing I could hear the voice on the other end. His eyes widened, then he swiveled in his chair, turning away from us. I heard him mumble into the phone: "Where?"

The hairs on my neck tingled. Had they found more evidence of my aunt's possible guilt?

The detective abruptly hung up the phone and looked directly at my aunt. I felt a flash of heat envelope my body.

This was it.

But instead of reading her her rights and whipping out a pair of handcuffs, he simply said, "Sorry to have bothered you, Ms. Warner." Then he closed his notepad, rose from his chair, and walked out, leaving the three of us stunned.

Chapter 8

The three of us remained slumped in our chairs for a few moments after the detective left, not sure how to react.

"What just happened?" I finally asked Jake, dumbfounded at the detective's sudden dismissal of my aunt and subsequent departure.

Jake shrugged and rose. "Apparently, the interrogation is over. No suitcase needed." When Aunt Abby started to get up, he reached over and helped her. She looked as dazed and confused as I felt.

"Why?" I asked, rising to my feet. "I mean, I'm thrilled he didn't take her away in chains, but I wonder why. It must have something to do with that phone call he got."

"Maybe telling the truth about being at the restaurant actually helped her case. Or maybe they caught the real murderer and that's what the phone call was about."

"Well, I say we lock the door before the detective changes his mind and comes back," Aunt Abby said.

"I'll take you to your truck," I said to Jake.

"I'll come too," Aunt Abby said. "I need a few things from the bus."

We piled into my car and headed back to Fort Mason. Aunt Abby hummed to herself in the backseat as we drove. Jake was quiet, and I caught him gazing out the passenger window, almost trancelike. I wondered what he was thinking

I wanted to grill Aunt Abby about the container of poison the police found that possibly had her fingerprints, but I decided to save my questions until we were alone. The less Jake knew, the better. Since he wasn't actually her lawyer, she and Jake didn't share attorney-client privilege, and as they say on TV, anything she said could be used against her in a court of law.

Curious as to what was on Jake's mind, I finally broke the quiet.

"Thanks again for your help," I said to him.

He nodded, still staring out the passenger window.

I tried again. "So why did you quit being a lawyer?"

He turned to me and frowned. "I didn't exactly quit."

"Really? I thought you said you gave up practicing law."

"I did. But not because I quit. I was . . . disbarred."

Oh my God.

The car swerved slightly in response to my surprise. Granted, I hardly knew Jake Miller, but he didn't seem like the shyster type to me. Then again, I hadn't suspected my ex-boyfriend of being a liar and a cheater either.

The question slipped out before I could stop myself: "What happened?"

His brows relaxed and a small smile broke through. "You sure get to the point, don't you?"

"I'm sorry. That was rude—and it's none of my business. Guess I went into reporter's mode. I'm just glad you were able to be there for Aunt Abby." I glanced at the mirror to check on my aunt. Her head lay back on the top of the seat and her mouth hung open like a dead fish's.

She was sound asleep!

Jake continued. "I did what I felt was right at the time, but the state bar thought otherwise."

"What did you do, if you don't mind my asking?"

He took a deep breath before answering. "I was a corporate securities attorney for a big firm. I discovered one of my clients—the head of a major corporation—was bilking investors out of their money. Kind of an Enron thing. Anyway, my client disclosed the privileged information to me in confidence."

"But you didn't keep it secret?"

"No, I told someone that I wanted to protect. One of the investors." Jake paused for a moment. "My girlfriend, actually."

Ah, so he had a girlfriend. I felt a wave of disappointment.

"Half of her portfolio was company stock, so I told her to pull out her money, as well as her parents' retirement nest egg."

I glanced at him, but he didn't look at me, just stared straight ahead. "That doesn't seem so bad," I said. "You stopped them from losing a lot of money."

"Yeah, well, I was indicted for securities fraud . . . disclosing insider information. The feds eventually dropped the charges, but they referred the case to the state bar. When the bar found out I had breached the attorney-client privilege, I was brought up on charges and eventually disbarred."

"Wow," I said. Remembering the reporter's oath not to disclose a source—even if it meant going to jail—I thought I probably would have done the same thing. Luckily, I'd never been put in that position. Most of my stories involved secret recipes, not secret knowledge.

"Couldn't you have gotten reinstated after a while?"

"I didn't even try. I actually felt relieved afterward, like a prisoner who's been set free. I never really enjoyed working in an office every day, wearing a suit, kissing up to clients, doing all that paperwork, tracking those billable hours. I used to bake when I was stressed—something my mom taught me. So when I lost my job, I decided to go into the dessert business, be my own boss, make people happy. Crazy, huh?" He finally looked at me.

I smiled at him. "Not crazy at all. Your cream puffs are so yummy! Almost better than sex," I blurted, then blushed. Did I just say that out loud?

He grinned at me, raising a speculative eyebrow.

I felt my face grow hot and sensed it was the color of a Dungeness crab's shell. I hoped he couldn't tell in the dim light of the streetlamps. "I just meant . . . you know . . . I'm glad you're making cream puffs now."

"Me too. I never thought losing everything—my career, my reputation, my girlfriend—would turn out to be the best thing for me."

My ears pricked up. "Your girlfriend? After all you did for her, you broke up?"

"Yeah. She dumped me for the prosecutor. At first I thought she was just kissing up to him to avoid becoming involved. But she ended up marrying the guy. Ironic, isn't it?"

Hmm, I thought wickedly. Perhaps there would be a lot more cream puffs in my future.

•

* * *

It was nearly eleven p.m. by the time we reached the food trucks at Fort Mason. I pulled the VW Bug into the area behind the food trucks and parked next to Aunt Abby's Toyota, figuring it was too late at night to get another ticket.

"Thanks again," I said to Jake.

"No problem. Wish I could have been more helpful. I'd recommend meeting with a criminal law attorney, to be on the safe side. I can put you in touch with a good one. Just let me know." He reached out and touched my arm, sending a jolt through me. Then he turned and headed for his cream puff truck.

I watched him for a few seconds before waking Aunt Abby. I helped her out of the car and followed her to her School Bus. She was unusually quiet as she picked up a few items and put them in a box. I wondered what was on her mind. She should have been relieved that the detective had let her go, but she seemed more preoccupied than ever. As she reached into a cupboard to retrieve some supplies, I had a thought. I pulled open the high cupboard overhead and peered inside.

"Aunt Abby, where's that container of rat poison that was here earlier?"

My aunt turned to me, her eyes wide. "It should be there. Why?"

"I don't see it."

"What do you mean? Let me look." She pulled up a stool and stepped on it to get a better view inside the cupboard. After moving around a can of cleanser, a bottle of disinfectant, and some bars of soap, she pulled her hand back, blinking those thick lashes several times.

"Aunt Abby? What's wrong?"

"The rat poison. It's . . . gone."

"Did you throw it away?"

"No . . ."

"Did you use it after I left this afternoon?"

"No! No! It was right there!" Her face flushed, she motioned toward the cupboard. "If the cops find it, covered with my fingerprints, they'll think I poisoned him with it. I think someone is trying to set me up!"

This was not good. Was it Aunt Abby's? Covered in her fingerprints?

"Jameson! It had to have been him. . . ." She drifted off, looking bewildered and glancing around the inside of the School Bus.

"You think he stole the poison from you and killed himself? That doesn't make sense." I looked at my aunt. "Aunt Abby, are you sure you didn't just misplace it?"

"Of course I'm sure!" she snapped. "I may be old, but I'm not senile. That container was there and now it's gone!"

If Aunt Abby's suspicions were right—that someone had somehow sneaked in and taken that box of poison—then it was quite possible that someone was trying to frame her for the murder of Oliver Jameson. But who would do that? And why?

I helped my aunt load up her car while I pondered the missing poison. Had she made other enemies besides Oliver Jameson? Granted, she was eccentric, but she wasn't malicious. Why would anyone want to get her into such serious trouble?

When she'd settled behind the wheel, I asked through the driver's window, "You sure you can drive?"

"Of course. I'm completely sober." I was pretty sure the alcohol had worn off, but I could tell that something still bothered her. Maybe the seriousness of everything that had happened was sinking in—not to mention this latest development regarding the missing poison. The only saving grace at the moment was the fact that she hadn't been arrested. But that didn't necessarily mean she was off the detective's suspect list.

"To tell you the truth," she said suddenly, "I'm a little worried about Dillon. I haven't heard from him for hours. It's not like him to disappear for so long."

"I thought you said he does this all the time."

"Yes, for short periods, but not this long. At least not without calling in. I hope nothing's happened to him—like before. . . ."

I assumed she was referring to his trouble with the university. He'd dropped out, moved home, and still didn't have a real job other than working at his mother's food bus.

"I'm sure you'll find him in his room when you get back home, working on some online project, oblivious to the outside world," I said.

Aunt Abby nodded, but I knew she wasn't convinced. Maybe she was right. Maybe something had happened to Dillon. What with all that was going on, anything was possible. The truth was, there was a killer on the loose, and no one would be safe until that person was caught.

"Are you sure you can drive yourself home?" I asked my aunt again. While she had sobered up from the alcohol, I wasn't sure about her emotional state.

"Of course, Darcy. I've been driving since I was fourteen. I'll see you at home."

Fourteen? Reluctantly, I waved her off and headed for my own car, parked a few feet away. At the moment it was blocked by the Meat Wagon delivery truck, so I glanced around for a sign of Tripp, the driver. It seemed awfully late for a drop-off, I thought, seeing no one.

I headed for the Road Grill truck next door, the Meat Wagon's usual customer. Suddenly I heard loud, heated voices coming from that vicinity. Alarmed, I stopped and pulled back behind Aunt Abby's bus. Slowly I peered around the corner.

Chef Boris was leaning out of the truck's service window and shouting at a skinny man in a black jacket, jeans, cowboy boots, and a knitted cap pulled over the top of his head. He was illuminated only by a light shining from inside the truck, but I saw the man's scruffy dark hair sticking out from under his cap, his ragged goatee, and his irregular sideburns.

Odd. What was Tripp doing dropping off a shipment of meat so late at night?

"I'm telling you, I'm done!" Boris said fiercely in his heavily accented voice. "I did what you wanted, and I'm finished. You got that? Done. Now, leave me the hell alone!"

Tripp leaned in toward Boris. I caught a glimpse of a toothpick protruding from his mouth. He pointed his finger at the chef but spoke so softly I couldn't make out his words. Then, reaching into the front of his jacket, he pulled out a package wrapped in butcher paper, about the size of a loaf of bread; he pushed it through the open window toward the chef.

"I said, no more!" Boris shouted. He shoved the package back. The delivery guy said something I still couldn't make out. Finally the chef snatched up the package.

"All right! But this is the last time. The last! Now, get out of here!" He slammed the window closed.

The delivery guy glanced around, no doubt checking to see if anyone had overheard them. I pulled back out of sight and ducked down, hoping he hadn't spotted me. From my vantage point, I could see his ornate cowboy boots as he stood outside the chef's window. The toothpick he'd been chewing on landed on the ground at his feet, followed by a wad of spit that caught the light. Moments later I watched as the boots moved around the side of Boris's truck and headed for the Meat Wagon truck.

I rose, hearing Boris's angry words ring in my head: *"I'm telling you, I'm done! I did what you wanted and I'm finished. You got that? Done. Now, leave me the hell alone!"*

So what had Boris "done" for the delivery guy? And why was Boris "finished" with whatever it was? I had a sneaking suspicion it had nothing to do with a meat delivery.

But did it have anything to do with Oliver Jameson?

I remembered Boris talking about receiving poison-pen letters he thought were from Jameson.

Was it possible that Boris murdered Oliver Jameson?

Surely not just because he'd received some letters. Letters, by the way, that *supposedly* were no longer available as evidence. Had Chef Boris really received such letters? Or was there something else behind Boris's dislike for Jameson?

Something that involved the deliveryman?

My cell phone rang, startling me out of my muddled murder theory. The "It's a Small World" theme song told me it was Aunt Abby.

I froze. Uh-oh. Had Tripp just heard the ringtone?

"Hello?" I whispered into the phone, still hiding behind Aunt Abby's bus.

"Darcy! Where are you?" Aunt Abby said, her voice strained.

"I'm about to leave here. Why? What's wrong? Where are you calling from?"

"Hurry, I need you!"

The line went dead.

"Aunt Abby?" I said into the phone. I cursed and slipped the phone back into my purse. Aunt Abby sounded as if she was in trouble—again. Was she already at home? If so, I needed to get over there before anything else happened to my poor aunt.

Checking to see if the Meat Wagon was gone, I peered around the corner—and froze again. The truck was still there. The driver's window was down, and in the dim light I caught a glimpse of Tripp's face. He was sitting in the driver's seat and staring in my direction, a frown creasing his brow.

He must have heard my cell phone ring.

That meant he probably knew I'd overheard him arguing with Chef Boris. I wondered if he knew what a big Disney fan Aunt Abby was. If so, he might have figured out who called me from the ringtone.

I peeked again. The window was up, and Tripp had started the motor. But before backing out, he turned to the passenger side.

Someone was in the truck with him.

I waited, hoping to get a glimpse of the passenger when Tripp finally pulled out. Instead, the passenger door opened, lighting up the interior of the delivery truck. To my surprise, Cherry Washington, Boris's assistant chef, stepped out and closed the door behind her.

Instead of returning to Boris's truck, she headed toward the overflow parking lot adjacent to the food truck area. Tripp opened the driver's side door. For a moment I thought he was going to come looking for me. Instead, he slammed the door shut and sped off. The sound of screeching tires filled the air.

So what was Cherry Washington doing with Tripp the delivery guy?

I didn't have time to think about it at the moment. Aunt Abby needed me.

I got in my car and drove to my aunt's Victorian home, arriving in record time.

"Aunt Abby?" I called after letting myself in the open back door. "Where are you?"

"In here," she called from down the hall. Her voice sounded raspy. "Dillon's room."

I headed for her son's room and found her sitting on Dillon's unmade bed, reading a note written on binder paper.

I eyed Dillon's pet rat, then went in cautiously, giving the cage a wide berth. Rats seemed to be a common theme with this family. "What happened? Where's Dillon?"

Her eyes filled with tears. "He's gone!"

"What do you mean, gone?"

Aunt Abby pulled a tissue from her pocket and wiped her nose. "He left this note. Something terrible has happened, I just know it." She held out the torn slip of paper for me to read.

Mom, got into a bit of trouble and have to lay low for a while.

I'll be in touch.

—Bugbyte

I looked up at her. "Bugbyte?"

"That's his avatar name."

I shook my head, puzzled at the message. "What kind of trouble is he in?" And how bad could it really be for a twenty-five-year-old man-child with no responsibilities? Was it nonpayment of student loans? Overdue cable bill? Video game addiction?

Aunt Abby glanced at Dillon's dark computer screens. "Darcy, there's something you don't know about Dillon."

Uh-oh.

"He didn't actually drop out of the university. He left because he was caught hacking into their computers. The truth is, he was being investigated by the FBI. I think he's in serious trouble this time."

"The FBI?" I said, stunned.

"He said he only did it to prove a point. He wanted to show the school officials how vulnerable their computers were. He was hoping to be hired as their IT guy. But the feds were called in and they didn't see things the same way he did. He was kicked out of school and placed on probation for a year. He's lucky he didn't go to jail. But he's not even supposed to go near a computer."

"Obviously he's ignored that," I said, rolling my eyes.

Fresh tears formed in Aunt Abby's eyes. "But this sounds even worse," she said, sniffling. "Now he's really disappeared!"

I rested a hand on Aunt Abby's shoulder. "You said he's done this before. Any idea where he might have gone?"

Aunt Abby shook her head. Tears spilled from her eyes. "I just hope he's all right."

I sat down next to Aunt Abby on the crumpled comforter and put my arm around her. "I'm sure he's fine. He'll probably check in soon. He's smart—at least, techwise. He'll figure out a way to deal with whatever the problem is. Who knows? Maybe the FBI or the DOD will hire him after all."

Aunt Abby pulled another tissue from her pocket and dabbed her eyes. "I hope he hasn't done anything really stupid. But whatever it was, I know he was only trying to help me."

I looked at Aunt Abby. "What do you mean? Does this have anything to do with Oliver Jameson?"

She pressed her lips together, then finally answered. "He . . . He said maybe he could remotely break into Jameson's personal computer and dig around, see if Jameson was hiding something. I told him not to do anything illegal. . . ."

Wow. Had Dillon actually hacked into Oliver's computer? More importantly, had he found anything? So what had caused him to disappear? And where the hell was he?

After reassuring Aunt Abby and putting her to bed, I returned to the RV and fell into my own bed like a zombie. Things would look better in the morning, my dad always used to say. Of course, he was high most of the time, which probably helped.

The theme song from *Jeopardy* woke me from my dream about food. The call wasn't from Dillon or Aunt Abby. I checked the caller ID but didn't recognize it.

"Hello?"

"Darcy?"

The warm, low voice was familiar. "Jake?" I smiled, then had a thought. How had he gotten my cell phone number?

"Are you all right?" he asked.

"Uh . . . sure. Why?"

"What about your aunt?"

"She's fine—as far as I know." I was growing alarmed. I decided to check on my aunt and grabbed my robe. "Why? What's wrong, Jake? You're starting to scare me. Is this about Dillon?"

Dead silence on the other end.

"Jake? Jake!"

"Sorry. Things are crazy over here. I just wanted to make sure you two were safe."

"Jake! What's going on?"

I heard him take a deep breath, then: "There's been another death."

Oh God, no.

"Dillon?" I whispered, praying I was wrong.

"Chef Boris. He's been murdered."

Chapter 9

When we arrived at Fort Mason at the crack of dawn, a crowd had already gathered around the perimeter of the police tape. The cops had cordoned off the area near Boris's truck, along with three trucks on either side of him, including my aunt's Big Yellow School Bus. Curious chefs and customers were being kept at bay, no doubt dying to know more about this second murder. All I knew was that Chef Boris had been murdered sometime during the night. I wanted to know more too.

While I was relieved that it hadn't been Dillon they'd found dead, I was still concerned about my nephew, and I knew Aunt Abby was too. He hadn't come home last night and there'd been no word from him this morning.

Where could he be?

Was there any chance it had something to do with him looking into the murder?

The parking area behind the food trucks was blocked by yellow police tape, and the adjacent lot was full, so I parked my car in the Safeway grocery store lot across the street and escorted Aunt Abby to the blocked-off area, now a crime scene. There was no sign of Jake, but I spotted Sierra and Vandy standing shoulder to shoulder outside the yellow caution tape. I headed in their direction to see if I could find out more information about Boris's death. Maybe they had heard or seen something suspicious before they left their vegan truck last night.

"Come on," I said, dragging my bewildered aunt by the hand. "Let's see if the vegans know anything."

"Oh dear," Aunt Abby mumbled as she trailed along. "This is not good. Not good at all."

Sierra turned around just as I stepped up beside her.

"What's going on?" I asked, playing dumb.

"Chef Boris was murdered last night," she said. She began chewing on a fingernail that had already been bitten to the nub.

"Wow," I said. "How was he killed?"

Sierra shrugged and glanced at Vandy. Vandy shot her partner an ambiguous look and began playing with the necklace around her throat. It was a picture of a cow inside a red circle with a line through it. On the back of Vandy's hand was a tiny tattoo—the letter *V*. For Vandy? Or for vegan?

I turned my attention to the activity behind the police line. Uniformed officers and a few men and women in suits were talking to one another, some holding baggies of what I assumed was evidence, others just guarding the crime scene. Even with his back to me, I recognized Detective Shelton immediately, dressed in a black suit and shiny black wingtips, his curly black hair hatless and glistening in the morning light. He appeared to be questioning someone, but his sizable frame blocked my view. When he finally shifted his weight, I caught a glimpse of his interviewee.

Jake Miller.

Dream Puff Guy looked as if he hadn't slept. He wore what appeared to be the same jeans and Dream Puff logo T-shirt he'd had on yesterday, and his blondish brown hair was disheveled. I wondered how long he'd been here.

"Why are they talking to Jake?" I asked Sierra. She pulled her fingernail away from her mouth long enough to answer. "I don't know. It seems like they're questioning all of us food truckers."

Out of the corner of my eye, I saw Vandy let go of the necklace she'd been playing with and nudge her partner. Sierra jerked her head around to face the woman. "What?" she snapped, clearly irritated.

Vandy shook her head. "Let's go! We don't have time to stand around here all day and wait for the cops to ask more questions."

"Then go!" Sierra barked.

Vandy's eyes narrowed. She abruptly turned and disappeared into the crowd of looky-loos. Sierra didn't watch her go, too interested in the goings-on by the trucks. She returned to her nail biting and continued to watch the crime scene drama.

"Any idea what happened?" I asked, hoping she'd talk more with her partner out of the picture.

"He was murdered, Darcy!" Aunt Abby piped up next to me. "Remember?"

I rolled my eyes. I was trying to play ignorant to gain more information from Sierra, but Aunt Abby hadn't caught on. I started to whisper to her, but she had already returned to her conversation with another gawker beside her.

I turned back to Sierra and smiled. "So, any idea how it happened? Or who did it?"

She shrugged and nibbled again on her nail. I wondered if fingernails were on the list of approved vegan foods. They were certainly organic.

"I heard he was killed right there in his food truck," came a voice behind me. I glanced back to see a teenage girl holding up her cell phone and taking pictures of the scene. I wondered how quickly she'd Instagram them and post them on Facebook.

"Prob'ly poisoned," said another bystander holding a Coffee Witch paper cup in his hand.

"How did you get that coffee?" I asked, dying for a much-needed jolt. "I assumed the Coffee Witch was temporarily closed."

He nodded at Willow's truck. Sure enough, it was just outside the cordoned area. Her line was at least twenty people deep. I'd have to get my Witch's Brew later when things died down—and see if I could find out what Willow knew about the murder.

"Poisoned. That's what I heard," said a hefty man nearby, talking into his cell phone and to the general crowd around him at the same time. "I knew these food trucks were health hazards."

"No, stabbed, I heard," came another rumor from a middle-aged man wearing a Giants baseball cap.

"Huh-uh," said the woman with him, wearing a matching Giants cap. "That black lady over there next to the cop—she said he was killed with a meat cleaver."

I looked over to see whom the woman was referring to. Cherry Washington, Boris's assistant, stood just outside the Road Grill truck, talking to a man in a suit. "You heard her actually say that?"

"Sort of," the woman said. "I read her lips."

Sierra shook her head, clearly disgusted by the wild guesses. She turned to me and said, "Obviously no one knows anything yet. The cops haven't told us what happened. They're asking a lot of questions, but they're not giving out any answers. It's been totally frustrating. I'd like to know when I can get back to work."

"Did the cops talk to you already?" I asked.

Sierra nodded. "Like I said, they asked a bunch of questions."

"Such as . . . ?" I prompted.

"The usual. Where were we between the hours of midnight and five a.m.? How well did I know Boris Obregar? Did I have any 'beef' with him—the cop's words, not mine. Did I know who might want him dead? Typical TV cop show stuff."

"What did you tell them?"

"The truth, of course," she said flatly. "Neither of us saw anything, heard anything, or had anything to do with this."

I noticed how aloof, almost angry, Sierra seemed. I wondered if it was the inconvenience of the murder and how it might affect her business. Or was it connected with that nudge/look Vandy had given her before she stormed off? I had a feeling Sierra wasn't sharing everything she knew. What could she be holding back?

"Who found him?" I pressed on.

"I heard it was Jake," she said, nodding toward Dream Puff Guy. He was still talking with Detective Shelton.

So Jake had found the body! He hadn't mentioned that when he'd called. Then again, maybe it wasn't the appropriate time.

"When did he find him?"

Sierra sighed. "I don't know. You'll have to ask him. All I know is this is going to suck for business. The Vegematic can't afford bad publicity, not the way things have been going lately."

Before I could ask her what she meant, I heard Sierra's cell phone chirp. She pulled her phone out of her pocket and read the text. "I gotta go." With a last glance at the crime scene crowd, she walked off in the direction her partner had gone.

That was odd. No, *they* were odd—Sierra and Vandy. It was clear I wasn't going to get any more information from the vegans at the moment. But I had a hunch those two were hiding something—I just wondered what it was.

I searched the crowd for other familiar faces, hoping I could glean a few more details about the crime. The murder had occurred right next door to my aunt's School Bus. If this was random, the victim could easily have been her. And if not, who knew? Maybe she was next on some killer's list.

I spotted Livvy Jameson from Bones 'n' Brew standing on the sidelines and away from the curious masses. Today she was wearing her chef's whites.

"Stay here!" I said to Aunt Abby, adding for emphasis, "Don't move!" My aunt nodded absently and returned to her conversation. I headed over to see Oliver Jameson's sister.

"Livvy?" I said, approaching her. She appeared to be

engrossed in the crime scene activities and hadn't noticed me until I said her name.

She turned to me looking puzzled, frowned, then smiled when she recognized me.

"Oh, hi. . . ." she said, no doubt searching for my name. I could tell she'd forgotten it.

"Darcy," I reminded her "We met yesterday when I came by your restaurant."

"Of course. Sorry. This whole . . . situation . . . It's been . . ." she stammered, then collected herself. "Well, it's all too familiar."

I nodded sympathetically. "I know how you must feel. First your brother, now Chef Boris. Any idea what happened?"

"Not a clue," she said. "What about you?"

"Not much," I lied. "Only that Boris was murdered."

"Well, his death shoots my theory all to hell," she said.

"You had a theory?"

She shrugged and continued to watch the crime scene area. "I thought Boris had something to do with my brother's murder."

I blinked, surprised at her revelation. "You thought Boris might have killed Oliver?"

"Boris hated Ollie," Livvy said. "Everyone around here knew that."

Odd. Boris was certainly unpleasant, but I thought Oliver was the one everyone hated, after all the things he'd done to the other food truck owners—including my aunt Abby. But as a reporter, I'd learned to ask questions, not give out my own theories.

"Why did Boris hate your brother?" I asked.

"Competition," Livvy said. "Boris was trying to run

Ollie out of business and corner the market with his bizarre meats. He accused Ollie of buying cheap cuts and calling them prime. I think he was afraid Ollie might get into the exotic-meat business in order to attract more customers."

I frowned, puzzled at this latest tidbit. "But I thought I heard Boris say that your brother had threatened *him*. He'd even written poison-pen letters telling Boris to move his truck elsewhere or he'd put him out of business—permanently."

Livvy stared at me, openmouthed. "That's ridiculous! Bones 'n' Brew is a landmark in this city. Everyone knows that! Ollie had no reason to threaten Boris, or anyone else. Yes, my brother could be surly at times—and stubborn—but that was just his personality. He was so much like our father. But it was Boris who was doing the threatening, not Ollie. I overheard him telling my brother that he'd get even with him someday."

Wow. This was a surprise. The pot was calling the kettle black. So who had really been threatening whom?

Livvy glanced at her watch. "Listen, I gotta get back. I still have a lot to do before we reopen." She started to go, then turned to me. "Will you let me know if you hear anything? Anything at all?"

"Of course," I said. She nodded, satisfied with my answer, and headed across the street to her restaurant. *Poor woman,* I thought. *Her brother is dead, and now another chef has been murdered*—one, she said, who had threatened Oliver. She had to be as interested in finding out the truth as I was.

I wandered back to where I'd left Aunt Abby but found her AWOL when I arrived. No surprise, really, knowing her attention span. I glanced at the crime scene area and saw Detective Shelton, but he was no longer talking to Jake. I wondered what Jake had told the detective. And what had he learned from the detective about the murder.

I was concentrating so hard on finding my aunt that I didn't notice someone running toward me until just before he rammed smack into me. He hit me hard, knocking the breath out of me. I slammed against the rough pavement, landed on my side, and gasped for air. As I fell, I managed to catch a glimpse of the man's shoes as he ran off: ornate black cowboy boots with gold trim and silver tips.

I'd seen those cowboy boots before. Tripp, the Meat Wagon guy.

Someone bent over and tried to help me up, but my shoulder ached and my arm stung from the pain. The woman helped me to a sitting position.

"Are you all right?" she asked.

I nodded, too winded to talk. After a few recovery breaths, I managed to whisper, "My arm . . ."

She and the man next to her eased me up to a standing position. I glanced at my arm and grimaced. My shirt was torn at the shoulder and blood had seeped through the cotton fabric where I'd scraped it on the pavement. Tiny dots of blood freckled my bare arm.

"You need to have that looked at," the woman said.

"That jerk who hit you didn't even stop to find out if you were all right," the man said.

"I'll be okay. Thanks for your help."

I had to find Aunt Abby and make sure she was all

right. From seeing those boots, I was pretty sure Tripp had knocked me down.

On purpose?

Why? I didn't know. But I had a feeling Aunt Abby might be in real jeopardy.

Chapter 10

I was suddenly panicked, and my heart raced as I scanned the area. Aunt Abby *had* to be here somewhere. I just hoped Tripp didn't get to her before I did—if that was his plan. Now I was certain that he'd overheard me talking on the phone last night. And that meant he knew I'd overheard *him* too, arguing with Boris only hours before the chef was murdered. He probably figured we'd be here, once we heard about the murder, and came looking for us.

Cradling my scraped and bloodied arm, I slipped through the crowd and made my way around the periphery of the crime scene. In spite of the fact that Aunt Abby probably couldn't hear me over the noise, I repeatedly called out her name and searched for her red curls in a sea of mostly brunettes, blondes, and baldies.

Finally I spotted her—in the last place I would have expected. Somehow she had made her way to the middle of the crime scene area and was talking to Detective Shelton!

I let out a sigh of relief. At least she was safe. But then another disturbing thought came to mind: What was she blabbing to the detective?

"Aunt Abby!" I yelled as I ducked under the caution

tape. I broke into a jog, ignoring the pain in my arm. "I thought I'd lost you! You were supposed to stay where I left you!"

Detective Shelton turned to me and said, "I called her over. I needed to talk with her." He paused and took a good look at me. After appraising my hurt arm, he raised his eyebrows in surprise. "What happened to you?"

"Uh, someone pushed me down," I said, holding my aching arm close to my chest. The bloodstain on my shirt had grown larger. "I'm fine, really." I turned to my aunt. "Are you all right?"

"Of course, Darcy," Aunt Abby said, frowning at my injury. "Better than you, it would appear. You're bleeding, you know." She pulled some tissues out of her purse and pressed them onto the wound. The bleeding had actually stopped, but dark red dots of drying blood covered the wound. Throbbing had set in, and it hurt to move my shoulder. Still, at the moment, there were more important issues than my scraped arm.

"You need to have someone look at that," Aunt Abby said.

I ignored her and said to Detective Shelton, "Listen, Detective, I have information you might be interested in."

"And what's that, miss?" the detective said. His condescending tone was clear. Whatever I had to say couldn't possibly interest him. Nodding at my tissue-covered arm, he added, "Your aunt is right. You need to get that looked at."

"I will!" I said, exasperated. "But I need you to listen! I overheard someone arguing with Chef Boris last night."

That got his attention. He studied me. "Really? Who?"

"It was one of his delivery guys. Tripp . . . something. After he and the chef argued, the guy left in his delivery truck."

"The Meat Wagon?" Aunt Abby asked.

I nodded.

"Yeah, that's Tripp," Aunt Abby added. "Shaggy looking. Needs a haircut and a bath and some teeth whitener and dental work and—"

"Got a last name?"

Aunt Abby shrugged.

"What did they argue about?" the detective asked me.

"I'm not sure exactly, but I heard Boris say something like he was done with whatever it was he was supposed to do. I couldn't hear the delivery guy very well—he mumbled, had a toothpick in his mouth—but he gave Boris a wrapped package about the size of a man's shoe. At first Boris refused to take it, but then he did, and then he slammed the window shut, and then Tripp left." I had to take a deep breath after getting all that out.

Detective Shelton clicked his pen. "When did you say this was?"

"It must have been around eleven or so. I was headed for my car when I heard them talking."

"And how were you able to see and hear all of this?" The detective eyed me.

"Uh . . . I was sort of standing behind my aunt's School Bus."

"Sort of standing?"

"Well, listening. And kind of hiding . . ."

"Eavesdropping," the detective confirmed.

I nodded and felt myself blush.

"Did he say anything else?"

"That's about it. After I hid, all I could see were Tripp's fancy cowboy boots."

"Cowboy boots?" The detective clicked his pen again.

"Yes. I was kneeling on the ground behind the bus and I could see the boots from underneath. Really fancy ones, with gold trim."

"The boots were under the bus?"

"No! They were on the *other side* of the bus, but I could *see* them from where I was kneeling."

Detective Shelton pursed his lips. I had a feeling I was losing credibility. "What about Obregar?" he asked.

"As far as I know, Boris was still in his food truck."

"Did you see or hear anything else?"

"Yes," I said. "There was someone else in Tripp's truck."

"Who?"

"Cherry Washington. She's Chef Boris's assistant."

"Cherry?" Aunt Abby said, eyes wide with surprise. I knew my aunt and the woman were casual friends.

The detective wrote something on his pad. "That's it?"

"Yes. I mean, no! I think the guy who knocked me down a few minutes ago was Tripp, The Meat Wagon guy."

Aunt Abby blinked several times. "Oh goodness, Darcy!"

"Why do you think that, miss?" the detective asked.

"Well, I'm not absolutely positive it was him, since I didn't actually see his face when I fell. But like I said, I did see his cowboy boots as he ran off. They were black with gold trim. Very ornate."

"You think they belong to this Tripp?" the detective asked.

"I'm pretty sure."

Detective Shelton frowned. "Why didn't you tell me right away about this guy bumping into you? He's probably long gone by now."

"I . . . I was worried about my aunt. I thought she might have gone off looking for her son—ouch!"

I shot a look at Aunt Abby. Had she just kicked me in the back of my ankle? On purpose?

The detective looked at me curiously. "Is something wrong?"

After giving Aunt Abby the stink eye, I shook my head. I wanted to reach down and rub my aching ankle, but I sucked it up. Apparently, my aunt didn't want me saying anything to the detective about Dillon's sudden disappearance.

"Well," he said, closing his notebook, "Thanks for the information. I'll contact you if I have any more questions."

"That's it?" I asked, surprised at his lackluster response.

"I'd advise you both to be careful," he added.

"Detective," Aunt Abby said, "do you think Tripp Saunders came back and killed the chef?"

He shrugged. "We really don't know what we're dealing with yet, Ms. Warner, but if the same guy who killed Jameson also murdered Obregar, he may kill again. You should keep your bus locked and your eyes open." He turned to leave.

"Just one more question," I said, catching him before he escaped. "How exactly did Boris die?"

"Sorry, I can't give out any more information." He shook his head and walked away. Apparently this question-answer thing was a one-way street.

Aunt Abby and I headed for the crime scene tape and ducked under it, freeing ourselves from the cordoned area. Just outside the periphery, Aunt Abby leaned over and whispered, "I know how Boris died."

I looked at her. "What? How?"

"Blunt-force trauma caused by bludgeoning—a blow to the head. They won't know for sure until they do an autopsy and see how localized the damage was."

Blunt-force trauma? Autopsy? Localized damage? My aunt had been watching too many CSI shows. "How do you know all this?"

Her eyes twinkled as she pointed to a young uniformed officer behind the yellow tape who was keeping curious onlookers from breaching the crime scene. "See that hunk over there? He said I remind him of his grandmother."

"Oh my God, Aunt Abby! You were shamelessly flirting, weren't you? What did you say to him?"

She smiled. "Oh, I just asked him what was going on and told him I was a possible witness. Then I chatted him up for a few minutes, told him I owned the Big Yellow School Bus next to Boris's truck. I offered him a complimentary grilled-crab-and-cheese sandwich next time he was in the area; then I batted my eyelashes at him and asked if he thought I had anything to worry about, what with a murderer on the loose and all. He sort of let the details slip out."

Whoa. My aunt was more devious than I ever imagined. I could learn from her.

"Did he tell you what the weapon was?"

"Not yet. But wait until he tastes my cooking. . . ." She grinned and batted those Kewpie-doll eyelashes again.

"Aunt Abby, you're shameless!"

"I know, but enough talk about me. You need to have that arm cleaned and bandaged. Let's go to the Safeway across the street and pick up some first aid supplies, since I can't get into my bus at the moment. I'll have you fixed up in no time."

As we headed for the store, I imagined all the kitchen equipment a murderer could use to off somebody like Boris—a tenderizing hammer, a meat grinder, a lead-filled rolling pin . . .

I shuddered.

The list seemed endless.

Aunt Abby shopped for supplies while I went to the restroom and gently washed my arm. She arrived moments later and took on nursing duties, patting the affected area with antiseptic, which stung, applying some sort of salve, which numbed the pain, and wrapping my arm with gauze and tape. When she was finished, we headed for my car.

As we crossed the street, I spotted my ex-boyfriend, Trevor the Tool-Head from the *Chronicle*. We'd broken up a few months ago, after I found out he'd cheated on me with my competitor at the "other" newspaper. At the moment, he was talking to one of the officers on the sidelines. What was he doing here?

"Wait a minute!" I said, and took a sudden detour, pulling my aunt by the hand.

"Where are we going?" she asked. "I need to look for Dillon!"

"I have to talk to someone."

I waved to Trevor to catch his eye. We'd been cordial,

since we both worked at the newspaper and had to get along, but it was all fake on my part, and probably his too. He held up a finger, telling me to wait a minute, wrote something down in his reporter's notebook, then thanked the cop and headed over to where I stood a few feet away.

"Darcy!" he said with a false grin. "So good to see you! What are you doing here?" He tried to hug me, but I stiffened, and he got the message and moved back.

"You too!" I lied. I could outfake him anytime, anywhere. But I had to admit, he still looked every bit the rugged journalist in his comfy jeans, button-down camp shirt, and well-worn athletic shoes. Tall, tan, and lean, he always appeared camera ready, like one of those intrepid reporters who covered dangerous missions in war-torn countries. For some reason, he'd never made it to the big leagues, and to his dismay he continued to cover local news. I wondered how many other reporters he'd cheated on over the years.

"So, Trevor," I said, crossing my arms in front of me, "are you reporting on the murder?"

"Yeah, this is going to be a big case," he said, brushing his tousled hair off his forehead. "I can smell it. It might be my ticket to the front page." He reached out a hand and placed it on my shoulder. "Hey, sorry about you losing your job. Have you found anything yet? I hear there are openings at that little online weekly."

The lack of sincerity in his voice was clear. My pride kept me from telling him I was working for my aunt in her food bus. I changed the subject.

"I saw you talking to that cop," I said. "Did you find out anything about the murder?"

He eyed me suspiciously. "Why? You trying to scoop my story and sell it to the *Examiner*?"

I forced a laugh. "No, no, I'm working on a book now."

"Really? A novel? Something literary, no doubt."

I so wanted to slap the smug off his face. Instead, I forced a smile. "A cookbook, actually. I've collected a lot of recipes over the years doing this job. But back to the murder. Did the cop tell you anything?"

"Why do you want to know?" Trevor asked, raising an eyebrow.

"Just curious. Must be the reporter in me. Plus, my aunt knew the dead guy." I nodded toward Aunt Abby.

Tripp looked at my aunt, then frowned. "Nothing much. They're being very closemouthed about it, keeping it under wraps, you know."

Yeah, sure, I thought, laughing inside at his verbal clichés. His writing wasn't much different. But he made his point—he had no intention of telling me anything.

Well, two could play that game.

"That's what I heard too. But my aunt was talking to some of the other food truckers and she heard the guy was hit over the head with something heavy."

It didn't take ESP on my part to figure out "bludgeoned to death" meant "hit over the head with something heavy."

Trevor took another look at Aunt Abby and asked, "How did you get that information? Who's your source?"

"Oh, I don't want to get anyone in trouble," Aunt Abby said, smiling sweetly. I'll say one thing for her—she caught on fast.

"Okay, listen," Trevor said, leaning in conspiratorially. "I'll tell you what I know—*if* you'll give me a name."

I glanced at Aunt Abby. She nodded.

"You first," I said. "How exactly did Boris die?"

He glanced around at the milling crowd and lowered his voice. "This is what the cop told me. They think Obregar left his truck for a few minutes, probably for a bathroom or coffee break. His assistant, Cherry"—he looked at his notes—"Washington. She was gone for the night. When he came back, he must have discovered someone inside waiting for him. Cops found the place turned upside down. They think the killer was going through Obregar's stuff, but they don't know why. When Obregar caught him, the killer grabbed a can of ground pepper and threw a handful at the chef's face, blinding him. Cops found pepper all over him. They figured the chef bent over, probably in pain; then the killer beaned him."

"With what?" I asked, picturing a meat hammer or even a small appliance.

"Get this," Trevor said, almost laughing as he spoke. "It was some kind of frozen animal! The cop wouldn't say what exactly, but they found a wrapped-up package of meat lying next to him on the floor when Obregar was discovered. Bizarre, right?"

I hadn't seen the morbid streak in Trevor when I was dating him. Interesting what a murder will bring out in someone.

"You sure it was meat?" I asked, remembering the package Tripp had passed to Boris.

"Yep. Pretty clever."

Not so clever that Roald Dahl hadn't already used that method in one of his books. Alfred Hitchcock had even featured a similar story in his TV show. A leg of lamb, I think it was. The murderer cooked it and served it to the police investigating her. Talk about clever.

"That's it?" I asked.

"Hey, that's a lot," Trevor said. He flipped a page of his notebook, ready to take down my words. "So spill your intel. Who's your source? And I'll want a number."

This time I leaned in and lowered my voice. "Call Wellesley Shelton. He's full of 'intel.' You can reach him at the SFPD, or dial nine-one-one."

I took Aunt Abby's hand, and we made a hasty retreat to the Coffee Witch. I could only imagine the angry look on Trevor's face as I left him standing there with his open notebook.

After all the times he'd lied to me, it served him right. They say revenge is best served cold—as in cold-blooded. They were right.

Chapter 11

"That wasn't very nice, Darcy," my aunt said as I led her to the Coffee Witch for a jolt of caffeine. She protested, saying she wanted to search for Dillon, but I told her he'd show up when he was ready. Besides, it was around eight thirty and I needed the caffeine. Plus, my aunt could use the distraction.

"You don't know Trevor, Aunt Abby. I wasted two years of my life with him before I realized it was all about him. He'll do anything to get a story, even step on his own girlfriend. I just outsmarted him this time, but I'm sure he'll get even somehow. He's not one to forget when he's been dissed."

"I always thought he was kind of cute. But looks can be deceiving, I guess."

"You got that right," I said. What I didn't say was that my aunt's innocent face also hid another side of her personality. Beneath that Betty White smile and those Shirley Temple dimples lay a savvy senior citizen with a mind as sharp as a kitchen knife.

"Well, I think he's still sweet on you. After all, you're the one who broke up with him. I'm sure he carries a torch for you."

"Oh God, please, Aunt Abby! The only person he's sweet on is himself."

Aunt Abby looked at me with those twinkling eyes. "Speaking of being sweet on someone . . ."

I shot her a glance. "What?"

My aunt shrugged. "I'm just saying, you've been eating a lot of cream puffs lately."

"Are you saying I'm getting fat?"

Aunt Abby gave me a sly grin. "You know what I mean."

"Listen, I'm not ready to even think about anyone in a romantic way, Jake Miller included."

"Uh-huh," Aunt Abby said.

"Stop it! I just happen to love his cream puffs."

"I noticed." Aunt Abby stepped into the coffee line behind a half dozen other caffeine addicts.

"You're . . . despicable!" I said, quoting Daffy Duck, only without the lisp. It was the only word I could think of at the moment, and it fit her perfectly.

Several coffee worshippers around us eyed me as if I'd just confessed to murder. Aunt Abby flashed them a toothy smile. I wanted to wipe that silly grin off her face, but I bit my tongue, afraid the mob nearby would accuse me of elder abuse. She was *so* working this innocent act.

"Speaking of Jake," my aunt said, "I wonder where he's disappeared to. I haven't seen him since he finished talking with the detective."

"Yeah. I wonder what he learned from his chat with Detective Shelton," I added. "Maybe he went back to his cream puff truck."

"No," Aunt Abby said, shaking her head. "The cops aren't letting us back in yet. I don't know how they expect us to make any money, but they're taking their sweet time removing that crime scene tape. Those crab mac and cheeses don't make themselves, you know."

I turned to her. "So what did you tell the detective when you talked to him?"

"Just that I was home at the time of the murder," she said with a casual wave of her hand.

Home alone, I thought. *With no alibi. Again.* I wondered how she remained so unconcerned.

"Nothing else?" I asked, sensing there was more behind her casual attitude.

She sighed. "He told me he'd have more questions for me later, but I really don't know what else I can tell him."

"Any chance he told you who found the body?" *Like Jake Miller?*

She shook her head and moved forward with the line.

"He asked me if I had any idea who killed Boris. I mentioned the poison-pen letters he'd received. I told him that if he found the writer of those letters, he'd probably have his murderer."

The back of my neck prickled. "What did he say to that?"

"He said anyone could have sent those letters—even me."

Great, I thought. My aunt still wasn't off the hook. Before I could respond, we reached the front of the line and Willow the Coffee Witch was asking for our orders. I ordered a Spirited Mocha—two shots of espresso—and turned to my aunt. "What would you like?"

"Do they have Sanka?"

I frowned at her. "No, Aunt Abby. They only have real coffee. How about a Cara-Magical-Cino or something?"

"That's just an overpriced chocolate milk shake," she replied.

I returned my attention to Willow. "She'll have that magical one. Make it decaf, please."

"Now it's an overpriced *impotent* chocolate milk shake," Aunt Abby grumbled under her breath.

While Willow made our drinks to order, I turned back to Aunt Abby. "Think for a minute. Did the detective say anything more about how Boris was killed or what exactly happened?" I wanted to see if she could confirm the information I'd already learned.

"No, but while we were talking, one of the technicians brought over something in a plastic lunch bag and showed it to the detective. Said she found it in the trash."

A chill ran down my back. A clue? "Did you see it?"

Aunt Abby nodded. "When she held it up, it looked like a small container. I couldn't read the label, but—"

Willow reached through the window and handed me my extra-spirited drink along with Aunt Abby's impotent potion. I took both of them, paid, and led my aunt to one of the benches nearby. We sat down and I gave Aunt Abby her "coffee."

"But what?" I said, after taking a sip of the soothing hot coffee mixture. I felt my insides wake up.

"What?" Aunt Abby said, licking the froth from her lip after several gulps of her chilly drink.

"You were saying something about what they found."

"Oh yes. I said I couldn't read the label, but it had a skull and crossbones on it. I assume it was some kind of poison."

The warmth inside me turned cold.

Poison?

I remembered that Aunt Abby's container of rat poison had gone missing from her truck. What were the odds it was the one the tech had found in the trash? If it was hers, then it probably had her fingerprints all over it.

So how did it end up in the nearby Dumpster?

I sipped my coffee, but suddenly it tasted like poison and I set it down. While Aunt Abby had no trouble slurping down her drink, we sat in silence and watched the police and technicians continue to do their work. I noticed the crowd that had gathered earlier had dissipated considerably, probably because the drama was over and the cops were being tight-lipped about the details—except to my aunt, who seemed to know all kinds of confidential information.

A man holding a small paper bag and a newspaper sat down next to me on the bench. He looked like one of the several homeless people who shuffled around the area, hoping for monetary handouts from the tourists and leftover morsels from the food trucks. He wore a tattered and dirty Columbo-style trench coat over baggy jeans, and a frayed Giants baseball cap adorned his head. A pair of taped-together sunglasses covered his eyes and a scraggly two-day growth of stubble seemed more a shaving oversight than a deliberate style statement. When he coughed, it was all I could do not to run away from the germs he'd just expelled.

Then I looked down at his feet.

It was the shoes that gave him away: Reef thongs. The kind with the hidden church key in the sole.

"Oh my God! Dillon!" I blurted.

Aunt Abby looked over. "Dillon?" she repeated, blinking as if to clear her eyes.

"Shhh!" Dillon hushed us, then glanced around. "I'm undercover. I don't want anyone to recognize me."

I almost laughed at his cloak-and-dagger disguise. All he needed were some Groucho glasses and a fake mustache to complete the look. "What are you *doing*?" I asked, shaking my head.

Aunt Abby got up and moved to the other side of the bench to sit next to him. "Dillon! Where have you been?" she whispered loudly. "You had me frantic! And why are you dressed like a hobo?"

"I don't want the cops to see me."

"Then why are you here?" I asked, relieved he was okay but still amused at his getup. "The cops are crawling all over the place. There's been another murder—right next door to your mom's bus. She's been worried sick!"

"I know. That's why I'm here," he said mysteriously.

"What do you mean, you 'know'?" I asked.

"I heard it on the police scanner."

"You have a police scanner?" I asked.

He nodded and pulled out his cell phone. "There's an app for that."

Of course. If only I had the "Solve a Murder" app.

"So you must know what happened to Chef Boris," Aunt Abby said to him.

He took my coffee from my hand and downed a gulp, then made a face as if he'd tasted a lemon. "How can you drink this stuff?"

"It's better than those energy drinks you pour down your throat," I said, taking back my coffee, even though I didn't have the stomach to finish it. "Dillon, what's going on with you? Does your recent disappearance have anything to do with Chef Boris's death?"

"God, no! Are you psycho?" He pulled down the sunglasses and looked at me as if I were crazy. I'd gotten a lot of odd looks today.

I shrugged. "No, but I'm beginning to wonder if you are."

"I've been doing some undercover work on the Net," he explained, his voice low.

"What did you find out?" Aunt Abby said, leaning in.

"Well, it seems that Chef Boris has a little history."

My skin prickled. "Like what?"

"Like he's got a record," Dillon said.

Aunt Abby's eyes lit up with excitement. "What did he do? Was it murder?"

"No," Dillon said. "But he spent time in prison a few years ago for dealing drugs."

I sat back. It wasn't the bombshell I thought it might be. Then again, drug dealing wasn't exactly nothing. Did Boris's past life have something to do with his murder? Maybe he was back in the business again, selling drugs through his food truck, and things went sour, as they say on TV.

But if that were true, how did it tie in with the death of Oliver Jameson?

Before I could ask more questions, someone tapped me on my shoulder. I jumped a foot, wrenching my sore arm and shoulder, and cried out in pain.

"Sorry, Darcy. Didn't mean to scare you."

"Jake!" Aunt Abby said. "We've been looking for you. Where did you disappear to?"

I rubbed my sore shoulder. Out of the corner of my eye, I noticed that Dillon had slunk down, like a turtle trying to pull its head into its shell. He was staring at the ground.

"Dillon?" Jake said, peering at him.

I laughed. "What, the 1950s spy disguise didn't fool you, Jake?"

Dillon looked up from under the brim of his ragged cap and glared at me.

"Shh," I said, mocking Dillon's earlier attempt to remain undetected. "He's undercover."

"Shut up, Darcy!" Dillon said. "This is serious! If the feds find out I've been hacking again, I could go to prison for a long time. I'm just trying to help my mom. Jeez."

I hung my head apologetically. "I'm sorry, Dillon. It's just that you look so funny in that disguise. Maybe next time you could lose the Columbo trench coat and Giants baseball cap, and wear a Sherlock Holmes cape and deerstalker hat. To tell you the truth, it was your shoes that gave you away. Reef sandals? Seriously?"

"Jake," Aunt Abby interjected, "Dillon was just telling us about Boris Obregar's criminal history. Did you know he was a—"

"Drug dealer?" Jake said, finishing her sentence and stealing her thunder. "Yeah. I have a friend who's a cop. He mentioned it."

Dillon looked downright crestfallen to hear that Jake already knew about Boris. All that work illegally hacking the Internet, risking arrest and imprisonment, and Jake had gotten the information from a cop friend.

"Well, that's not all I learned," Dillon huffed. "Did you know his assistant, Cherry Washington, has been in and out of rehab for years?"

Jake shook his head. "Interesting. I don't know her that well, but a frequenter of rehab facilities working for a former drug dealer doesn't sound like a good mix. I assume the police talked to her."

Judging from the blank faces, it appeared no one knew. I wondered if Cherry might have a motive to kill Boris but had no idea what it might be. And again, what was the connection to Oliver Jameson? Did he have anything to do with dealing drugs?

"Jake, what else did your cop friend have to say?" I asked.

"Only that he heard Boris was killed with a hunk of frozen meat from his own freezer," Jake said. He eyed me. "You don't seem surprised, Darcy."

"She already knew that," Aunt Abby said. "Her old boyfriend told her."

"Old boyfriend?" Jake asked, raising an eyebrow.

"Ex-boyfriend. Trevor O'Gara," I said.

"He's a hotshot reporter at the newspaper," Aunt Abby added. "Apparently he found out about the weapon from one of the cops at the scene."

"Hardly hotshot," I mumbled.

Jake said nothing.

Hmm, I thought. Was there a hint of jealousy in those dark brown eyes? Maybe Aunt Abby was right. Maybe Jake didn't give out his special cream puffs to just every girl. Or maybe I was reading way too much in those eyes of his.

"Oh, I almost forgot!" I said, breaking out of the brief daydream. "So did your cop friend happen to know who found the body?"

"Nope," Jake said. "But I do."

"Who?" Dillon asked.

I waited for Jake to confirm the rumor.

He pressed his lips together, then said, "You're looking at him."

Less than an hour later the police tape was lifted from around the perimeter of the food trucks. The only tape that remained circled Boris's Road Grill truck. Aunt Abby and Jake returned to their mobile businesses to prep for customers who still lingered in the area. As a former reporter, I knew that news like a murder can work two ways. The notoriety can taint businesses and even kill them, or the publicity can attract customers and make the businesses flourish. We'd have to see how the food trucks survived after the double homicides, but my guess was the vendors would have a record sales day. There's nothing like a taste of crime to bring out the hungry ambulance chasers and thirsty rubberneckers.

Naturally, Dillon disappeared again, claiming he had more "investigating" to do, but he promised to keep in touch so his mother wouldn't worry. I spent the rest of the day helping Aunt Abby by taking orders from the onslaught of the festival crowd. By seven o'clock, my feet hurt from standing, my neck ached from craning out of the School Bus window, and my arm throbbed from the pain of my earlier fall, giving me little time to ponder the murders. But by the time I got back to the RV, my mind was spinning like a whisk with all that had happened.

My reporter habits kicked in, and my first thought when I arrived home was to write up what I knew. The events over the past couple of days were a story waiting to be told. In fact, I thought if I could scoop Trevor and find out why the two men were murdered, I could write it up for the *Chronicle* and maybe get my old job back. At the very least I'd be paid a much-needed wad of cash for being first with the news.

I poured myself a glass of bargain merlot and opened my laptop. I'd spent so many years writing restaurant reviews, I was afraid I'd lost my touch for front-page headliners. But I was no crime writer; I was a food critic. Did the two have anything in common? Could I gather the ingredients for a good story, build it into a compelling, step-by-step narrative, and actually have it turn out as meaty as a perfectly grilled filet?

Or was I so rusty it would be more of an undercooked pile of mush?

My phone rang, disrupting my vision of an above-the-fold byline.

"It's a Small World." Aunt Abby.

"Darcy? Come in the house! The cops are here!" She hung up before I could say hello.

I glanced out the back window of the RV and saw the back of a black-and-white car parked in front of Aunt Abby's house.

Uh-oh.

I rushed out of the RV and around the side of the house to the front, where I found not one but two cop cars. Two officers from each car were getting out of the official vehicles.

"What's going on?" I called to them.

One of the officers had a hand on the gun that hung from his belt. His other hand rested on the handcuffs that dangled down. He looked like he was ready for anything.

Receiving no answer, I said again, "What are you doing?" My voice rose as panic set in.

"Step back, ma'am," the officer next to him said. He raised a warning hand, gesturing for me to halt.

I tried to scramble up the steps ahead of the two officers, but the second cop stopped abruptly and I bumped into him, hitting my sore arm.

"Ouch," I cried out, cradling my arm.

"Stand back," he said again, this time more forcefully.

I took a step back. "Wait a minute! This is my aunt Abby's home. What do you want with her?"

Even as the words came out of my mouth, I had a feeling why they were there. That container of poison they'd found in the trash behind Boris's truck earlier. I was sure it had my aunt's fingerprints all over it.

Keeping my distance, I followed the two officers to the front door, while the other two stood back by their cars.

"This is harassment!" I said, blurting out the first thing that came to mind. "I'm calling my lawyer!"

Ignoring me, the first cop pounded on the door. "Police! Open up!" he commanded.

Seconds later Aunt Abby appeared at the door. She looked as white as cake flour. I stepped around the cop and stood next to my aunt, who seemed about to faint.

"Can't you leave her alone? She's innocent!" I said.

The first cop turned to Aunt Abby. "Are you Abigail Warner, the owner of this house?"

Eyes as wide as saucepans, Aunt Abby bit her lip and gave a slight nod.

"We have a warrant to search your home." He looked at the second cop, who held up a handful of papers.

Aunt Abby slowly took the papers and scanned them. She gazed up at the cops with tears in her eyes.

"Step aside, ma'am."

Aunt Abby did as she was told, but I didn't move from my spot.

"What are you looking for?" I cried as the two officers stepped around me and entered the foyer.

Cop number two nodded toward the sheaf of papers Aunt Abby held limply in her hand. Her hand fell open and the papers floated to the floor. I knelt down to gather them up and froze. While one of the sheets was indeed a warrant to search Aunt Abby's home, the other caught me by surprise.

I looked up at the officer, shaking my head. "What the hell is this?"

"That is an arrest warrant for Dillon Edward Warner."

Chapter 12

"Dillon?!" I said, not expecting this turn of events at all. "But . . . but . . ."

But what? I'd been so ready to defend my innocent aunt, I had nothing to say about my cousin.

The two cops shouldered past us and began searching the house. While we waited in the foyer, I whispered to Aunt Abby, "Do you know where Dillon is?"

She shook her head and twisted the ring on her finger. "I haven't seen him since I left Fort Mason. He wasn't here when I got home."

Worry lines creased her forehead, and I squeezed her hand, trying to comfort her. I knew she was concerned about her son, but this time I was glad he'd gone missing. Was this about Dillon's computer hacking? After all, that was the reason he gave for going AWOL and wearing a disguise.

Or did it have something to do with the murders?

Of course not! What was I thinking? Dillon had been using the Internet to find out more about the two victims so he could help his mother.

So what did the police want with him?

The two officers emerged from Dillon's room, carrying what looked like most of his computer equipment. In spite of everything he had, I'd only seen him use his laptop, which he carried with him everywhere. At the moment, that laptop didn't appear to be among the stuff the cops had confiscated.

No doubt Dillon had it with him. And hopefully there wasn't anything incriminating on the computers he'd left behind. Surely Dillon was too smart for that.

Or was he?

After the police headed out the door with their loads, I turned to Aunt Abby and whispered, "Any idea what they're going to find on those computers?"

"Nothing," she said matter-of-factly. "He uses hard-drive encryption. Even if the cops try to open his files, it will immediately boot and ask for a password. No password? No access."

I stared at my aunt. "How do you know all this?"

"Dillon told me after he got in trouble with the university. He said the encryption he uses is military grade, so he should be safe."

I was surprised and impressed by her tech savvy. "Wow. Can they get his password?"

"Nope. Even if they catch him, they can't force him to give up his password."

"Really!"

"Yeah, but that only works with the police. If someone like the mob wanted his password, they'd use the 'type in your password or lose a finger' method of recovery."

Yikes. Good thing the mob wasn't after him. At least, I hoped that was the case.

The two officers returned and headed back down the hall to Dillon's room. Moments later they came out with more of the electronic equipment. At least they left Ratty.

As soon as they were outside again, I said, "The cops probably have their own computer geeks who can figure this stuff out."

Aunt Abby shook her head. "Dillon always copies his files onto a thumb drive and then uses a hard-drive cleaner to wipe all traces of the files. Something called DBAN. Apparently that and Sledgehammer Crusher are the standards for hard-drive destruction, along with Sledgehammer Manual Crusher."

I couldn't believe all the techno-words coming out of my aunt Abby's pert little mouth. And here I thought her vocabulary was mainly limited to "stir," "braise," and "sauté."

We spotted one of the officers about to get into his squad car. Aunt Abby ran out to him and cried, "Hey! Where are you taking my son's computers? You said you had a warrant to search my house, not to steal stuff!"

I grabbed my aunt's arm and held her back, afraid she might do something stupid like threaten one of the cops with a carving knife, like she'd done to Oliver Jameson. Assaulting the police would only make things worse, and arguing wouldn't help either. I'd done enough of that for the both of us.

The officer stuck his head out of the driver's window and handed Aunt Abby a piece of paper. "Here's a receipt for everything. But I'd advise you, Ms. Warner, if you know where your son is, you should tell us. Withholding information or harboring a fugitive is a felony."

"I told you—I haven't seen him for several days," she replied, lying through her perfect white teeth.

"Well, if you do, you need to contact us. Understand?"

Aunt Abby's mouth dropped open as if she were about to say something else, but she pressed her lips together and nodded. She glanced at the receipt and added, "When can I get my son's stuff back?"

"We'll be in touch," he tossed back. With both vehicles loaded with computer equipment, the police officers drove off, leaving my aunt and me standing at the curb, wondering what had just happened.

We walked back inside and I closed the front door behind me. Aunt Abby led the way to the kitchen. It looked like she'd been in the midst of preparing mini potpies for her food truck when she was interrupted by the police. Dozens of dough-lined foil bowls sat on the counter, filled with what looked like a mixture of meat and vegetables.

Instead of returning to her work, Aunt Abby plopped down on a stool and let out a big sigh.

I rubbed her shoulders for a few minutes, then opened her cupboard and pulled out a bottle of chardonnay. Filling two glasses nearly to the rim, I handed one to Aunt Abby and joined her on the second stool. After a long sip, I set down the glass and reached for my aunt's hand. She stared into her wineglass as if in a trance.

"Aunt Abby?" I said gently.

She blinked and looked at me.

"Are you going to be all right?"

She nodded. "I'm just worried about Dillon." She took a sip of the medicinal wine.

"Any idea where he is?"

She shook her head.

I frowned. "Are you sure?"

"Honestly. I have no idea. I'm just glad he wasn't here."

My thoughts exactly.

She took another, longer gulp. Remembering how intoxicated she'd been the other night, I wondered if serving her wine was a good idea. I decided to get her talking more and drinking less.

"Why do you think the police want to talk to him?"

She took another sip. Apparently my questioning only made her want to drink more.

"I'm sure it has to do with his hacking. I told you, the feds have been watching him since he left college."

"But those weren't federal officers, Aunt Abby," I told her. "They were SFPD."

"They all work in cahoots together," she said.

I sat silently for a moment, hesitating to continue, not wanting to upset her—or cause her to drink more. But I wondered if she was holding back information about Dillon.

"Aunt Abby, is there any chance Dillon did something to protect you, maybe something involving Oliver or Boris . . . ?"

She looked at me as if I'd just thrown wine in her face. "Of course not! How can you ask that? Dillon would never harm anyone, not even to protect me. And besides, I don't need any protection! I can take care of myself."

Except for the fact that you were a suspect up until recently, I thought, *and maybe still are.* Instead, I said, "Any chance you're protecting *him*?"

"No! There's no reason to protect him. He didn't *do* anything."

"Except break into some computers."

"He only did that to help me when the cops thought I might have killed Oliver Jameson."

"All right, if you're sure, then there's something we need to do."

"What?" Aunt Abby asked, her tight face softening.

"We have to find who killed those two chefs. And we'd better do it soon, before Dillon finds himself in bigger trouble than computer hacking."

Aunt Abby's eyes lit up. She slid off her stool and opened a nearby kitchen drawer. Unlike the rest of her neatly organized cabinets, this was a mess of odds and ends—the classic junk drawer. After riffling through the chaos, she withdrew a Mickey Mouse pad of paper and a pen that read "Pirates of the Caribbean," and brought them back to the counter.

"All right, Darcy. Let's *do* this," she said.

I smiled. "Okay. Well, first we need some suspects. I've been trying to come up with a list of anyone who had a problem with either Oliver Jameson or Boris Obregar. Then we have to find some sort of connection between the two dead men."

Aunt Abby began writing down names as I called them out from my list, which included everyone from the Fort Mason food truckers to the delivery people to the restaurant owners nearby. She had nearly thirty names down before I stopped feeding them to her.

"I think we can move most of these to the bottom of the list," I said, glancing at her notes, "since it seems like only a handful of the food vendors had a problem with either Jameson or Boris. Tripp stays at the top of the list for his argument with Boris, but I wonder if he had problems with Oliver too. So what do we have?"

Aunt Abby numbered them as she read the names aloud.

"Number one is Tripp, for obvious reasons. Numbers two and three are Sierra and Vandy, because they were hassled by Boris for being vegans. And number four is Willow, since she'd had several run-ins with him as well."

"Really?" I asked. "Willow and Boris didn't get along?"

"Nope," Aunt Abby said. "She told me he was always hitting on her and wouldn't take no for an answer. Sleaze-ball. And the rest had problems with Oliver, since he wanted to get rid of the food trucks."

"I wonder if Tripp made deliveries at Bones 'n' Brew too," I said.

Aunt Abby shrugged.

"Well, anyway, we're off to a good start. Anyone else?" I asked.

Aunt Abby tapped the counter. "What about Cherry Washington, Boris's assistant?"

"Right! I saw her in Tripp's delivery truck that night."

Aunt Abby added Cherry's name to the list.

"Something's going on between those two," I said. "Any idea what Cherry's motive might be?"

Aunt Abby thought for a moment, then said, "Maybe she was having an affair with Tripp and Boris was jealous!"

I almost laughed. "I doubt it, Aunt Abby. An attractive young woman like Cherry Washington would hardly be interested in a bore like Boris. Anyone else?"

Aunt Abby tapped the counter again.

I hesitated, then offered, "Uh, what about Jake Miller? Did he have any problems with Boris?"

"Don't be silly!" Aunt Abby said. "Jake wouldn't hurt anyone! He's a sweetheart. . . ." She suddenly drifted off.

"Aunt Abby?" I said, wondering where she'd gone. "I know that look. You just remembered something, didn't you? Something about Jake?"

She took another sip of wine.

"Aunt Abby! Spill it!" I demanded.

"It's nothing. Really."

"Then tell me!"

Aunt Abby turned to face me and took a deep breath. "All right. This one time, Boris asked Jake why, if so many cops frequented his cream puff truck, he didn't sell doughnuts. Jake told him that he had a lot of friends at SFPD because he used to be a lawyer, and not all cops eat doughnuts. Boris made some kind of rude remark—a pig reference—and after that, it was like Boris avoided Jake and vice versa. That's what Jake said, anyway."

Remembering what Dillon had found out about Boris's arrest record, I wasn't surprised he'd avoided Jake. But that hardly gave Jake a motive to kill Boris. Was there something more to it than that? Something Jake hadn't shared with Aunt Abby? Had he had another run-in with Boris we didn't know about? Or with Oliver Jameson?

"Well," I said, "maybe he had a beef, so to speak, with Boris, but it doesn't sound like anything that would lead to murder."

Aunt Abby took another sip of wine. It was such a tell. I narrowed my eyes at her.

"Aunt Abby?"

"What?"

"What!"

"Nothing," she said. "It's just that, well, another time I overheard Oliver threatening Jake about his cream puffs. He said something about offering a new menu item—cream puffs—and accused Jake of stealing his secret recipe. Jake just blew him off. At least, as far as I know."

Either that or he blew him away, I thought.

"Did you ever ask Jake about this?"

"Of course not. It was none of my business. Besides, Jake would never steal recipes. I told you. He's a sweetheart."

I took the pen from Aunt Abby's hand and wrote down "Jake Miller."

Maybe there was something more sinister hidden inside that cream puff we knew as Jake Miller.

Chapter 13

Tired from the day, I headed for the RV around eleven and fell into its welcoming bed after barely pulling on the Cinderella pajamas Aunt Abby had bought me. I'd offered to spend the night in the house with her, but she'd insisted I get a good night's sleep. She'd promised to do the same. When I left her, she was still sitting at the counter, jotting down notes and sipping wine, tomorrow's potpies waiting in the fridge to be finished.

I startled awake at seven fifteen, when my phone played "It's a Small World."

My first thought was that Dillon had returned.

"Aunt Abby?" I said into the phone.

"Come here! Quick!" she said. Goose bumps rose on my arms.

Grabbing my robe, I hurried over to the house and let myself in through the unlocked sliding door at the back.

"Aunt Abby?!"

My aunt was sitting at the kitchen island where I'd left her the night before. She was wearing the same green warm-up suit and fuzzy socks, and her mascara had left shadows beneath her eyes. Her curly red hair was a little flatter than usual, and there was an imprint of inked letters on one cheek. Spread around her were several dozen recipe cards.

"Your phone call scared me," I said to Aunt Abby, patting my chest. "What's up? Is Dillon back?" I glanced around the kitchen and dining area.

"Sit down," she said calmly, patting the other stool.

I pointed to her face. "You have something on your cheek." I took a detour and headed for the cupboard, then pulled down two mugs. One read "Drink Coffee. Do Stupid Things Faster with More Energy," and one read "Be Nice to the Lunch Lady. She Knows How to Poison Your Food." Filling the cups, I reheated the coffee in the microwave and brought them to the counter. I grabbed a paper towel and moistened it, then handed the towel to my aunt. She rubbed the side of her face so much that she smeared the ink, making one cheek look sunken and bruised.

"You haven't been to bed all night, have you?" I asked, sitting down and surveying the spread of recipe cards. The ink on the cards matched the ink on her cheek.

"I couldn't sleep. Too worried about Dillon and too worked up about finding the killer." She swiped at her cheek again. "I guess I dozed off at some point." She picked up the pen and wrote something on one of the recipe cards. I'd never seen her look so excited about a few ingredients.

"Have you been writing recipes ever since I left you last night?"

I took a sip of coffee and set the cup down.

"Careful!" Aunt Abby said, pulling a card away from my mug.

Touchy? It sounded like my crabby aunt needed this coffee more than I did.

"You need to get some real sleep, Aunt Abby. Aren't you supposed to head over to the School Bus soon? Why are you sitting here writing recipes?"

"These aren't exactly recipes," she said cryptically.

I picked up one of the cards. Next to the phrase "From the Kitchen of Abigail Warner" was the name "Oliver Jameson."

I looked up at my aunt, then back down at the card. Was she planning to cook up a new dish called Oliver Jameson Potpie?

Curious, I read the ingredients, hoping there was nothing cannibalistic about them.

1 container rat poison
1 serving crab bisque

I glanced up at my aunt again. She was busily filling out another recipe card. I couldn't wait to read that one. "What is all this, Aunt Abby?"

"They're recipe cards, dear."

"I *know* that, but what are you doing with them? Why did you write Oliver Jameson's name down and then list poison and crab bisque?"

"It's the way I think, Darcy. Systematically. Using that list you drew up last night, I started with the name of the recipe, only in this case, the person. Then I listed the ingredients, essentially the facts. And finally, I added the step-by-step instructions, only there I jotted down what happened, chronologically. I made up a recipe card for both of the dead guys and all our potential suspects."

She waved her hand over the display of cards that covered the island counter. I read the "instructions" for Oliver Jameson's recipe card:

> OJ found dead in his office Friday afternoon.
> Cup of poisoned crab bisque found nearby.
> Container of poison missing from crime scene but found in the trash (perhaps stolen from AW's School Bus?)

Down at the bottom, under the word "Tips," she'd written:

- Had several enemies (see additional recipe cards)
- Poor reviews recently, business was struggling
- AW falsely suspected

The AW obviously stood for Abigail Warner. I smiled at my aunt. "You've written up a recipe card for all of them?"

"Yes. Of course, some of the information is still missing because I don't know it yet. Whenever you see 'TBD,' it means 'to be determined.' "

I picked up the next card. "Boris Obregar" was written at the top where the name of the recipe should have been.

"Interesting," I said, intrigued by her method, if not her madness. "Let me have a couple swallows of coffee and I'll see if I can fill in any of the gaps."

After fortifying myself with a dose of caffeine, I reread the card Aunt Abby had written for Boris. It took me a few seconds to get used to her style, but if it worked for her, then maybe it would work for me too.

Ingredients:

1 bludgeoning (aka method)
1 frozen packet of meat (aka weapon)
Secret ingredient: Suspect served time for dealing drugs

Instructions:

Found dead in his truck by Jake Miller
Pepper found at the scene
Weapon (frozen meat) left behind

To which I added: *"wrapped or unwrapped?"*
Under "Tips" she'd written:

- Back to dealing drugs? (felony record discovered by Dillon)
- Didn't get along with the vegans (they protested his use of meat)
- Threatened by Jameson (poison-pen letters)
- Avoided Jake (friends with SFPD)
- Argued with Tripp the Delivery Guy (overheard by Darcy)

I went over the rest of the "Recipe for Murder" cards that listed facts about the victims and our suspects, and filled in information, supposition, and questions here and there. After an hour, we'd completed cards for Sierra, Vandy, Willow, Tripp, Cherry, and "Unsub"—a word Aunt Abby insisted on using because she'd heard it on *Criminal Minds*. Apparently it meant "unknown subject." In other words, the list was open to anybody.

That narrowed it down.

I picked up one more blank card and wrote the name *"Jake Miller"* at the top.

Aunt Abby shot me a look. "What are you writing his name for? I told you, Jake is completely innocent."

"He probably is, but let's include him anyway. He's certainly a part of this investigation. He found the body. And he had his own problems with Boris—or at least Boris had a problem with him."

"None of that makes him a killer," Aunt Abby said. I was beginning to wonder if she was the one who had a small crush on the cream puff guy.

"No, but it doesn't rule him out either," I countered.

"Well, you're wrong. And I'll bet he doesn't have a secret ingredient."

"What do you mean?" I asked.

"Most people have a secret or two, Darcy. Like Boris and his drug record, Cherry and her rehab stints. I just don't think Jake has one."

Did she know about Jake being disbarred? I suppose if she did, it wasn't a secret. But I was beginning to wonder if Aunt Abby had some secrets she hadn't shared with me, when her phone chirped. The ringtone—the theme from *Mission Impossible*—sent a chill down my spine. Aunt Abby grabbed the phone from the countertop and whispered into the speaker, "Dillon?"

She listened, then said, "I know. I whispered just in case someone might be listening."

I glanced around the room for spies, but it was just the two of us. I hoped she hadn't meant me.

"Yes, she's here," Aunt Abby said. "Okay." She clicked the speaker icon and set the phone down on the counter.

"Dillon?" I said, leaning in to make sure he'd hear me.

"Yeah, it's me," the low voice said. Obviously he was trying to talk quietly. I wondered where he was.

"Dillon, the cops were here!" Aunt Abby said breathlessly. "They took all your computer stuff."

"I know, Mom. No worries. Everything's been wiped clean. And I still have my laptop. Is Ratty okay?"

"Ratty's fine. How did you know about the cops? Where are you, son?"

"I'm safe. For now. Are you all right, Mom?"

"Yes. The cops searched the house and they weren't very polite. Rude, in fact. I'm going to talk to Detective Shelton about that. But there was no police brutality or anything. They were looking for you, not me. They said they had a warrant to arrest you. Dillon, I'm so worried!"

"Calm down, Mom. I'm fine. Believe me. I just want *you* to be careful."

"Dillon," I spoke up, "you didn't have anything to do with Boris's—"

"Jeez, Darcy, give me some cred. I know you think I'm an epic fail, but I'm no killer."

"Sorry, Dillon," I said, and quickly changed the subject. "Have you found out anything more?"

"Obviously the murderer has to be someone who knew both those guys—and had a reason to kill them," Dillon said. "I've been trying to find a connection, but so far, nothing. The only thing that linked them was that they were both chefs, and their businesses were across the street from each other. Plus, they hated each other, but that would only account for Jameson's death, because he was too dead to kill Boris. So the question is, who killed Boris?"

I tried not to say, *"Duh."* Instead, I said, "And why? I think our best bet is to find out what Tripp was delivering to Boris that night—and what their argument was really about."

"Maybe it had something to do with Cherry Washington," Aunt Abby spoke up. "Darcy, you saw her in the truck with Tripp. Maybe they were lovers. Boris was always coming on to pretty young women. Maybe Tripp got angry."

Dillon broke in. "Maybe she was playing both of them to get what she wanted—whatever that was. Girls do that, you know."

Like he'd know. "Look, we've got to stop imagining all the possibilities and get some facts," I said.

"Then do it," Dillon said simply.

"Easy for you to say. Got any suggestions?" I asked.

"Listen, I'm just the computer geek," Dillon said. "I'm doing what I can from this end. You two are my field ops. Figure it out."

"You're taking this James Bond stuff a little too literally," I said. "This isn't a game, Dillon."

"Oh, it's *on*. Oops. Gotta run," he said, his voice low again. "I'll be in touch."

"Wait!" I said. "See if you can find out anything on the other food truckers."

"You mean like Willow and those vegans?"

My ears pricked up. "Did you learn something about them?"

"Well, Willow isn't her real name. It's Christine McLaughlin."

"Why did she change it to Willow?"

"I'm not sure yet. And I'm working on the vegans."

"Thanks, Dillon," I said. "Hey, aren't you risking getting caught when you use your cell phone?" I asked.

"Nah. The cops can't trace my calls."

"Why not?"

"There's an app for that."

The line went dead before I could call him a smartass.

"Thank goodness he's all right," Aunt Abby said with a sigh. "Now I can finish those potpies and get to work."

"And *I* can take a shower, get dressed, have breakfast, and try to keep you propped up at work, since you've had too little sleep and too much wine."

"I'll be fine now that I know Dillon's okay—and not in jail," she said, retrieving more dough from the double-wide refrigerator. "Got any idea how you're going to find Cherry Washington, now that the Road Grill truck is closed due to murder?"

"Me? What about you?"

"I've got a food truck to run."

"And I work for a tyrant of a boss who expects me to help her out in her food truck all day," I countered.

"You'll have plenty of time on your frequent and overly long breaks."

I was tempted to stick my finger in one of her finished potpies, just to be ornery, but instead I headed out the back door for the RV. During my shower, I tried to come up with a plan to track down Cherry so I could ask her a few questions—and find out more about Tripp. Unfortunately, I had no idea where she lived or how to get ahold of her. I figured Dillon could find out in a matter of seconds using his computer skills, but for an ordinary newspaper reporter who didn't turn into a superhero by stepping into a phone booth and putting on a disguise, it would be a challenge.

So what did I know about Cherry Washington? She'd been working with Boris for the past year or so, she'd been in and out of rehab, and she was a huge flirt. But I rarely saw her out and about. She didn't hang out at the Coffee Witch, she hadn't stopped by the School Bus for a snack, and she didn't seem to sample foods from the other trucks when she was on a break.

I wondered if she had a sweet tooth. Maybe Jake's cream puffs were her Achilles' heel. Like they were mine.

Note to self: Talk to Jake ASAP. And eat a cream puff.

Chapter 14

I arrived at the Fort Mason food trucks a little past nine, planning to speak to Jake before the crowds started lining up for their late breakfasts. Although the Crab and Seafood Festival was over, most vendors, including Aunt Abby, still kept some of the more popular fish-related items on their menus. My aunt planned to continue offering her Crab Potpies, Crabby Cheerleader Mac and Cheese, and Crabtown Fry until she ran out of crab.

I noticed that a few new trucks had pulled into the back lot, no doubt hoping to join the food truck circle once the Road Grill truck moved out. The semipermanent sites were at a premium, and the few transient sites were booked up months in advance. I spotted one truck called the Gluten-Free Glutton, another called the Quinoa Queen (which I continually mispronounced as *quinn-oh-wa* instead of *keen-wah*), and another one called Grill 'Em All, no doubt the closest replacement for Boris's fare. I wasn't surprised to see these trendy new trucks already vying to replace the dead man's truck, since Fort Mason was one of the most popular spots for "road food." I wondered which one would get the coveted parking site. Personally, I was hoping for a chocolate truck, since everything could be enhanced by a few ladles of melted chocolate. Even a cream puff.

I spotted Jake talking to the chef at Porky's and wondered if he was planning to substitute bacon bits for candy sprinkles on his cream puffs. He caught me waving, said something to the porky chef leaning out the ordering window, and moseyed back to his cream puff truck, where I stood waiting for him. Unlike Aunt Abby and me, Jake looked as if he'd had a great night's sleep. He wore a bright white T-shirt and clean relaxed jeans, and his thick, sun-bleached hair looked freshly washed, a stray lock dangling over his forehead.

"Morning, Darcy," he said, grinning.

"You sound chipper," I said, glancing over at the line for the Coffee Witch. "I need caffeine—or at least jumper cables."

Jake laughed. "Not quite awake, eh? What with everything that's going on, I'm not surprised."

"I managed a few hours of sleep, but I think my aunt was up most of the night." I explained about the police coming to search her home, the warrant for Dillon's arrest, and Dillon's latest call and disappearance.

Jake's smile turned to a frown. "Why didn't you call me when the police came?"

I thought of Jake's name on my suspect list. I'd put him there because Boris might have given him some trouble and Jake had been the one who'd found Boris's body. Plus, I didn't know Jake all that well.

"Oh, uh, it was all so sudden and hectic—I didn't even think of it. I'm sure you would have been a great help." I bit my lip, trying to look sincere. "Have you heard anything more about Boris's murder?"

"Nah. I talked to most of the other food truckers. They all said the police questioned them but none of them saw or heard anything. Apparently you're the only one who witnessed the argument between Boris and Tripp."

That's because no one else was there that late at night, I thought, *other than Boris, Tripp, Cherry, and me.* "Have the police talked to Cherry or Tripp?"

"I don't know. The cops aren't updating me on their investigation, unfortunately. They're keeping it close to their Kevlar vests. Even my friends in the department are being tight-lipped. Your guess is as good as mine."

Was it really? I wondered.

"Hey, want to try one of my new cream puffs? Tiramisu." He gestured toward his truck. But I had a few more questions for him first. "Sure, but—"

"Come on. I'll show you how I make them."

I glanced at Aunt Abby's bus. I could see her moving around inside and figured I still had a little time before she needed serious help. Why not? The cream puff sounded delicious, and I could ask my questions in the privacy of his truck.

I followed him inside. The smell of freshly baked pastry shells made my mouth water. I scanned the equipment. Hot ovens at the back, large refrigerator on the far side, cooling racks nearby. Everything stainless steel and sparkling clean. Jake put on a fresh white apron with a cream puff pictured on the front and the words "Dream Puffs" lettered above, then pulled a bowl of filling from the fridge and a couple of shells from the rack. It took him only seconds to slice open one of the puffy shells, generously scoop in the creamy mixture, replace the top, and drizzle on chocolate sauce. I had to restrain myself from grabbing it out of his masterful hands.

He picked up a napkin and handed over the cream puff. I took a bite, closed my eyes, and shivered. The pastry crust was as light as a cloud, crispy, with just a hint of coffee flavor. The creamy filling slid over my tongue, cold and smooth, and tasted like a mascarpone-chocolate-coffee blend. The whole thing melted like cocoa butter in my mouth. If Jake could do this to me with his cream puff, I wondered what—

"You all right?" Jake said, startling me from my brief fantasy.

I opened my eyes and felt a flush of heat envelop my face and body. "Oh . . . yeah," I said, then coughed and patted my chest. "Just went down the wrong pipe. It's incredible!" I popped the rest in my mouth and licked the chocolate sauce from my lips.

"Well, it's easy enough to make. The French call it *choux à la tiramisu*."

Oh my God, he speaks perfectly accented French, I thought. *I'm doomed.*

"You just make the basic pastry puff—water, butter, sugar—bring it to a boil, and add the flour and stir for a couple of minutes. Then add the eggs and coffee, spoon the batter, and bake them for thirty minutes. While they cool, you beat cream and sugar, then fold in mascarpone and chocolate. I drizzle a little Ghirardelli chocolate sauce on top, then dust it with powdered sugar. That's it."

That's it, eh? Might as well try to teach me how to hack into a computer or solve a murder mystery. I smiled. At least it would make a great recipe for my food truck cookbook.

"Well, it's amazing. Thank you."

He looked pleased and began filling more shells with the creamy custard.

"So," I said, trying to sound nonchalant, "I saw you chatting to that bacon truck guy. Anything new?"

"We were just talking about the new trucks that want Boris's site. I think they'd kill to get in here."

I frowned.

"Sorry," he said. "Bad choice of words."

"What do you think will happen to Cherry Washington now that the truck is closed?"

Jake returned about a dozen freshly filled cream puffs to the fridge and pulled out another tray of shells. I tried not to drool.

"She mentioned something about taking over his truck, if she could get some cash together quickly. I think she was hinting for me to lend her some dough, but I'm still paying off the loan for my own truck. She talked about hitting up Willow from the Coffee Witch and a few others to invest."

Hmm. So Jake *had* been talking to Cherry. And he'd been talking to Willow. I briefly wondered if there was something going on between Jake and Cherry or Willow. He was hot, and they were both attractive in their own ways.

Not my concern at the moment, although I felt a wave of something resembling jealousy pass through me. *Focus, Darcy,* I told myself. *You're trying to figure out who murdered Boris Obregar and Oliver Jameson, not who's dating whom.* Willow seemed unlikely for the murder, since I couldn't come up with a motive for her, but Cherry might have had a motive, since she apparently wanted to take over Boris's truck.

Enough to kill Boris?

Then how did Oliver fit into all of this?

"When did you talk to Cherry?" I asked, tempted to stick my finger in the bowl of melted chocolate.

Jake continued scooping spoonfuls of tiramisu cream into perfectly shaped pastry puffs, one after another, in a smooth and precise rhythm. "Yesterday, after the police were done questioning us."

"Any idea where she is now?"

Jake dropped the spoon in the nearly empty bowl and wiped his fingers on his apron. He turned to me. "Not really. I assume she's in Boris's truck, cleaning up the place. You still trying to figure out who killed him?"

I ignored his question and added a couple more of my own. "What about his truck being a crime scene?"

"I guess you didn't notice. The police took the tape down last night, after they'd finished collecting all the evidence."

It was true—I hadn't noticed. Some sleuth wannabe I was. "That was quick."

"The amount of time varies," Jake said. "Most crime scene techs get what they need the first time around. They pretty much cleaned the place out and hauled everything away. I assume Cherry is free to collect whatever she needs. I'm sure she has a key to the place."

I peered out the window at the Road Grill truck. The yellow tape was indeed gone. I wondered if Cherry Washington was inside at this very moment. If so, I definitely wanted to talk to her. I straightened up and pulled my purse up over my shoulder.

"Thanks for breakfast," I said. "I'd . . . better go help Aunt Abby open up the School Bus. Come by later for a complimentary Crab Potpie—today's specialty. I owe you."

"You don't owe me anything," Jake said, smiling. That smile was as infectious as his cream puffs. "Wait a sec," he said, reaching for a spotted and stained notebook. He opened it and pulled out a stained sheet of paper. "I've got a copy of the tiramisu recipe if you want it for your cookbook. You'll probably want to try it before you put it in your book."

I didn't have the guts to tell him I didn't cook. "Thank you," I said. I folded up the recipe. I opened my purse to stuff it inside and caught the purse strap on the edge of the counter. My bag fell to the floor with a thud, spilling the contents on the black-and-white-checked linoleum. We both knelt down to retrieve the fallen items. I gathered up my keys, wallet, makeup bag, pens, and mints, while Jake collected my ChapStick, cell phone, tissue pack, and reporter's notebook.

He waited as I stuffed the first wad back into my purse, then began handing me the rest of the items. He was about to give me my notebook when he paused.

I looked up at him. He was staring at the notebook, frowning.

I glanced down. It was open to the page where I'd written the word "Suspects."

Jake's name was at the bottom of the list.

And now he knew it.

I pulled the notebook from his hand and forced a fake laugh. "I can explain," I said as I rose. *Oh really, Darcy? This should be good.* "Of course I don't consider you a *real* suspect, but, uh . . . since you were the one who found the body, I added your name—more to rule you out than anything else. Plus, I'd had a lot of wine, so I was putting down all kinds of names—even Dillon's."

Oh my God, I was rambling on and going nowhere, except maybe digging myself deeper into a black hole.

Jake nodded, but by the frown on his face, I could tell he was not convinced. I decided to make my escape before I caused any more damage.

"Anyway, I'd better run. Thanks again for the cream puff. It was awesome!"

I leapt down the steps and fast-walked toward the Coffee Witch, nearly bumping into the maintenance man who was sweeping litter into a pile nearby. I needed a jolt of coffee more than ever. I wondered what Jake was thinking at the moment. That I suspected him of murder? That I didn't trust him? That I was an idiot? Probably the latter.

I glanced back to see if he was watching me. He was. And the frown was still on his handsome face.

I checked my cell phone for any texts from Dillon, but the only message I had was from Aunt Abby asking if I could bring her more napkins on my way back to the School Bus. When I reached Willow's truck, I ordered a Witch's Brew—double espresso latte—making a mental note to question her about her name change when she wasn't so busy. After helping myself to a handful of napkins from her condiments shelf—and telling myself it wasn't "really stealing"—I headed for Aunt Abby's bus, swinging by a few other trucks to "borrow" more napkins. When I reached the Road Grill truck next to my aunt's place, I tried to peer in through the drawn shades to see if there was any sign of life.

I heard a loud thump come from inside and froze.

Someone was in there. Cherry?

I set down the coffee and napkins on the School Bus ledge nearby and headed for the door of the beef truck. I knocked and called out, "Cherry? Are you in there?"

No answer.

I listened. More bumps and thuds. I knocked again. Still no response. Maybe Cherry didn't feel like talking right now. Maybe she was in the middle of something important. Maybe she was being murdered.

"Cherry!" I yelled. "It's Darcy from the Big Yellow School Bus next door! Are you all right?"

The door flew open, slamming against the side of the truck.

"What?!" Cherry Washington stood in the doorway, dressed in tight short-shorts beaded with rhinestones and a tank top that did nothing to hide her large breasts, her sleek mocha-colored abdomen, or the belly-button ring that dangled from her navel. Her spiky black shoes could easily put an eye out if used the right way. She certainly wasn't dressed for success—or for working in a food truck.

"I . . . I thought I heard noises coming from inside. I wanted to make sure you were all right. Is everything okay?"

"Yeah, I'm just picking up a few things, trying to clean the place up now that the cops are done with it." She brushed her hands against her shorts, wiping off little black flecks.

Pepper.

She started to pull the door shut. I reached for it and held it open, feeling decidedly at her mercy since I was standing at least three feet below her. Make that four, with the heels.

"I was wondering . . ." I said.

"What?" she said, frowning.

"Uh, Jake mentioned that you might be taking over Boris's truck. Is that true?" I tried to keep my tone light, as if I were rooting for her rather than trying to root out information.

"Yeah, maybe," she said, shrugging.

"Oh, well, if there's anything I can do to help . . ."

"Who're you again?"

"Darcy. I've been helping out in Abby Warner's Big Yellow School Bus next door."

"Oh yeah. I seen you around, haven't I? You always over at Jake's place. Got a thing for cream puffs, doncha." She eyed me as if waiting for my reaction to this deep, dark secret.

"They are pretty delicious," I said. "So, are you going to keep the menu the same if you take it over? Or do something else?"

She stuck out a hip. "I wanna do my own thing, you know, but I haven't decided what, yet. Maybe Cajun. I'm from N'Awlins. I'm thinking I'll call it Creole Voodoo. My *grand-mère*'s got some magical recipes that'll cast a spell on anyone who tries them. But I'm looking for a silent partner, you dig? You interested?"

"Oh, no, sorry. I'd like to help, but I just lost my job. That's why I'm working for Aunt Abby."

"She your aunt, eh? Maybe she interested?"

"I doubt it. But good luck. I hope you find a backer. Maybe one of Boris's contacts?"

I was hoping she'd mention Tripp, the delivery guy I'd seen her with, but she raised a well-drawn eyebrow and just nodded. When she started to close the door again, I held it fast. "Hey, what about Tripp, from the Meat Wagon? Didn't I see you talking to him the other night? Maybe he could invest a little?" It was a long shot, but I had to find a way to get her to talk about him.

Her eyes narrowed. "Yeah, maybe. Look, I gotta get back to cleaning up. Lemme know if your aunt's interested in a good business deal, y'hear?"

"Will do," I said as she closed the door.

I turned around and nearly bumped into the maintenance man I'd nearly bumped into earlier.

"Whoa!" I said. "You startled me!"

Avoiding eye contact, he mumbled something under his thick gray mustache that I couldn't make out and shuffled off, sweeping the surface as he went. I collected myself and headed next door, mentally summarizing what I had learned to share with Aunt Abby. One, Cherry Washington was interested in owning the truck. Good motive for killing off your boss. And two, she had raised a telltale eyebrow and had abruptly ended the conversation when Tripp's name came up. Why? Because the two were in on something together and he killed Boris for her?

I had to talk to Tripp—if I could find him. Meanwhile, I could have used some help from Dillon. I had a feeling he could get on the computer and find out all kinds of things about Cherry Washington and Tripp Saunders, not to mention everyone else on my list.

Where was a computer nerd when you needed one?

Chapter 15

"Aunt Abby?" I called as I stepped into the Big Yellow School Bus. I didn't want to startle my aunt. There'd been enough of that lately.

"About time," she said, busily sprinkling a dash of paprika on the tops of her crab potpies, which she'd named "Coach Crabbies." "We open in twenty minutes. Where've you been?"

"Snooping around," I said, helping myself to a slice of cheddar cheese that sat waiting for the onslaught of grilled-crab-and-cheese sandwich orders that were sure to come.

Aunt Abby stopped what she was doing and looked me over. "What did you find out?"

"Well," I said, slipping on an apron. I tried a couple of times to tie it the way Aunt Abby had taught me, but I only managed to wad it up around my waist. It was a lost cause. "First I stopped by Jake's to get some breakfast."

Aunt Abby's Kewpie doll eyebrow shot up. "I'll bet."

I took an air-swipe at her. "Stop that! Actually, he was full of information. I found out Cherry Washington wants to take over Boris's truck. That could be a motive for killing Boris."

Aunt Abby indicated the loaves of fresh bread on the

counter, then handed me a large, familiar knife—the one she'd waved at Oliver Jameson just before his death. The way things were going, I was surprised the police hadn't confiscated it for evidence.

"But that wouldn't explain Oliver's death," Aunt Abby said, making a sawing gesture so I'd start slicing.

"No, but if I do a little more digging, I might find a connection. I've only talked to her once."

"How'd you find her?" Aunt Abby asked. She began placing the paprika'd pies in the oven.

"Jake saw her going into Boris's truck. The crime scene tape is down. She was inside cleaning up. At least, that's what she said she was doing."

Aunt Abby pulled out another rack of pies and proceeded to "decorate" them with the red-orange spice. "Huh. I assumed that truck would close and another truck would replace it."

I nodded. "I saw a few vying for the spot, but they may not have a chance if Cherry finds a backer for her plan."

Aunt Abby's eyes lit up. "She needs a backer?"

I nodded and replaced the slices of bread back in the plastic bag.

"I have an idea," Aunt Abby said. "Why don't I offer to be her backer?"

"What? I thought you barely made enough to keep this place running."

"That's true, but I could at least *offer*. That would give me a chance to ask her some questions, like what's her credit record, does she have any criminal history, stuff like that. Of course, Dillon could do all that online . . . if he were here." Her face fell at the mention of her absent son.

"I'm not so sure that's a good idea, Aunt Abby. What

if Cherry turns out to be a murderer? If she thinks you're looking into her background, she may try to stop you."

"Who? Little old innocent me?" Aunt Abby batted those eyelashes again.

"Yes, you. You're not as invincible as you think you are." I pulled out another loaf and began whacking away again.

"Did Jake say anything else?"

At the thought of how the meeting had ended, a heat wave seared through me. "Uh . . . not really." I busied myself with the loaf of cheese bread.

Aunt Abby stared at me, hands on her hips. "Darcy. What did you do?"

"Nothing!" I shrugged. "My purse . . . fell open. Accidentally. Jake may have seen my suspects list. . . ."

"Oh, Darcy, no! He was our only real ally besides Dillon. Now he thinks we suspect him of murder?"

"I'll fix it," I said, sawing at the bread. Sawing, sawing, sawing.

"Oh, really? How?"

"I don't know yet. But I can't live without those cream puffs of his, so I'll make it better."

We worked in silence for a few minutes. The clock was ticking and in less than five minutes it would be time to open the service window and greet the growing line of customers for their late breakfasts or early lunches.

Finally, Aunt Abby finished wiping the counter and turned to me. "Well, we still don't have our killer. So what do we do next?"

"I need to talk to Tripp Saunders and find out what he and Boris were arguing about—and what's up with him and Cherry."

"Oh, is that all? How do you expect to do that?" Her words dripped with sarcasm.

"I'm a reporter, remember?" I said. "Or at least I was until a few days ago. I'll pretend to interview him. I don't think he knows that *I* overheard him. He just knows *someone* did—someone with a personalized 'It's a Small World' cell phone ring." I shot her a look. I really needed to change that tune.

Before I could continue, Aunt Abby opened the window and began taking orders. I filled them as fast as I could and made only four mistakes the whole morning. Most of the customers wanted the Custodian's Special at this hour—bacon, egg, and hash browns on a biscuit. How people could eat such a loaded combination of fat, salt, and cholesterol was a mystery to me. I liked my breakfast food simple—like a cream puff.

The rush kept us both busy until around two, when things settled down enough for me to take a break and get a coffee.

"Want anything?" I asked my aunt.

She raised her bottle of peach Snapple, took a swallow, and shook her head, then went about cleaning up the latest mess.

I headed for the Coffee Witch, walking slowly past Jake's truck, hoping to catch a glimpse of him, judge his mood, and see if he could take a coffee break. Unfortunately, he was still dealing with a line of customers, mostly women. Attractive women. Oh, well. After putting Jake on my list of suspects, I could pretty much cross him off my list of future dating material—a list of one. So much for that list.

There was only one person in line for Willow's coffee

truck—the maintenance man. As I stood behind him, I wondered if he'd seen anything related to Boris's murder. I hadn't really thought of him before, but then, people who work in the service business are often invisible. They become part of the background, overlooked or ignored. Yet they're often in a position to see and hear all kinds of things the rest of us miss.

"Excuse me?" I said to his back.

No response.

I tapped his shoulder. He turned around. He had a thick, unkempt mustache that matched his bushy eyebrows, and deep lines in his weathered, dark-skinned face. A cap that read "SF Maintenance" was pulled over his graying hair.

"Hi, you're the maintenance man, right?" I asked, stating the obvious.

He mumbled something I couldn't understand, then turned back to the coffee window to await his turn.

Was he speaking another language? He looked somewhat Middle Eastern, so maybe he hadn't understood me. I moved up beside him and tried again, speaking slowly and using gestures. "I'm Darcy," I said, pointing to myself. "I work at the Big Yellow School Bus with my aunt." I waved an arm toward the bus. "I noticed you work here and I wondered if you might have seen or heard anything about the murder the other day. I'm doing a story for the newspaper—" I gestured writing with an invisible pencil in my palm.

The man turned his back on me and stepped up to the service window. Moments later Willow handed him a black coffee. He reached into his deep overall pocket, pulled out a wadded handful of dollar bills, and placed them on the counter. Willow gave a "no charge" wave of her hand. The man collected his money, nodded, and shuffled away.

Leaving my place in line, I ran over to him. "Excuse me, sir. Did you hear what I said?" I was becoming irritated at his rudeness. Even if he didn't speak English, he could have said something. Once again, he turned away.

I stood there, openmouthed. "What a jerk!" I said loud enough for the man and everyone around me to overhear me. I returned to the Coffee Witch, garnering odd looks from the people in the recently formed line, but the maintenance man didn't even turn around. I shrugged and said to no one in particular, "I just wanted to ask him some questions."

When it was my turn to order, I looked up at Willow and asked, "Do you know that guy?"

Willow slid a rumpled note over to me. The words were scrawled in block letters and read: *"Deaf. Black coffee. How much?"* Apparently he'd handed her the note when his back was turned to me.

I felt my chest tighten. Crap. I had been trying to talk to a deaf man and had even called him a jerk. I could only be glad that he hadn't heard me say that.

"I feel like an idiot!" I said to Willow.

"You didn't know," she said. "Your usual? Or do you want to try my new tiramisu-flavored frap? I call it Jake's Bane. Jake gave me the idea."

Oh, really? I thought. Maybe there really was something going on between Willow and Jake. Even with all the piercings, tattoos, and hair art, she was attractive, but I had a hard time seeing her with ex-attorney Jake Miller.

"Oh, you talked to Jake today?" I asked casually.

"Yeah, he came by this morning for his usual."

"Are you two pretty good friends?" It was hard trying to sound uninterested.

She shrugged. "We went out a couple of times, if that's what you're asking. But I was seeing someone else at the time, so it got to be too complicated. You know how it is."

I didn't, but my ex-boyfriend probably did.

Willow's grin suddenly spread, revealing her pierced tongue. "OMG, you're totally hot for him!"

"No, I'm not!" I said, glancing around, hoping no one heard her. "I was just asking. I'm trying to find out more about the people who work around here. Somebody's got to solve these murders and the police don't seem to be doing anything but falsely suspecting my aunt and my cousin."

"Uh-huh," she said, clearly not convinced. "Well, I doubt it was Jake. He's too nice a guy."

I shrugged. "Sure, but everyone has a skeleton or two in the closet." I wondered if Jake's disbarment was his only skeleton.

"If Jake has one, I'd be surprised. You're more likely to find skeletons in the other food truckers' closets. . . ."

My eyes lit up. "Really? Like who?"

Willow glanced behind me. "Can't talk now. I've got customers."

I turned around. More than half a dozen people had lined up to get their favorite concoctions from the Coffee Witch. I quickly ordered the tiramisu frap on her recommendation, then paid her and waited for the drink while scanning the circle of food trucks, wondering what secrets they all held.

I thought about stopping by Jake's truck and apologizing again, but this time the window was closed and a BE BACK IN 5 MINUTES sign was pressed against it. I wondered where he'd gone. And when he'd be back.

Moving on, I made a mental note to chat up the vegans as soon as possible and check in again on Cherry Washington. And I still needed to find Tripp Saunders. There were fast becoming too many cooks in the kitchen. I wondered which ones were just red herrings.

I headed for the School Bus with my drink. Maybe my aunt knew more than she realized about everybody's business.

"Aunt Abby?" I said as I stepped inside. "What do you—"

I stopped cold.

Aunt Abby stood facing me in the narrow bus aisle, holding her favorite knife.

Opposite her, with his back to me, was the deaf maintenance man.

He held something in his raised hand. It looked like a large can of black pepper.

I screamed, nearly forgetting the deaf man wouldn't hear me.

I only hoped someone would.

Chapter 16

The deaf man spun around and looked at me aghast, as if offended that I had interrupted him while he was about to pepper my aunt.

"What the hell!" the man said, sticking his fingers in his ears and wiggling them around. "You're going to make us deaf with all that screaming!"

"Dillon?!" I said, recognizing his voice and finally seeing through all the theatrical makeup, fake mustache, and maintenance man getup. "What are you *doing*?"

"I'm talking to my mom, Darcy. What does it look like I'm doing? Why did you scream like that?"

"You scared the crap out of me! I thought you were the murderer, getting ready to attack her with a can of pepper like you—like he did Boris. Why are you holding it like that?"

"We were just trying to figure out what happened—"

Before he could finish his explanation, the doors to the School Bus burst open. Jake bounded in, his eyes wide. He was holding a rolling pin and he looked like he meant to use it, but not for rolling out dough.

"What's going on?" he said, ready to rumble. After a second he seemed to realize no one was about to get murdered and he lowered the floured weapon. "Darcy?

Abby? Are you all right?" He eyed the costumed Dillon.

"We're fine, Jake," Aunt Abby said. "It was all a big misunderstanding. Darcy thought this nice maintenance man was going to hurt me and she overreacted, didn't you dear?" Aunt Abby shot me a look that said *"Back me up, here."* Obviously she was trying to keep Dillon's identity a secret.

"Uh . . ." was all I could manage. I glanced at Jake.

He was staring at the intruder, his eyes narrow. "Dillon? What are you doing in that ridiculous costume? Your Inspector Clouseau act isn't helping things."

"Shhh!" Aunt Abby whispered, moving protectively next to her son. "He's undercover. The cops and the feds are after him, remember?"

"How did you know it was me?" Dillon asked Jake, seeming more concerned about being recognized by Jake than about being pursued by law enforcement.

I glanced down at Dillon's shoes, a dead giveaway the last time he tried to "go undercover." But this time he wore a pair of tattered athletic shoes. I wondered where he'd gotten them. Goodwill?

"Well, first of all, your hands and fingernails," Jake said. "They're too soft and clean to belong to someone who deals with the dirt around here. Although the disguise is a pretty clever way to gather some dirt, I suppose."

Dillon held up his hands and checked his nails. Jake was right. Those were the hands of a computer guy, not a maintenance guy. How could I have missed recognizing my own cousin? And how come Jake recognized him so quickly?

"I think it's a brilliant disguise, son," Aunt Abby said, beaming up at Dillon with parental admiration. "And so far the cops haven't made you."

Made him? Who was this woman I called my aunt Abby?

"How long have you been around here?" I asked Dillon, still nonplussed at his appearance.

He shrugged noncommittally and glanced at the back of the bus. I followed his look and spotted an open cupboard. Inside, next to a bunch of cooking supplies, was a rolled-up sleeping bag.

"You *slept* here last night?" I asked, stunned that Dillon would actually hide out in his mother's food bus with the police looking for him. Then again, maybe such an obvious place was easy to overlook, just like a maintenance man was easy to overlook in a food truck lot.

Aunt Abby gave Dillon's arm a motherly pat. "I found him this morning, lying there on the cold, hard floor, poor thing. You don't know how relieved I was."

"Dillon!" I cried. "The police are going to think you're guilty because you're hiding out!" I turned to Jake. "Isn't that right, Jake?"

He didn't answer.

"Jake?" I said, irritated at his lack of focus on such a serious development.

"What?" Jake said.

"Never mind!" I snapped. I turned back to Dillon. "So, Clouseau, did you learn anything playing maintenance man?"

"As a matter of fact, I did." Beneath all that dark makeup, Dillon still managed to look smug. "You know those vegans?"

"Vandy and Sierra?" I said. "Yeah, what about them?"

"You know how they didn't get along with Boris and kept putting up those 'no meat' signs?"

"You think their vegan beliefs are strong enough to make them murder a meat lover?" I asked. "Seems a stretch."

"Not when you hear what I found out about them," Dillon said, trying to sound mysterious. He helped himself to one of his mother's caramel brownies.

"Well? Tell us!" I said, exasperated.

"They're fanimals."

"Huh?" I was too confused to say anything.

Jake asked, "What's a fanimal?"

"It's this bizarre subculture where people dress up and act like animals. There are all these conventions and Internet sites and stuff for people who really, *really* like animals."

"So, Sierra and Vandy love animals and like to dress up." I looked Dillon over. "Sort of like you in your various costumes. But that doesn't make them potential killers."

"Let me finish!" Dillon said, rolling his eyes. "Gosh!"

"Go on, Dillon," Aunt Abby said, after shooting a daggered look at me.

"Well, fanimals started at a sci-fi convention about ten years ago, when fans started dressing up as animal characters, like Wookies and Ewoks, and it took off. There are all these Internet sites like Animorphs and FanimalCity and FurNation you can join where you can chat with other fanimals. There's a bunch of pictures of them wearing everything from ears and tails and paws to full-on fur suits, like bears and raccoons and foxes, with heads and everything."

"So basically it's Halloween whenever they feel like it," I said.

"Well, to each his own," Jake said, shrugging. "It may be embarrassing for them if word gets out, but it's hardly a motive for murder."

"No," Dillon said, "but it got me curious about Boris. Did he have something on his computer that would be a problem for them?" He paused.

"Well, did he?" I asked.

"I found some pictures of Vandy," Dillon said.

"Sex pictures?" Aunt Abby said, raising her eyebrows.

Dillon shook his head. "No, nothing like that."

"Then what?" I asked.

"There were pictures of her . . . alone . . . at a restaurant . . . eating a big, juicy hamburger," Dillon answered.

"You're kidding!" I said. So vegan Vandy was cheating on vegan Sierra with a carnivorous hamburger. If Sierra found out, it would probably ruin their relationship.

But was that motive enough for murder?

As I watched Jake walk back to his truck something caught my eye.

The door to Boris's truck opened. I expected Cherry to step out but was surprised to see a man exit. A man wearing cowboy boots.

Tripp Saunders.

I peered through the window, watching until I saw him walk behind Boris's truck and disappear.

I grabbed my purse. "I've got to go. I'll be back as soon as I can."

"Where are you going?" Aunt Abby cried, her eyes wide.

"Dude, you're leaving?" Dillon said. "Aren't you going to ask those vegans some questions or anything?"

"Later," I said, and fled the bus for my car. Today it was parked in the lot beyond the circle of food trucks. I jammed the key in the lock, opened the door, slid in, and started the engine.

Tripp's Meat Wagon was easy to spot, thanks to the ginormous sign and bright red paint job. I pulled up to the lot exit and waited for the truck to pass me on the street, keeping my head down to avoid being spotted. Traffic was heavy along the marina, as usual, but that made it simpler to tail the truck, since Tripp couldn't go any faster than the rest of the other cars on the road. I followed him as he zigzagged through the city, keeping my distance and allowing a couple of cars in between us.

I followed him for fifteen minutes, until he turned south near the freeway, into the warehouse district of Potrero Hill. I pulled over and parked on the street several yards away, being careful not to appear obvious. Slinking down in the seat, I watched as Tripp got out of the meat truck, locked it, and headed toward an old warehouse that had seen better days. The faded sign painted on the outside read WHOLESALE MEATS.

Several of the windows were boarded up with wood panels. The rest were embedded with chicken wire. Some were cracked; all were filthy and opaque. Tripp unlocked the door, glanced around, then spat out the toothpick he'd been gnawing on. He pulled open the double doors and slipped inside, closing them behind him.

I got out of the car, ignoring the fact that I was in a twenty-minute loading zone, and headed for the warehouse, rehearsing what I'd say if Tripp caught me. He might recognize me from Aunt Abby's bus, so I couldn't use the "Gee, I'm lost, can you help me?" ruse. I had to come up with something better if I found myself face-to-face with this possible murderer.

Then again, I could just call the police and let them figure out what was going on behind those locked double doors. And what would I say? *"Hi, Detective Shelton. I followed the Meat Wagon guy to a warehouse near Potrero Hill and I think something bad is going on inside."*

Yeah, that would bring him running.

I had to see for myself what was going on inside first before I called the cops and made a complete fool of myself. Plus, if I blew this—and Tripp *was* guilty—I might ruin the only chance I'd have of finding out the truth.

By the time I reached the double doors, I had the only plan that I knew would be foolproof: don't get caught.

I tiptoed up to one of the windows that wasn't boarded over and tried to scratch off the grime that had collected over who knew how many years, but I only managed to blacken my hand and fingernails. The wire-paned windows seemed to have just as much grit on the inside as on the outside. When I looked closely, I realized it wasn't dirt that blocked my view, but gray paint. The windows had been painted over on the inside to keep snoops like me from peeking in.

There were scratches and holes here and there, but nothing large enough to allow me to see inside. I made my way along the row of panes, searching for a chip in the paint that would give me a glimpse into the warehouse. After trying all the windows on the left side of the double doors, I moved to the right side and searched again. About half a dozen panes down, I found a small hole in the paint about the size of a nickel. I pressed my eye to the dirty pane and strained to see inside.

The warehouse was brightly lit, something I couldn't tell from the outside, thanks to the blocked views. There were no hanging animal carcasses, no signs of refrigerators, no butcher table, nothing to indicate a meat-processing plant. Instead, in the middle of the mostly empty room were several large tables filled with electronic equipment—mostly computers and printers. I also spotted what looked like a thermal laminator—we had a couple at the newspaper office—along with a few digital cameras, paper cutters, and stacks of paper.

Tripp Saunders was perched on a stool, bent over some loose papers, peering at them closely with something like a jeweler's loupe.

What was the meat delivery guy up to?

Chapter 17

My phone played "It's a Small World." Aunt Abby!

Dammit! I'd forgotten to turn off the ringer!

I *had* to change that ringtone.

I peered into the peephole to see if Tripp had heard the ring, hoping the walls were too thick for the song to catch his attention.

He was staring in my direction. Frowning.

Crap! I had to get out of there—fast, before he caught me. He must have recognized the tune—the same tune he'd heard the night Boris died. Not good.

Starting to panic, I ran around the side of the building. The weedy area was cluttered with old machine parts, broken-down signage, rotting two-by-fours, and probably lots and lots of rats. I tried to step over any loose boards and watch for upended nails, but in my hurry, I scratched my arm on a sharp piece of metal sticking out of what looked like a discarded mattress. Apparently I had escaped into a local dumping ground for everything from broken tools to disused furniture.

I ducked under an old door with the paint peeling off in large flakes. No doubt lead paint, with my luck. If I didn't get tetanus, I'd surely come down with brain damage in a few years. Curling myself into a human ball, I slowed my breathing and prayed Tripp wouldn't find me in this garbage heap.

In the distance, I heard the double doors slam open against the metal walls.

"Who's out there?" Tripp yelled loud enough that I could hear him and so could anyone else within half a block. "I know you're here! I heard your phone."

I held my breath.

Silence.

Seconds later I heard footsteps crunching over gravel. The crunching grew louder as Tripp rounded the corner; then it stopped abruptly.

What was he doing? No doubt scanning the area, looking for any sign of the Peeping Tom with the Disneyland cell phone ring. Or readying his weapon of choice. Or alerting his minions for backup.

Which reminded me. I *still* hadn't turned off my phone. Aunt Abby was sure to call again. Slowly I snaked my hand into my pocket and flipped the tiny switch with my thumbnail to silence the ringer. I only hoped my aunt hadn't called earlier because she was in some kind of trouble.

The crunching started up again. And grew closer. Sweat broke out on my forehead and I felt a trickle down my back. Tripp was nearing my hiding place. A few more steps and I'd surely be discovered. My heart beat so loud I was sure he could hear it.

A loud thud, only a few feet away.

Then another. Even closer.

I knew exactly what Tripp was doing—searching through the refuse, piece by piece. It would be a matter of seconds before he came upon the discarded door that hid me. As soon as he heaved it over, I'd be caught.

I was trapped like a rat in a—

An ear-piercing scream filled the air, followed by a long string of swearwords.

"Get away from me, you filthy rats!" Tripp yelled. Only he didn't say "filthy."

I heard him throw down whatever heavy piece of trash he'd been holding and take several steps back, cursing as he retreated. With a last f-bomb, I heard him scramble back around the corner. You'd have thought he was being chased by giant rats.

I peeked out from behind my hiding spot. No sign of Tripp.

I stayed scrunched down for a few minutes, waiting to hear the comforting sound of the warehouse doors closing again before making a dash for my car.

Seconds later a rat the size of Godzilla ran across my foot.

I gave a silent scream, cupped my mouth, and was out of that garbage heap, down the street, and back in my car faster than an Olympic runner on steroids.

After my breathing returned to near normal, I tried calling Aunt Abby as I headed back to Fort Mason. No answer. That couldn't be good. I left a message that I'd called and would be back at the School Bus soon. I hoped Dillon was still with her, and that the cops—or whoever—hadn't caught up with him. I needed to talk to him. He might be able to figure out what was going on with Tripp and all that computer equipment in that warehouse.

I smelled like crap, but there was no time for a shower. I'd wash up in the sink, put on a fresh apron, and hope the cooking smells covered any unpleasant odors. When I arrived, I parked the car in the lot adjacent to the food trucks again and headed directly for Aunt Abby's Big Yellow School Bus. At four o'clock, the serving day was pretty much over for her comfort food, but the lights were still on in her bus—a good sign, I hoped. I bounded inside and was relieved to see her and Dillon still aboard. Dillon, not surprisingly, had changed into yet another disguise. This time he wore a pair of white overalls and a white cap. The words sewn onto the front of the uniform read "San Francisco Health Department."

Where did he get these outfits?

"You're kidding me," were the first words out of my mouth. "Health inspector? Why not Inspector Gadget?"

"Who?" Dillon said.

"I think it's brilliant," Aunt Abby commented. "He blends right in. No one will recognize him dressed like a health inspector."

I shook my head, then felt a burning on my arm. I held it up to check the spot where I'd scratched it earlier. It was in nearly the same spot as the wound I'd collected when I'd fallen, but on the other arm.

"What happened to you?" Aunt Abby asked, her eyebrows raised to an alarming height. "And your hair? It looks like a rat's nest. What have you been doing?" She reached into a cupboard for the first aid kit and pulled it down, then went to work on my scratch.

Did she have to say "rat's nest"?

"It's nothing. Could have been worse," I said, reminded of the rats. Black plague. Hantavirus. Ugly teeth marks. Not to mention nearly being caught by Tripp Saunders. Who knew what he would have done if he'd found me. "But I did find out where Tripp works. It's no meatpacking plant—that's for sure."

"How did you find him?" Dillon asked. "I tried to find his business online but came up empty."

"That's because his business is bogus. I followed him." I winced as Aunt Abby dabbed alcohol on my wound.

"Sweet. What'd you find out?" Dillon asked

I described the equipment I'd seen through the hole in the covered window.

"Anything else?" Dillon asked.

"A bunch of papers," I said.

"What kind of papers?"

"I don't know. White. Some were cut into the size of business cards. There were a few photographs of people—head shots. Small. Oh, and something that looked like squares of sandpaper.

Dillon nodded. "He's making fake IDs."

"What?" I said.

"Fake IDs."

"You mean, like, so underage kids can buy beer?" I asked.

Dillon shook his head. "I doubt it. He's probably making them for illegals and selling them for megabucks."

"Seriously?"

"Sounds like it, from what you described," Dillon said. "Fake IDs are big business these days. Against the law, of course, but there's a huge demand for all kinds of fake documents, especially for illegal aliens. And they're pretty easy to make."

"You know how to make fake IDs?" I asked as Aunt Abby placed a large Band-Aid over the scratch on my arm. She would have been a great nurse.

He shrugged. "You don't need to be a genius or anything. The easy way is to just scan an ID into your computer, open it in Photoshop, insert a photo, change the text fields—name, birth date, hair, eye color, stuff like that—then print it on heavy cardstock, cut it out, and laminate it."

"That's the easy way?" I asked, realizing I could never enter the fake ID business if my life depended on it.

"Yeah, but from what you described, it sounds more like Tripp is using professional equipment. The initial setup costs a bunch, but the results look totally real, and the payoff can be huge."

"What's the professional method?" Aunt Abby asked. I wondered if she was thinking of starting up a side business.

"Same as the easy way, but you also need Teslin paper, butterfly pouches, a laminator, and a magnetic strip encoder, just to get started. You have to find a template for your state on Internet sites like Peer-2-Peer file sharing or BitTorrent. Then use Photoshop to change the text fields—that's standard. Scan in the photo and signature image files. If you have a passport photo, that works best. Change the background and color variance, then add a PDF417 bar code. You can find those online too. Last, you'll need to encode a magnetic stripe so it's scannable. They aren't cheap, but there are discount suppliers online if you know where to look. Then just print everything on synthetic microperforated paper with an inkjet printer, laminate it in the butterfly pouch, add a hologram, and you have a whole new life." Dillon grinned, proud of his questionable knowledge.

I was sorry we'd asked.

"Who *are* you?" I asked, shaking my head.

"Where do you get a hologram?" Aunt Abby asked.

"Like everything else—online," Dillon said matter-of-factly.

Ha. I wondered if Amazon carried them. They sold everything.

"A generic one is fine," he continued. "Most people don't bother looking at it. But if you really want it to look pro, you use the shield-and-key hologram—it's a transparent rainbow, and pretty much impossible to tell that it's fake."

"And this really works?" I asked, finding it hard to believe that making fake IDs could ever be a simple task for someone like me.

"If you know what you're doing. There are tricks, like sanding the edges a little to make the card look worn."

Hence the sandpaper I'd spotted on one of the tables.

"Dillon," Aunt Abby, said, "you haven't made any of these fake IDs, have you?"

"No way. It's totally illegal," Dillon said.

As if that had stopped him from hacking into computers.

"But I know a few people who do, and they're making hella cash," Dillon continued. "They sell them through a bunch of different outlets. I'll bet Tripp sold his through places like Boris's food truck. It would be pretty easy to buy, say, lunch, then pay a little extra for it and get a fake ID along with it."

Hmm. Could be the connection to Boris's death we'd been looking for. "How much do people pay for fake IDs?" I asked.

"Anywhere from a hundred to a grand, depending on what kind and how many."

A grand! "Can these friends of yours make any kind of ID you want?" Aunt Abby asked.

"Yep. Driver's licenses, green cards, social security cards, credit cards, library cards, just for starters. There was this big ring in New York last year that was finally busted. They were making around two mil a year. People ordered the IDs in the morning and had them by afternoon. They were distributed by pawn shops, street food carts, knockoff jewelry shops, places like that. I'm telling you, identity theft has become big business."

"So really, Dillon, how do you know all this stuff?" I asked. "Who are these 'friends' of yours?"

Dillon shrugged.

"Darcy, he knows all of this because he's supersmart," Aunt Abby answered for him.

He's more like a savant, I thought. I'd read about Asperger's syndrome when I'd first met Dillon years ago. He had so many of the characteristics—lacking social skills, fixated on routine, avoiding eye contact, preoccupied with computers, talks a lot about his favorite subject, prefers the quiet of his bedroom. But no one had ever approached Aunt Abby about his possible disorder. To her he was simply "supersmart."

"So if Tripp is making and selling these fake IDs, and using places like Boris's truck to distribute them, why would he kill Boris?" I asked.

"I dunno. Maybe Boris didn't want to do it anymore," Dillon said. "Didn't you say you overheard him say something like he was finished with whatever? Maybe he threatened to rat on Tripp and Tripp killed him to shut him up."

I thought about Cherry Washington. "How does Cherry fit into all of this?"

"You said you saw her with Tripp," Dillon said.

I nodded. "And she seems quite eager to take over Boris's business. But again, there's no connection to Oliver Jameson's death."

"Maybe Oliver was selling IDs for Tripp too," Aunt Abby suggested, packing up the first aid supplies.

I turned to her. "You think Oliver might have been involved in this? But why?"

"You said his business was dying," Aunt Abby suggested. "Maybe he needed the money."

"And you think Tripp is going around killing all his middlemen?" I said. "Seems unlikely."

"Maybe I can do some digging on Cherry Washington—see if there's a connection to Jameson we might have missed," Dillon offered.

I nodded. "While you're at it, see what you can find out about Tripp Saunders. Is your laptop here?"

Dillon nodded.

"Okay, tomorrow I'll go back to Bones 'n' Brew and see if I can find out anything more about Oliver from his sister—what's-her-name." I said. "Maybe if I ask the right questions, she can provide some kind of link between these two chefs and/or Tripp. As soon as we get cleaned up here, I'm heading home to take a long hot shower and get the smell of rat poop off me. If I never see another rat in my lifetime, it'll be too soon. And that includes your rat, Dillon."

Dillon shot me a look. I made a face at him.

I spent the next half hour helping Abby and Dillon clean up, so we'd be ready for the next day's customers.

"You smell!" Aunt Abby said. "Go on home and take a shower. Dillon and I will finish the rest."

I took off my soiled apron and dropped it in the laundry bag. "Okay, See you at home," I said as I headed down the School Bus steps.

"I'll be right behind you, dear," Aunt Abby called to me.

"Lock up tight," I called back to my aunt and Dillon. "Tripp may have figured out it was me snooping around his warehouse, so we need to be extra-careful."

I stepped out of the School Bus and shuddered as a cold, damp bay wind blew across my face. I glanced around the food truck area and focused on Boris's truck. No sign of life. I checked Jake's place. The lights inside appeared to be on, but I didn't see Jake through the windows and wondered where he was.

As I walked toward the parking lot, I got the eerie feeling I was being watched, and I tried to shake it off as paranoid jitters. When I arrived at my car, I noticed a ticket on my windshield and snatched it off.

"Damn!" I said aloud. "I paid the parking fee!" I was about to curse the faceless parking attendant when I unfolded the white paper and saw the words scrawled inside in black marker.

"Mind your own business, or you might find a little rodent meat in your next potpie."

Chapter 18

I glanced around the parking lot for any sign of trouble, peeked in the backseat of my car just to make sure no one was hiding inside—including a rat—then quickly got in and locked the doors.

I shivered. Someone was on to me. Someone knew where I worked, which car I drove, and no doubt a lot more about me than I realized.

Was it Tripp? Was he watching me now? Did he mean to follow up on his threat and taint my aunt's food with a dead rat?

Or did he know about Dillon's pet rat?

I pressed the button to turn on the engine and headlights and backed out of the spot. My sweaty hands slipped on the steering wheel. As I pulled up to the parking lot exit, I thought about the other people on my suspects list. They all knew I was looking into the murders. If one of them was the killer, then he or she had good reason to try to stop me. The question was, if it wasn't Tripp, who was it? Or had I overlooked someone not on my list?

The car idled at the exit as I waited for a break in traffic to pull out. So much for a fast getaway. Good thing no one was chasing me at the moment.

Or was someone following me and I just didn't know it?

I tapped Aunt Abby's number on my cell phone. If the killer knew about me, then he surely knew about my connection to my aunt. After all, he'd just left a threatening note relating to a rat in Aunt Abby's food. I had a feeling she wasn't safe either.

"Hello?" my aunt said brightly.

"Aunt Abby? Are you all right?"

"Of course, dear. Why do you ask?"

"Someone left a nasty note on my car. I think it might have been the murderer, and he knows where I live, so to speak. I'm worried we both might be in danger."

"Oh goodness, Darcy. What about Dillon?" I hadn't thought to worry about my cousin. I decided not to mention the reference to rodent meat, in case the note referred to Ratty. "Oh, I'm sure he's safe after using all of those disguises. But tell him about the note and make sure he keeps an eye on you, will you?"

"Dillon's not with me, Darcy," my aunt said. I heard alarm in her usually cheery voice. "I'm already on my way home. I left him in the bus. It's locked, but now you've got me worried."

Aunt Abby was never a fan of the hands-free cell phone law.

"Listen, I'll give him a call. Just take care of yourself. Go straight home and lock the doors. I'll be there soon."

"All right," Aunt Abby said, "but you'll call me if Dillon's in any kind of trouble, won't you?"

"Yes, of course. I'll talk to you soon." I ended the call, then tapped Dillon's cell phone number. He answered on the fourth ring, just when I was about to panic.

"'S'up, Darce?" Dillon said. I could hear his laptop keyboard clicking in the background.

"Dillon, I'm worried about your mother. I found a threatening note waiting for me on my windshield when I got to my car. Whoever left it knows I've been digging into the murders. And I think he made a veiled threat involving your pet rat."

The clicking stopped. "What? What did the note say exactly?" Dillon asked.

"Just that if I didn't stop snooping, there might be a little rodent meat coming our way. I told Aunt Abby to go directly home and lock the doors."

There was a long pause on the other end. Goose bumps rose on my arms. "Dillon? Are you there?"

I heard some noise; then he answered, "Yeah, I'm on my way."

"But, Dillon, the cops are after you! They're probably watching the house. And if they are, they're sure to spot you."

"Don't worry. They won't see me. Gotta go. Later."

Dillon hung up, leaving me holding a dead line.

I set down the phone. I had mixed feelings about Dillon going home. I was glad that he'd be there to protect his mother, but I didn't want him to get arrested.

I was just about to pull into the street when I heard a knock on the hood of my car.

I jumped a foot, accidently hitting the horn and managing to kill the engine.

A dark figure hovered outside my side window.

"Get out of here!" I screamed and fumbled for my phone. "I'm calling the police!"

The figure stepped back into my headlights, his hands raised in surrender. One hand held a small bag.

"Jake!"

"Just me. Sorry if I startled you."

I lowered the window. "You didn't startle me—you scared the crap out of me! Who goes around parking lots knocking on people's hoods? No one! You nearly gave me a heart attack."

He moved closer to my window and leaned in. "Why so jumpy? Something happen?"

How did he know?

"Nothing . . . I just . . ."

"Pull over. You don't look like you're in any condition to drive at the moment. Besides, I've got a surprise for you."

"How did you know where I was?" I asked.

"Saw you leave the bus and head this way. I hoped I'd catch you before you drove off."

I hesitated, then felt foolish that I was still worried this guy might be a murderer. He was just too cute to kill anybody.

I thought about Aunt Abby alone at her house and figured Dillon would be there soon. Restarting the car, I backed out of the exit and over to a nearby slot, then turned off the engine, deliberately this time. Pushing a button, I unlocked the doors. Jake let himself into the passenger seat and held up the bag.

"What's that?" I asked, hoping it was a cream puff and not a weapon of some kind. Of course, if anyone wanted to try to kill me, they didn't need to leave threatening notes. All they had to do was distract me with a cream puff and get it over with.

Jake opened the bag. In such close quarters, he smelled of chocolate. What had he been doing? Bathing in it?

Worked for me.

"Here. I'm trying another new recipe. See what you think."

He lifted out a delicate mini cream puff concoction and held it in his open palm.

I eyed it suspiciously. How would I know if poison was one of the ingredients? "What is it?"

"A cream puff," he said smartly.

"I *know* that. What *kind*?" I tried not to openly drool, but the heady aroma of dark chocolate practically made me swoon. I felt like Dorothy under the influence of a poppy field.

"S'mores," he announced proudly.

"Seriously?" I said, recalling the flavor of my favorite Girl Scout camp dessert. "How do you make S'mores Dream Puffs?

"Simple. I added graham cracker crumbs to the shell batter, then filled it with a marshmallow cream mixture and covered it in melted Ghirardelli chocolate bars. I want to know what you think."

It sounded so tempting I wanted to swallow it whole. *But that would be crass,* I thought. I accepted the culinary artwork from his large hand and took a bite, savoring the combination of sweet flavors as they melted in my mouth.

"Mmmmmm," was about all I could manage after that first bite. I finished the rest in a single bite, wishing he'd brought a dozen more. I could have easily downed

them without a thought about the billions of calories in each one.

"Wow," I finally said. "Heaven."

Jake grinned. "Thanks." He pointed to the side of my cheek. "You've got a little . . ." He leaned in and used his finger to wipe off the bit of cream puff that had managed to escape my mouth. My breath caught. His dark eyes held my gaze. He leaned in closer and put his warm hand on my cool cheek.

And then he kissed me.

It was almost as good as the cream puff.

I pulled back, surprised at myself. I had just let a suspect kiss me! That was not a good thing for a person investigating a murder to do. What was wrong with me? I could claim I was under the influence of chocolate marshmallow and dark brown eyes. No jury of women would ever convict me. But this was not cool.

Jake must have recognized my reaction. "Sorry," he said.

With that little smile on his face, he didn't look so sorry.

"Oh, no . . . I . . . uh," I stammered. "I should be getting home to my aunt. I'm worried about her."

Jake frowned. "Something happen?"

I sighed. Now that he'd kissed me—and I'd let him—I figured I might as well tell him about the note—and maybe cross him off my suspect list. I pulled the crumpled paper out of my purse, switched on the dome light, and showed it to him.

"Someone left this on your car?" he asked after reading it.

I nodded. "That's why I'm worried about Aunt Abby. Whoever wrote that probably knows I've been looking into the murders. And he somehow knows that Dillon has a pet rat. I have a feeling he's been following me."

"Darcy, this is serious. You need to call the police."

"You're right. I will. It's just that with Dillon hiding out in Aunt Abby's bus, I don't want to get him into more trouble, you know?"

"It sounds like Dillon can take care of himself. Right now you need to protect yourself and your aunt. And that means calling Detective Shelton, you hear?"

Jake sounded genuinely concerned, and it touched me. Almost as much as that kiss had.

"I will."

"Now," Jake ordered.

I sighed and dialed the detective's number. He answered on the first ring, and I explained about the note I'd found on my car. He asked me several questions—Did I see anyone around my car? Did I have an idea who left the note? Had something else happened he didn't know about? After fifteen minutes on the phone, I finished answering his questions and hung up.

"Happy?" I asked Jake.

He nodded. "What did Shelton say?"

"He told me to go home, lock the doors, and watch my back."

"Good advice," Jake said.

"And I'll do that, right after I check to make sure my aunt's okay."

"How about I follow you?"

"No need. Really. Dillon will be there."

Jake nodded. "All right, but call me when you get there. I want to know you're safe."

"Okay," I said.

He started to open the door, then turned back to me. "Listen, I've been doing a little digging myself, mostly to get my name off your suspect list." He shot me a glance.

I felt myself blush. "Did you find out something?"

"I don't know if you've heard, but when I first opened for business here, I went out with Willow a couple of times. I just wanted to get that out in the open. She kept asking me to these clubs, but they weren't for me. Then she met this guy who worked for Boris a few months ago—someone named Ivan, I think his name was. Turns out he was an illegal."

"You mean, an illegal alien?"

Jake nodded. "Willow said that Boris said he was going to help get Ivan legal status because he worked for him. But the deal fell through after Willow began seeing Ivan. It turned out Boris had a major crush on Willow and was jealous."

"That's what Aunt Abby said."

"She *is* pretty cute, if you overlook all her tats and piercings."

I narrowed my eyes at him.

"Just not my type," he added, grinning.

"Do you think Willow might have killed Boris for getting what's-his-name sent back to wherever he came from? Or hired someone to do it for her?" I was thinking of Tripp.

"Don't know, but Willow told me she'd once been an exotic dancer and had been in trouble with the law for beating up a guy who tried to force himself on her."

"She beat *him* up!?" I was stunned that my friendly coffee source had that kind of muscle in her. And that kind of background.

"Kicked his ass, is what she said. She said his eyes were solid red and his face looked like it had been run through a coffee grinder. She was kind of proud of that."

"Wow. Did she go to jail?"

"Got probation. Called it self-defense. She said if she'd had more than pepper spray and her cell phone with her, she could have easily killed him."

"She used her cell phone?"

"Smacked him with the corner of it."

"Wow." Who knew a cell phone could be used as a weapon?

"And pepper spray?"

"She said all the girls carried pepper spray."

We were back to pepper again.

"Do you think she could have killed Boris?"

"I don't know, but she's got a temper—that's for sure."

I thought for a moment, taking it all in. "Thanks for telling me."

He reopened his door. "So, you'll call me, right?" He reached into his jeans pocket and pulled out a business card with the name of his company and his cell phone number.

I took it and put it in my purse. "As soon as I get home."

"All right. Night, Darcy."

"Good night, Jake. And thanks for the cream puff."

"Glad you liked it. Thanks for the dessert afterward."

I felt myself blush again.

He got out of the car and stood watching me as I started up the engine and headed for the parking lot exit once again.

I was about to pull into the street when I noticed someone enter the back door of the Bones 'n' Brew restaurant across the street. Moments later, the figure came back out carrying two large bags of trash. I couldn't tell if it was a man or a woman in the dim light, but the person was strong enough to open the heavy Dumpster lid and heave over the two bags before slamming the lid shut. With a last glance around, he—or she—reentered the restaurant.

Hmm. Was business getting back to normal at Bones 'n' Brew already?

I thought a moment, weighing my options. I was sure Dillon was at home by now, keeping Aunt Abby safe. In fact, Dillon was a lot better protection than I would have been. I let curiosity get the better of me. Who was tossing out garbage at Bones 'n' Brew?

I pulled into traffic, made a left turn at the first opportunity, then drove into the Bones 'n' Brew customer lot, making sure to park in a well-lighted section just in case I was still being followed. I hadn't come up with a connection between Oliver Jameson and Boris Obregar yet, nor had I talked to Oliver's sister since Boris's murder. If she was the one taking out the trash, this might be a good time to ask her a few more questions and see if I could figure out the link between the two dead chefs.

And if anyone tried to follow me inside and attack me, there would be plenty of knives around to use to defend myself. After working in Aunt Abby's School Bus kitchen for the past couple of days, I was beginning to know my way around sharp instruments.

I got out of the car, made sure to lock it, then started for the back door. I paused a moment when I reached the Dumpster, still wondering what was in those bags of trash that had just been tossed. Maybe something that would offer a clue to the mystery? But I wasn't about to go digging around in there alone, now that it had gotten dark. Not with a killer on the loose.

Maybe tomorrow.

I knocked on the door and waited.

No answer.

Glancing around to make sure my stalker wasn't stalking me at the moment, I turned the knob.

It opened. I entered.

"Hello?" I called, walking down the small hallway toward the kitchen. The place was empty and deadly quiet, but the overhead lights were on. So where had the person I'd seen disappeared to?

I moved through the kitchen, passed the dining area, and headed to Oliver's office. The door was ajar. I pushed it open slowly and looked inside the room, lit only by a small desk light. I tiptoed in. The place was empty, but something felt odd. I stepped to the desk where Oliver had been discovered, slumped over his crab bisque. *Brr.* Had a ghost just passed through me or was it cold in here?

I scanned the desk. A mess of papers were scattered about. I walked around to the front of the desk and froze.

All the drawers were pulled open. Several of them had been dumped out onto the floor. There were papers everywhere.

Someone had obviously been searching through Oliver's stuff.

For what?

I heard the office door creak and whirled around.

A figure stood in the doorway, one arm raised, a large knife glinting in the upheld hand.

I was trapped like a rat in a dead man's office.

Chapter 19

"Get out of here!" the figure screamed, stepping into the room. "I have a knife!"

I recognized Livvy immediately. Apparently she hadn't recognized me.

I held my hands up. "Livvy, it's me, Darcy. We talked the other day, remember? I'm the one writing a story about your brother and the restaurant."

She squinted at me, then lowered the knife. "What are you doing here? You scared me half to death."

"I'm sorry. I knocked but no one answered. The door was open. . . . I saw the lights on and thought I could ask you a few more questions. I didn't mean to frighten you."

"Well, you did. I wasn't expecting anyone to just come waltzing in uninvited." She moved a few more steps inside and set the knife on the desk.

"I know. Sorry." I glanced around at the ravaged office. "What happened?"

She shrugged, then bent down, righted Oliver's overturned swivel chair, and dropped into it. "Someone tossed it, obviously. Probably looking for cash or employee paychecks. It was like this when I got here a few minutes ago."

A few minutes ago? Then who was the one I saw carrying out the trash?

"Did you call the police?"

"I was just about to. I thought I'd look around and see if I could figure out if anything is missing."

"Is there?"

"That's what's weird. It doesn't seem like anything's been stolen." She yanked out the already open top drawer and riffled through the contents. "Even his keys are still here." She held them up and twirled the key ring. It flew off her finger and landed at her feet. She slid off the chair and knelt to retrieve the keys. On her way up, she bumped her head on the open desk drawer and sat down again.

"Ouch!" she said, rubbing her head. "Stupid drawer!" She reached up and viciously shoved the drawer with the heel of her hand in an attempt to close it, but the drawer caught on something and didn't budge. This time she massaged her hand.

"You okay?" I asked, looking down at her.

She nodded and shook her hand. She started to get up but stopped and studied the drawer a moment. Frowning, she reached up with her other hand and gently tried to push the drawer closed. It still wouldn't budge.

"Something's stuck. . . ." After she'd run her hands under the drawer, her eyes widened. Suddenly she yanked the drawer out from the desk and turned it over on the floor.

Duct-taped underneath was a legal-sized manila envelope. Livvy dug at the tape and ripped the manila envelope from the bottom of the drawer. Peeling off the tape, she reached inside and pulled out a handful of loose papers.

"Oh my God," she whispered.

"What are those?"

She flipped through the papers, then looked up at me. "They're recipes! Ollie's secret recipes for all his signature dishes. He would never tell me where he kept them. He was so paranoid someone was going to find them and steal them. He had his chef memorize them so no one would be able to copy them. This must be what the thief was looking for!"

"Wow, he really was paranoid, wasn't he? Hiding them like that. Who was he afraid would steal his recipes?"

"Everyone, but lately he was obsessed with Boris Obregar. He was sure Boris wanted to put him out of business."

Oliver felt threatened by Boris? "Do you think Boris might have killed Oliver to get the recipes?" I asked.

"I don't know. I suppose he could have been the one who poisoned my brother, but stealing recipes doesn't seem like much of a reason to kill someone. And besides, how do I find out for sure, now that Boris is dead too?"

Was this the link I was looking for, the connection between Oliver Jameson and Boris Obregar? Hard to believe it was all about recipes. Were Oliver's recipes really that valuable? Or was there something more to it? And if Boris killed Oliver to steal them, then who killed Boris? I felt like a beater turning in circles in a mixing bowl, from Boris to Oliver to Boris. . . .

Who was the third ingredient in this bizarre recipe?

"What will you do with them?" I asked Livvy as she flipped through the recipes.

"Lock them in the safe, I guess. I wasn't planning to

use them when we reopen. I'm offering a whole new menu."

I was puzzled by the odd timing of the break-in and said aloud, "Well, Boris didn't break in here, because he's dead, and you said you just found it this way." I glanced around for signs that the lock had been damaged, the door had been busted, or a window had been smashed, but I saw nothing to indicate a break-in. While the office had been turned upside down, the door and windows seemed secure. Except for the back door, the way I'd come in.

"Livvy, was the office locked?"

She thought for a moment. "Uh . . . yes. After what happened to Ollie, I wanted to make sure his things were safe."

"I'm no cop, but I don't see any signs of forced entry. Are you sure you locked it?"

Livvy paused again. "I . . . suppose I could have forgotten this time. The door was open when I got here about an hour ago, and the room was a mess."

"Did you see anything or hear anything?"

She shook her head. "I went straight to the office to see if there were any phone messages and found it like this."

"Well, you need to call the police. Do you want me to call them?"

"No, I'll do it," Livvy said, retrieving her cell phone from her apron pocket. She stepped out of the room to make the call. At that moment, my phone played a familiar Disney tune.

Aunt Abby! Was she all right? Had Dillon arrived to make sure she was safe?

"Aunt Abby?" I answered, alarmed. "Are you okay? Is Dillon there?"

Silence.

"Aunt Abby!? Are you there? Has something happened?"

More silence.

"Aunt Abby! Talk to me!"

The line went dead.

I punched REDIAL. The call went to voice mail.

"Something's wrong," I said, more to myself than to Livvy as she stepped back in the office. I looked at her. "You called the police?"

She nodded. "They're on their way. What's the matter?"

"My aunt . . . I've got to go. Will you be all right by yourself until they get here?"

"Yes, I'm sure they'll arrive in a few minutes. Go."

I ran from the room and out the back door, headed for my car. I hoped Livvy would be safe, but my priority was Aunt Abby. And the way things had been going, I didn't want to take any chances. Even if Dillon was there, he was no Superman, unless it involved virtual fighting.

As soon as I arrived at my car, I knew something was off. I glanced down at the front tire. It was flat. I checked the back tire. Also flat. As I rounded the car, I was sure I'd find two more flat tires.

Obviously someone knew I was at the restaurant and had sent me another message, this time by disabling my car. Whoever it was had probably stuck a knife in the tires to flatten them.

Great. Now what? I could call AAA and get a tow, but that would take an hour or so, time I didn't have to spare. I could ask Livvy if I could borrow her car, but she was going to be dealing with the police. And if they came while I was here, I'd have to answer all kinds of questions. Again, I didn't have the time. My only other option was to hail a cab.

I walked down a couple of blocks, searching for a taxi, but all the ones that passed by were occupied, most likely by tourists. I finally caught one on Columbus and gave the driver directions to my aunt's house. We passed the bustling Fisherman's Wharf and North Beach areas, where the tourists were out in full force, sampling crab cocktails and checking out shops along the brightly lit street. I kept calling my aunt and Dillon, but the calls continued to go to voice mail.

Totally panicked, I dialed 9-1-1.

A voice came on the line. A recorded voice.

I was put on hold.

Seriously?

I hung up, frustrated, then had a thought. I could call Jake. He'd offered to help if I needed it. I pulled his business card out of my purse, flipped on the interior cab light, and punched in his number as quickly as I could. I misdialed twice; third time was the charm.

"Hello?"

"Jake! It's Darcy! I think my aunt is in trouble. . . . I just got a call from her and—*Watch out!*" I called to the cabdriver, who was trying to squeeze the car between a bus and a truck.

"Darcy?"

"Sorry. I'm in a cab headed for Aunt Abby's and . . . Never mind. Anyway, can you meet me there as soon as possible? I think something's seriously wrong. . . ."

"You sound out of breath. Slow down, and tell me what happened."

I took a deep breath and explained everything I knew—the phone call from Aunt Abby, the four punctured tires, the unanswered call to the police. "Can you come?"

"I'll be right there."

"Hurry!"

I hung up and told the driver to hurry too. He stepped on the accelerator and took the corners like Vin Diesel in one of those *Fast and Furious* movies. I felt the tires skid a few times and heard the squeals, but I said nothing, too frantic about my aunt's well-being. And Dillon's.

In spite of the cabdriver's race-car maneuvers, it was nearly seven when we reached Aunt Abby's house, thanks to the congested streets and crowds of pedestrians. All in all, I'd lost a lot of time.

I got out of the cab, paid the driver, and ran up the driveway of my aunt's home. The house was completely dark. Not good. Was there any chance Aunt Abby had decided not to go home? If so, then where would she have gone? Where was Dillon? And why had she called?

I debated about whether to call the police again, decided to try, and gave up when I was put on hold once more. I had no choice. If my aunt was inside, she could be in real trouble.

I tiptoed up to the front door, peering into the dark window. No sign of anyone.

Suddenly I heard barking. Basil!

I tried the door. It opened.

That wasn't like my aunt. Even though she left the sliding glass door in the back unlocked for me, she never left her front door unlocked. I supposed Dillon could have done it—he's that absentminded. But under the circumstances . . .

Slowly, I pushed the door open. Basil barked wildly until he recognized me, but he still seemed agitated.

"Aunt Abby?" I called before stepping inside.

"Mmmphlrph!"

At the muffled sound, I broke into a sweat, but I listened, trying to determine where the sound came from.

"Aunt Abby?" I called again, glancing around for a sign of an intruder. I glanced down at Basil. "Where is she, boy?"

A thud came from the kitchen area.

I switched on the entryway light and ran toward the sound, then switched on the kitchen light. Basil was at my heels.

The room was empty.

"Aunt Abby!" I screamed, looking around for her. Basil made a beeline around the kitchen island.

I heard a moan. From behind the island.

I sped around the corner of the island and spotted my aunt. She was lying on the floor, tied up with duct tape, bound to a kitchen chair, with a flour sack over her head. It looked like she'd fallen over backward. Basil continued barking.

"Hold on!" I said and knelt down, frantic to free her. I pulled off the bag and tugged the duct tape from her mouth, trying to reassure her. As soon as I cleared her airway, she coughed.

"Aunt Abby! What happened? Are you all right?"

She rolled her eyes, appearing dizzy and disoriented. Finally her eyes cleared and she spoke, "Darcy . . . Thank God you're here. Find Dillon!"

"As soon as I get you untied." I worked at the tape that bound her hands and legs to the chair, then grabbed a large kitchen knife and cut through the tape. Moments later I had her free. She reached over and picked up her small dog.

I helped her to a sitting position on the floor. With Basil on her lap, she rubbed her wrists, then massaged the back of her skull. "Oh, my head," she said. "I fell over trying to scoot to the phone." She lifted the dog and tried to get up. "I've got to find Dillon. Dillon!" she called.

We both heard a muffled noise coming from the hall closet.

"Help me up!" Aunt Abby said, putting the dog on the floor. I gave her a hand and she staggered for the closet. I followed, holding the knife in case I needed it for more than cutting through duct tape.

Aunt Abby pulled open the closet door. Dillon was seated on the floor, his arms taped behind his back, his legs folded and taped together. His head was also covered with a flour bag. As soon as I pulled off the bag to reveal his duct-taped mouth, his wide eyes spoke volumes. While Aunt Abby removed the tape, I cut through the bindings that held his arms and legs. We had him free minutes later.

"Dillon! What happened?" Aunt Abby knelt beside him, while Basil licked him.

"I'm fine, Mom," Dillon said as he pushed himself to standing. He helped his mother up and looked her over. "Did they hurt you?"

She rubbed her head. "No. I bumped my head when I fell over in the chair. I was trying to get to the phone."

"What happened?" I asked, relieved they were both alive and apparently well.

Aunt Abby looked down at her hands. "I . . . guess I left the back door unlocked."

"What? I told you to lock up!" I cried.

"I know, but I knew Dillon was coming over. Sometimes he doesn't have his key. . . . I didn't really expect . . ." Tears welled in her eyes. "Anyway, I thought it was Dillon when I heard the door slide open, so I called out to him. A few seconds later someone put a bag over my head and tied me up. Then they duct-taped my mouth. I was so scared."

Dillon gave his mom a hug. "It's okay, Mom. We're all right."

"Great watchdog you are, Basil," I said to the dog. I turned to Dillon. "You didn't see or hear anything when you arrived?"

"No . . . I came in through the back door and headed for the kitchen. That's when someone pulled that cloth bag over *my* head. I tried to wrestle with him but I couldn't see. He knocked me down and bound me with that tape and shoved me into the closet."

"At least he didn't hurt Basil," Aunt Abby said. She headed for the kitchen, Basil at her feet. "I think we could all use a glass of wine."

When we got there, I noticed a recipe card lying on the floor near where I'd found Aunt Abby. It must have blown off the counter at some point. I bent down and picked it up, flipped it over, and read the words scrawled in black marker.

"Remember the rat? Next time it'll be you."

"Oh dear God!" Aunt Abby said, spotting the message in my hand. She looked up at me.

Dillon blinked, then ran to his bedroom. He returned moments later, looking relieved. "Ratty's fine."

I shook my head. This was all my fault. If I hadn't been sticking my nose into these murders, Aunt Abby and Dillon wouldn't have been attacked. And if I hadn't dawdled so long in the parking lot with Jake or at the restaurant with Livvy, I might have been here in time to deal with the intruder. I could feel tears forming and blinked several times to keep them at bay.

"What's taking Jake so long?" I said to myself.

"You called Jake?" my aunt Abby asked.

"Yes," I said. "After I got your phone call. I was worried. I couldn't get through to the police, so I asked him to come."

Aunt Abby looked puzzled. "What phone call?"

"The one you made about thirty minutes ago. You didn't say anything when I answered and when I called back, you still didn't answer, so I had a feeling you were in trouble."

"I didn't make any phone call," my aunt said. "Not after I talked to Dillon and he told me he was headed home."

"But you had to have made that call," I said. "Who else would it have been?"

Aunt Abby ran into the kitchen. I followed her and found her digging through her purse.

"What is it, Aunt Abby?" I asked.

"My cell phone," she answered, withdrawing her hand from her purse. "It was in here."

"Uh-oh," Dillon said. He reached into his pockets. His

hands came out empty. "My phone's gone too. Whoever attacked us took our cell phones."

I shuddered. Why would someone do that?

Where had that call—the one I thought was from Aunt Abby—actually come from?

And who had made it?

Chapter 20

The doorbell rang, startling all of us. Basil barked. I jumped. Aunt Abby let out a little scream. And Dillon ran back to the closet, got in, and closed the door.

"That's Jake!" I said, rushing out of the room. At least I hoped it was Jake, I thought as I neared the front door. I slowed down and switched on the hall light, calling out, "Who's there?"

"It's me. Are you all right?"

I looked through the peephole and was relieved to find it was indeed Jake. I yanked open the door and pulled him inside, closing and locking the door behind him. Basil wagged his tail.

"You look like you've seen a ghost," Jake said, eyeing me. He took me in his arms—and I let him. It felt good to be held.

"Thank God you're here! Someone broke into the house. . . ." I led him into the kitchen, where Aunt Abby was waiting with the large knife in her hand.

"It's okay, Aunt Abby. You can put the knife down."

Aunt Abby lowered the weapon and set it on the island counter, then plopped onto a stool, looking exhausted.

"Dillon!" I called. "You can come out now. It's just Jake."

The closet door creaked open. An eyeball appeared in the crack. The eyeball scanned the area; then the door opened the rest of the way and out stepped Dillon.

"What's going on?" Jake asked, glancing around at the three of us.

I explained what I'd found when I'd arrived and showed him the note. Aunt Abby filled in the rest of the details. Dillon said nothing. Instead he helped himself to some leftover snickerdoodles Aunt Abby had brought home from her food bus.

"You called the cops, I assume," he said to me.

"I tried, but all I got was a recorded message, so I gave up. That's why I called you."

Jake pulled out his cell phone. I figured he was going to call 9-1-1, but he withdrew a business card from another pocket and tapped in a seven-digit number.

"Who are you calling?" I asked.

He didn't answer me. Instead, he said into the phone, "Yeah, Detective Shelton? This is Jake Miller. I'm . . . friends with Abigail Warner. . . ."

He paused, listening, then continued. "Right. I'm over at Mrs. Warner's house. Someone broke into her place a while ago and tied her up and threatened her. Can you send somebody over?"

I watched Jake's face as he listened to the detective, trying to read his reaction to Shelton's response, but other than the tight eyebrows, Jake's expression masked his emotions.

As soon as he hung up the phone, I asked, "What did he say?"

"He's coming over with a couple of crime techs. Said to stay put, keep the doors locked, and not touch anything."

Dillon swallowed the bite of cookie in his mouth, nearly choking on it, before managing to say, "I'm outta here." He mumbled something more through the remaining crumbs, but I couldn't make out his words.

Jake shot him a look. "Shelton's going to know you were here, Dillon. You're part of this. You can't go running off again."

"Oh no?" Dillon said, wiping his mouth with his sleeve. "Watch me."

"Dillon!" Aunt Abby cried. "What should I tell Detective Shelton?"

"Tell him I was here, but then I left and you don't know where I went," Dillon said. "Tell him I'm doing my own investigation since they obviously can't seem to solve these murders and want to pin it on you and me. Tell him to go—"

"Dillon! Watch your language," Aunt Abby said. In spite of everything that had happened, my aunt still believed in good manners, even from her grown son.

"Later, dudes," Dillon said. He gathered a handful of snickerdoodles, stuffed them in his jacket pockets, and ducked out the back door. I heard his little motor scooter buzz off into the night.

Aunt Abby glanced at me, then Jake. She threw up her hands in defeat. "Don't look at me like that. I tried. He had no choice. They have a warrant for him."

Jake and I said nothing, but we both understood. The only problem was, when we eventually told the detective what had happened—including the part about Dillon—would we be accused of aiding and abetting a wanted criminal?

Aunt Abby prepared some coffee and arranged the

remaining snickerdoodles on a fancy plate. Jake looked around the room for clues about the intruder, being careful not to touch anything. I sat on a stool, pulled out my notebook, and jotted down what had happened.

Ten minutes later there was a loud knock on the front door. Basil ran to the door and barked loudly.

"That was quick," Aunt Abby said. She checked her lipstick in the toaster reflection, fluffed her curly hair, and said, "I'll get it."

I didn't want her to answer the door alone in case it wasn't the detective, so I followed her. Jake was right behind us. Aunt Abby peeked through the peephole, then turned to us and said, "Remember, we don't know where Dillon is." With a last tug at her jersey top in an attempt to straighten it, she opened the door to Detective Shelton and two officers wearing white overalls and latex gloves.

I felt like part of a welcoming committee, standing there with Jake and my aunt.

"Oh, Detective Shelton!" Aunt Abby said. "I'm so glad you're here. It was horrible!"

For a moment there, I thought she was going to throw herself into the detective's arms.

And then it dawned on me. My aunt actually had a crush on Detective Shelton!

"Ms. Warner," the detective said, nodding in respect. "Ms. Burnett. Counselor," he said to me and Jake.

Jake started to say something but then just shut his mouth.

"Come in, come in," Aunt Abby said, opening the door wider. Once the cops were inside the entryway, she led them to the kitchen, where the plate of snickerdoodles sat on the island counter waiting for them. "Would you like some coffee? I just made it. And these snicker-doodles are homemade. My secret ingredient is nutmeg."

I stared at my aunt. She was blathering on as if these guys were party guests instead of police officers.

"No, thanks," Detective Shelton said curtly. He turned to the crime techs. "Look around, guys. See what you can find."

The two men immediately went to work, taking notes, snapping pictures, and examining the duct tape that had bound my aunt and nephew, along with the flour sacks.

The detective sat down on a stool at the counter and pulled out his notebook. "All right, Ms. Warner, tell me exactly what happened."

Aunt Abby poured coffee and brought the cups to the island counter. She set one near the detective and kept the other, then took a seat. Jake and I remained standing—and coffeeless—nearby.

"Well, I was in the kitchen," she began, "testing a new recipe for a seafood casserole made with crab instead of tuna—my secret ingredient. Anyway. I thought I heard Di . . . Someone come in the back door. I'd left it unlocked in case, uh, Darcy came home and forgot her key. Anyway. I called out and no one answered, so I kept working, and that's when someone came up from behind me and pulled that bag over my head."

"Did you get a look at him?" the detective asked. "Male or female? Height? Hair color? Anything?"

Aunt Abby shook her head and nudged the plate of cookies closer to the detective. "Like I said, whoever it was surprised me from behind, so I never saw him. I was so startled and disoriented. Before I could think straight, he grabbed my wrists and taped them behind me and jerked me over to that kitchen chair there and taped up my ankles."

She pointed to a chair at the small kitchen table located in the nearby nook. The detective looked at it, then nodded to one of the officers, indicating he wanted it checked out. Unfortunately, I had righted the chair after freeing my aunt. Hopefully any fingerprints the suspect might have left weren't smeared by my own hands.

The detective jotted down a note. "Then what?"

"Well," Aunt Abby continued, "after he tied me to the chair, naturally I started screaming. So he lifted up the bag partway and taped my mouth shut." The scrap of tape still lay on the floor where I'd dropped it after removing it from my aunt's mouth.

The detective continued his questioning. "Did the intruder say anything to you? Threaten you? Tell you to be quiet? Anything like that?"

"No, nothing. Not a word. At one point I heard him walk away and I thought he was leaving, but he must have heard Dillon—" Aunt Abby clapped a hand over her mouth. Did she really expect to keep Dillon's presence a secret from the detective?

"Your son was here?" the detective asked, eyebrows raised in surprise.

"It's all right, Aunt Abby," I said, laying a hand on her shoulder. "You have to tell him everything. It's obvious you weren't the only one attacked." I turned to the detective. "Yes, Dillon was here. He . . . happened to arrive soon after the intruder broke in. But the attacker surprised him too."

"Where is your son now, Ms. Warner?" the detective asked, looking around.

Jake answered for my aunt. "I'm afraid he's gone, Detective."

Detective Shelton frowned as he turned to Aunt Abby. "Any idea where he is?"

We all shook our heads.

The detective sighed. "All right, why don't you tell me what happened next, Ms. Warner?"

Jake and I shared a quick glance.

"Well," she continued, "like Darcy said, Dillon happened to drop by out of the blue. I would have told him you were looking for him, Detective, but at that moment, I couldn't say anything because my mouth was taped shut. Anyway, the guy did the same thing to Dillon—put a bag over his head, tied him up, and shut him in the hall closet."

The detective alerted one of the techs, nodding toward the closet.

"Did he take anything? Did he hurt you in any way?" Detective Shelton asked.

"I don't think he stole anything, but he left this note. Darcy found it on the floor." She handed over the message written in black marker: *"Remember the rat? Next time it'll be you."* She shivered.

"I think that note was meant for me, Detective," I said. "He probably thinks I live here. I'm just glad he didn't harm my aunt or Dillon."

"What's the reference to the rat?" the detective asked.

"Dillon has a pet rat. I think he was referring to that."

"And why do you think he's after you, Ms. Burnett?"

I dug into my purse and pulled out the note that had been left on my windshield earlier, then handed it to the detective. "Because of this."

He held it by the corner and unfolded it with his pen. If he was trying to save any fingerprints, it was probably too late for that. He read the note aloud: "*Mind your own business or you might find a little rodent meat in your next potpie.*"

"Why didn't you call me about this?" Detective Shelton asked.

"I was going to . . . but I got distracted."

The detective shook his head. "Why do you think he threatened you?"

"Isn't it obvious, Detective?" Jake said. "Because she's trying to save her aunt and her nephew by solving these murders."

Detective Shelton looked at Jake. "And what is your role in all of this?"

"I told you, he's helping us," I answered for him. "Besides, he's right. I found out something that might be connected to the murder of Boris Obregar."

The detective eyed me. "Like what?"

"I think Boris was part of some illegal business."

"Why do you think that?"

"Because I followed that guy from the Meat Wagon—Tripp—and found out he's printing up all kinds of documents in an old abandoned warehouse. I think he heard my phone ring and figured out I was spying on him, so he put that note on my windshield to scare me off. And to make sure I got the message, he came to Aunt Abby's and threatened her."

The detective clicked his pen. "Anything else?"

"Aren't you going to arrest Tripp?" I asked, surprised at his nonchalant response.

"We'll check him out," he said, rising from the stool.

"But look what he did to my aunt! She could have been killed!"

"We don't know it was him yet," Detective Shelton said. "I'll know more when my guys get this stuff back to forensics. Meanwhile, lock your doors and quit following possible murder suspects to empty warehouses. Leave that to us."

I was too stunned to reply.

"Oh, and one more thing," the detective said to Aunt Abby. "You mentioned your son was here but you said you don't know where he went?"

Aunt Abby looked at the plate of cookies. "That's right. He took off without telling us where he was going."

The detective had the hint of a smile on his face. I knew he knew she knew.

"When you see him again, tell him I want to talk to him. The longer he stays hidden, the harder it's going to be for him."

Aunt Abby bit her lip. "Oh! I almost forgot. The intruder took our cell phones! Maybe you can you trace them and find out where he is?"

"You mean track them," the detective corrected her. "Have you installed any antitheft apps on it?"

"No," Aunt Abby said.

I had a feeling Dillon hadn't either, since he didn't want to take the chance of someone finding him through his cell phone.

"You might be able to find it through your GPS," the

detective said, "unless it's an old phone or it's been disabled or it's turned off. You could also try the Find My iPhone app using a friend's phone. That sometimes works. But again, if the thief is tech savvy, he can make it hard to find."

Finding Aunt Abby and Dillon's phones was just another piece of the puzzle. The thief had used my aunt's phone to lure me to the house, where Aunt Abby and Dillon were tied up, so it had probably served its purpose.

But that led to the question: If it was me the intruder was after, why had he left before I'd arrived?

Chapter 21

"Well, if you'll excuse me, I'm off to bed," Aunt Abby said after the detective and his officers had left. She bagged up the leftover cookies and poured out the remaining coffee. "I didn't get much sleep last night. Not that I'll get any tonight either, what with everything that's happened. Darcy, would you mind staying in the house tonight?"

"No problem," I said, and gave her a hug good night.

"Thank you," Aunt Abby said. "You can sleep in Dillon's room or on the couch. There are sheets and blankets in the linen closet. Come on, Basil."

"I'll be fine on the couch," I said. No way was I going to sleep in Dillon's bed. With a rat—pet or otherwise.

"And I'll make sure everything's locked up before I leave," Jake added.

Aunt Abby padded down the hall to her bedroom, her dog following behind her, then switched off the hallway light. I heard her door close.

I looked at Jake and suddenly felt awkward. "Would you like a glass of wine or a beer?"

To my surprise, he answered, "Sure, I'll have a beer," and took a seat on one of the stools.

I checked the fridge and found a couple of Fat Tires—

Dillon's, no doubt—then joined Jake at the island counter. He twisted off the caps and handed me one of the beers. We both took a swallow, then both sighed as the alcohol began to hit our systems.

I laughed and felt the tension leave and my body begin to relax.

"What's next?" Jake asked. He took another swig of beer.

"What makes you think I'm going to do anything more? Nothing I've done so far has been of any help at all. In fact, it's just gotten my aunt and Dillon nearly killed. I think I'd better quit while we're still alive."

"I'm starting to get a sense about you, Darcy, and I *know* you aren't going to quit looking for the killer. I just want to know what I can do to help."

I smiled. From the earnest look in his eyes, I believed him. Jake was one of the good guys, no doubt about it—anymore. And while Dillon was doing what he could to dig into things, his help was limited, what with him disappearing all the time, not to mention being hunted by the cops.

"So what do we know so far?" Jake asked.

I reached for my purse and pulled out my notebook. Flipping to the page of suspects and motives, I made sure Jake saw the name at the bottom—his own—had been crossed out. He smiled.

I took a sip of beer before adding to my information. Then I wrote the following under Tripp's name, saying the points out loud for Jake's benefit:

"'Running some kind of illegal document printing at a warehouse. Making fake IDs? For illegal immigrants?' Anything else?" I looked at Jake. He shook his head.

" 'Must have heard my cell phone ring and knew I'd seen his operations'—which reminds me. I have to change that ringtone!"

"I can do that for you," Jake said. "Hand me your phone."

I dug in my purse and pulled out my cell phone. Jake took it, tapped the phone a few times, then handed it back.

"What song did you use?" I asked.

He reached over and tapped the phone again. A police siren filled the air. "Now you'll definitely know it's your aunt."

I grinned. "Very funny. That's going to drive me crazy." I set the phone down, making a mental note to have Dillon reprogram it. "Now, where was I?"

"You're pretty sure it was Tripp?" Jake asked.

I nodded, then continued.

" 'Stole their cell phones, then called me with Aunt Abby's phone to lure me to the house—why?' "

Jake frowned.

" 'Left before I arrived—why?' "

I looked up at Jake. "None of this makes any sense. It all seems so random. If Tripp is the killer, what's his motive? Why the threats?"

Jake shook his head. "Well, as a former attorney, I know one thing for sure."

"What's that?" I asked.

"Everybody has a secret."

"Oh really? What's yours?"

"You already know. I was disbarred. That's not something I'm proud of or share with just anyone."

I felt a little heat wave pass through me. Was I not "just anyone"?

"So, the question is . . ." Jake continued.

Uh-oh. He's going to want to know my secret. Am I going to have to tell him that I lost my job, my boyfriend, and my apartment and will probably be working in my aunt's food truck and living in an RV for the rest of my life? Being disbarred was nothing compared to the loser life I was headed for. At least Jake was doing what he loved—creating artisan desserts and making people happy. What was I doing? Slopping sandwiches together and trying to find a murderer in order to stay alive.

"Darcy?" Jake said, startling me out of my depressing thoughts.

"What? Oh, sorry!" Apparently Jake had been talking to me and I hadn't heard a word he'd said after, *"So, the question is . . ."* "Uh, you were saying something about secrets." I steeled myself for the end of his sentence, certain it would be *"What's your secret?"*

To my surprise, he asked, "Yes. The question is, what secrets were Boris and Oliver keeping that led to their deaths?"

Phew, I thought. "Of course!" I said. I looked at my notebook. "We know that Oliver hated the food trucks—that was no secret. And we know he threatened several of the owners. We also know his restaurant was in trouble. Was that enough to get him killed?"

Jake shrugged. "What about Boris?"

"We know he had a record for selling drugs. And he was working with Tripp in some way—maybe selling fake IDs through his truck? We know he and the vegans didn't get along because of his exotic meats and he had a crush on Willow. But again, was any of that enough to cause his death?"

Jake shrugged. "Who knows why people kill other people these days. Some of my best friends are defense attorneys who defended jealous boyfriends who murdered their girlfriends, drug dealers who killed other drug dealers, even guys who shot people over parking spaces. Maybe we'll never know the truth about those two."

"I can't accept that," I said. "All behavior is motivated. I learned that being a reporter for the *Chronicle*. It's just that some people keep their motives hidden better than others. And if I don't find out what happened to Oliver and Boris, the same thing could happen to my aunt or anyone else who had a connection to those two."

"So like I said, what do we do next?"

"We?"

"Why do you think I'm still here?"

"Oh, uh, well, I think we need to find out more about Tripp, maybe take a look in that warehouse. Get some evidence for Detective Shelton. Then find out how he distributes the IDs—if that's what he's doing—and who pays him, and how involved Boris was in all of this. We still need a connection to Oliver. Maybe I can find out more from his sister . . ."

Something suddenly occurred to me.

"Darcy? I know that look. What is it?"

I blinked. "I was just thinking. . . . I saw Livvy earlier tonight after I left you. When I was about to pull out of the parking lot, I spotted someone across the street at Bones 'n' Brew. Whoever it was—Livvy?—was taking out a couple of bundles of trash, so I drove over to talk to her. When no one answered the back door, I went in calling her name. She didn't answer, so I went on down the hall to Oliver's office—"

"Wait a minute. You went in there *alone*?" Jake asked.

"Yeah . . . like I said, I wanted to talk to Livvy."

"You realize that restaurant was the scene of a murder. Who knows what could have happened to you. Everyone knows the killer returns to the scene of the crime at some point—at least on TV."

I hadn't thought about that at the time. The only thing on my mind was finding out more about Oliver. I hesitated to continue telling Jake what happened.

"Go on," Jake urged, still frowning.

"Like I said, when I didn't see anyone, I went to Oliver's office." I glanced at Jake's disapproving face. "Don't worry. Nothing happened. The killer wasn't hiding inside, waiting for me."

"But Darcy, something *could* have been," Jake argued. "You should have called me. I would have gone with you."

I chugged the last of my beer. "Do you want to hear the rest of the story?"

"Yes," Jake said.

I took a deep breath. "The office had been ransacked. All the drawers were pulled out, some of them dumped over. Papers were everywhere. Someone had obviously been in there searching for something."

Jake groaned. "Darcy! They could have easily still been in the restaurant. I hope you got out—fast."

I pursed my lips, then said, "Not exactly."

Jake rolled his eyes.

"I would have," I explained, "but just then Livvy appeared. She said she'd found the office like it was and suspected the same thing—that someone had been looking for something. I asked her if she'd called the police and she said she was about to. Then she came in and shuffled through the papers. When she tried to shut the top drawer of Oliver's desk, it wouldn't close, like it was stuck on something."

"She shouldn't have touched anything," Jake said, his lawyer persona coming through.

"I know. But when the drawer wouldn't shut, she found out why. A packet was taped underneath the drawer and it had come loose. That's what was keeping it from closing."

"What kind of packet?" Jake asked, suddenly interested.

"A big manila envelope. She opened it, and it was full of recipes. She recognized them and said they were Oliver's secret recipes. Apparently he'd kept them hidden from everyone, including his own sister, because he was sure someone wanted to steal them. She thinks maybe those recipes were related to his murder."

"Killed over secret recipes?" Jake said, disbelief in his voice. "Sounds like an episode of *Castle*. Does she suspect anyone?"

"She didn't say. I told her to call the police. Then I got that phone call from my aunt—or at least, my aunt's phone. I felt bad leaving, but what could I do? I figured the police would be there soon."

"You both should have gotten out of there. The guy could easily have been hiding somewhere in the restaurant."

"I know, but obviously he wasn't, since we never saw him."

"That doesn't necessarily mean he wasn't there," Jake said.

Jake was right. But it was too late now to speculate. If I'd had time to think things through at that point I might have, but I'd been caught up in the moment.

"Then, when I got to my car, someone had flattened all four tires. I had to take a cab to my aunt's house."

Jake rubbed his forehead. "Darcy!"

A thought occurred to me. "That's odd."

"What? That someone deliberately stuck your tires?"

"Yes, but no. Something Livvy said. She said she'd only just arrived at the restaurant and found the office the way I had—turned upside down. But later she mentioned that she'd been there at least an hour or so. And I'm pretty sure she's the one who took out the bags of trash."

"So?" Jake asked.

"I don't know. It just seems like an odd mistake to make." *Why would she lie?* I wondered. I thought about the trash bags. Did she toss out something that might have been related to Oliver's death? Something she found in his office before I arrived? Something embarrassing for him? Maybe she ransacked the office just to make it look like someone broke in and was looking for something herself. The recipes?

I checked the clock: a little after ten. "I don't suppose you want to do a little investigating for me," I said to Jake.

"Like what?"

"I'm pretty sure Livvy took out those trash bags a few minutes before I arrived. Maybe there's something in there she doesn't want anyone to find."

"You want me to go digging through her trash? At *this* hour?"

"It's not that late. And it's not illegal—is it?"

"Depends on the ordinance. Usually, once the trash is outside the building, it's public property, but if it's still on private property, it can be questionable. Still, that's really not my concern. I'm just not big on Dumpster diving."

"Well, I'd go except I can't leave my aunt alone," I argued. "Besides, I thought you wanted to help."

Jake shook his head. "I was hoping you wanted me to stay over and help you protect your aunt."

I grinned. "Is that what you hoped?"

"All right, I'll do it. But if I don't find anything, you'll owe me."

"What'll I owe you?" I said, leaning in flirtatiously.

He cocked his jaw. "I'll think of something—don't worry. Now, lock up after I'm gone. Don't answer the door unless you know the person. And keep your cell phone handy. I want you to call me if anything—*anything*—happens."

"Thank you!" I said, pulling back in victory.

Jake got off his stool and sidled up to me. Looking down at me, his face inches away from mine, he stroked a strand of my hair back behind my ear and studied my mouth. The suspense nearly killed me as my heartbeat went into hyperdrive.

"Just answer me one question," he whispered. I could smell his delicious beer breath.

My own breath caught. "What?" I managed to say.

"What flavor of cream puff do you want in the morning?"

And then he kissed me.

The ring of the doorbell roused me from my dream about a witch cooking up a magical potion in her cauldron. I sat up on the couch, startled at first by my surroundings. Then I remembered. I had slept on Aunt Abby's couch to keep her company. To my surprise, Basil was asleep on my feet, unaffected by the ring of the bell. *Great guard dog,* I thought. I checked the clock. Six in the morning? Who comes calling at six in the morning?

It was either Jake or the police. I threw the comforter off and headed for the door in my Cinderella pajamas. After a quick check in the entryway mirror and a hair pat-down, I peeked through the peephole.

Jake. Thank goodness.

He held up a white bag like a police officer flashing his ID badge.

"Good morning," he said after I pulled open the door. "Cute pj's."

I glanced down at my sleepwear. I couldn't have looked more ridiculous unless I'd been wearing flannel pajamas covered with cats. Good thing I didn't own a pair of high-heeled bunny slippers.

"Do you know what time it is?" I said, running my fingers self-consciously through my couch hair.

"I'm on bakery time," Jake said. "My day usually starts at four a.m."

"Well, I'm in a completely different time zone, so I don't think this"—I started to say "relationship," then changed my mind—"friendship is going to work out."

He held up the bag again and headed for the kitchen. "A couple of these will wake you up. Got coffee?"

"Uh . . ." I said.

"Never mind," Jake said, seeing my deer-in-the-headlights look. "I'll make it. Go do whatever it is you do in the morning. Everything will be ready in a few minutes."

Shaking my head to loosen the sandman's leftovers, I said, "I could use a shower. . . ."

"Go!" He helped himself to the bag of espresso beans Aunt Abby kept in the fridge, then began handling the espresso machine as if he'd grown up around one. "By the way, how's your aunt?"

Oh my God! I hadn't even checked on Aunt Abby. I ran down the hall and quietly opened her bedroom door. Basil ran in and jumped on the bed. I tiptoed into the semidark room.

"Aunt Abby?" I whispered as I moved closer to the bed. The covers were in such a mess, I couldn't tell if she was still under there. I touched one of the lumps on the side. It caved in. I poked at another lump near where her head should have been. It fell flat.

"Aunt Abby!" I said loudly, placing both hands on the billowing covers and shaking them.

"Whaaa?" called a disembodied voice. Her bathroom door opened, lighting up the bedroom. Aunt Abby popped her head out, a foamy toothbrush in her mouth. "Wha's wong?" she said through the obstruction.

I let out a breath of air. "Nothing. Just checking on you," I said.

"Okay," she said, frowning. "Be out soon," I think she said. Sounded more like "Vee oud thoon."

I returned to the kitchen to find three mugs of coffee on the nook table, along with three plates filled with pastries that resembled puffy doughnuts. I started to tell Jake Aunt Abby was fine, but the sweet-smelling doughnut-thingies had taken control of my brain.

"Wow," I said, gazing at them. "I've never seen anything like these. What *are* they?"

"I call them dossants," he said, giving the word a French pronunciation. "It's croissant dough, layered and shaped into circles, then deep-fried like a doughnut and drizzled with glaze. They're pretty popular in New York, so I thought I'd try some. See what you think."

I wanted to lean over and suck the tray of dossants right into my mouth, but I knew that wouldn't be cool. Instead, I daintily picked one up and took a bite.

Suddenly I didn't care what time of day this guy got up or when he woke me, as long as he kept feeding me his awesome sweets.

Chapter 22

"Did you find anything in the trash?" I asked Jake after I finished gorging on the goodies he'd brought.

"I thought you'd never ask," Jake replied, handing me a much-needed napkin.

Aunt Abby padded into the kitchen, Basil at her heels. She was already dressed for another day at her food bus. Naturally everything she wore matched. Today's color choice was purple—purple blouse, purple slacks, purple crocs, and purple eye shadow. I was surprised she didn't have a wardrobe full of matching aprons, but at work she stuck with classic white, tinted here and there with various food stains.

"Good morning, everyone," Aunt Abby said. She gasped when she saw the coffee mugs. "Darcy? You made coffee?"

I laughed. "Sorry, Aunt Abby. That would be Jake's culinary expertise. You know I'm still working on heating water for tea."

"I should have known," my aunt said, settling in a chair at the table. She reached for one of the remaining pastries, studied it a moment, sniffed it, then took a bite, revealing the many layers inside. Her eyes lit up. "Yum! What's this?"

"It's a dossant," Jake said. "A cross between a croissant and a doughnut. Like it?"

"Love it," she said, reaching for the last one. "I must have the recipe."

"Over my dead body," Jake said, grinning. "Oops. Bad choice of words," he added, losing the smile.

That sobered us up. I asked Jake again about the trash. When Aunt Abby looked puzzled, I explained the errand I'd sent Jake on last night.

"I went through a couple of trash bags that were at the top of the heap," Jake began.

"Only the ones at the top?" I asked, interrupting him.

"Hey, no way was I going inside that thing, Darcy. I'm sure it's full of rats."

I nodded. While I should have been grateful, I found myself a little disappointed that he hadn't been as thorough as I'd hoped. Oh well. At least I didn't have to go Dumpster diving myself. I'd just have to settle for the bags he'd managed to retrieve. "What did you find?"

He shrugged. "Not much."

My face fell. "Are you sure? Did you go through everything?"

He nodded. "I found your basic trash, but that's about it. Old food. Wadded-up paper towels. A couple of dishrags. A bunch of old menus. Some recipes . . ." He threw out the last couple of words with a slight smile.

"You found recipes?" I said, sitting up. "What kind of recipes?"

"I didn't have time to go through them all," he said casually. "There was one for crab cakes, another for potpie—"

"Oh my God! Where are they?" I asked, interrupting him.

He glanced around as if looking for them. "Uh, I must have left them in my car. I'll go get them."

"Jake!" I wanted to smack him for teasing me. He got up and headed for the front door.

Aunt Abby turned to me. "What was that about a pot-pie recipe?"

Jake returned seconds later, a bunch of rumpled and stained papers in his hand. He set them on the table, then went to the sink and washed his hands.

I picked up the top one, a recipe for potpies.

"Let me see that," Aunt Abby said, reaching for it. I handed it to her. Her eyes grew wide as she read over the ingredients and instructions. "Hey, this is my Principal Potpie recipe! That rat must have stolen it somehow!"

"Are you sure it's yours?" I asked, figuring all potpie recipes pretty much looked the same.

"It's my handwriting, and it's definitely my recipe. No one else I know makes potpies with tartar sauce added to the mixture except me. That's my secret ingredient."

Aunt Abby scooped up a handful of the recipes and thumbed through them. "This is my Crabby Cheerleader Grilled Cheese! And my Gym Class Gyro! That thieving, conniving . . ." she sputtered, then threw the rest of the papers on the table in disgust.

Jake glanced down at one of the recipes, then picked it up. "Huh," he said after looking it over. "This is my Crème Brûlée Dream Puff recipe. How did it end up in Oliver Jameson's trash?" He began sifting through the rest of the recipes. "Here's one for a falafel burger with flax and tahini dressing. I'm pretty sure that's Sierra and Vandy's recipe. It's one of their most popular dishes. And here's another for rabbit stew from the Road Grill truck.

And Chocolate-Covered Bacon from Porky's. It looks like someone's been stealing recipes from all of our trucks, including mine."

"Maybe it was Oliver Jameson," I said. "If one of the food truckers found out what he was doing, that would make a possible motive for killing him."

"But it still doesn't explain Boris's murder," Jake added.

I agreed. It seemed as if there were two completely different murders here. The only link was that both were chefs, and they were in the same vicinity. We were still no closer to finding the killer.

Frustrated, I dropped my handful of recipes on the table. "I'm a reporter, not a detective. I feel like I'm trying to tie up a bunch of loose ends, but I'm all thumbs."

We were quiet for a few minutes, sipping our coffees and reflecting on the recent find. Then Jake spoke up, breaking thc silence. "Remember what you said last night?"

"No, what?"

"You said we should try to find out what's in that warehouse and collect some real evidence."

"So why don't the cops just go in there and get it themselves?" I argued. "I told them what I saw."

"They can't go in without a warrant. They need probable cause. A bunch of computer stuff inside an old warehouse isn't enough to go on."

I had an idea and looked at Aunt Abby. "How soon do you need me at the bus?"

She looked at her Mickey Mouse wristwatch. "I suppose I can get by until around eleven. If Dillon's back in the bus, he can put on one of his disguises and help out until you get there."

"What about your cream puff truck?" I asked Jake.

"I can open a little late if I have to," he said.

I met Jake's intense stare and said, with a renewed sense of energy, "All right. Let's do this." I was jazzed. But then again, it could have been the overdose of sugar talking.

I showered, did my hair and makeup, dressed in my usual khaki pants and a T-shirt that read "Will Work for Money," and was ready in record time—for me. Meanwhile Jake helped Aunt Abby clean up the kitchen and load her stuff into her car. We were all out the door a little before eight, which gave Jake and me plenty of time to snoop around Tripp's warehouse before heading for Fort Mason. Providing Tripp wasn't at the warehouse, of course. My guess was he was out making "deliveries."

"We'll have to take your van," I said to Jake. "Triple A towed my car to the auto shop for new tires."

We hopped into his white van and headed out. On the way, Jake and I developed a plan. I would be lookout while he searched for evidence. Luckily the Meat Wagon was nowhere in sight when we pulled up to the warehouse. Good sign.

In fact, the area was pretty deserted for a workday. Tripp's place wasn't the only warehouse that was in need of repair. Several others sat decaying on their weed-infested, junk-littered lots. Some of the buildings sported FOR SALE signs, while others were too decrepit to salvage. Even though land is expensive in the city, these plots apparently didn't hold enough appeal for investors yet.

Gentrification took time and money, and other parts of the city, like Dogpatch, Potrero Hill, and China Basin, were already in the midst of renewal transitions. Still others, like Treasure Island, were on hold for the present and near future.

Jake drove the van to an empty spot along the curb several yards down the street from Tripp's warehouse. The side of his van featured the logo of his cream puff business, and the colorful artwork stood out among the ordinary trucks and vans parked nearby.

I looked at the signage. "If Tripp sees your van, he'll know something's up."

"You're right. I've got an idea." Jake opened up the back and pulled out a white tablecloth.

"You carry around a tablecloth?" I asked.

"Just in case I want to have a spontaneous picnic," he said with a wink. "Actually, when I bring cream puffs to places in the van, I like to have something nice to set them on." He shook out the cloth a couple of times. Bits of leftover pastry puff went flying. He opened the driver's side door, let down the window an inch, inserted the top of the cloth into the opening, then rolled it up with a press of a button. When he closed the door, the cloth hung down over the sign.

"You don't think that looks a little weird?" I asked, impressed by his ingenuity.

"Better than shouting 'Dream Puff guy is here!,' don't you think?"

I shrugged. With a last glance around, we headed for the warehouse. I led Jake over to the scratched-out hole in the paint-covered window.

"This is where I peeked inside."

He leaned in close, squinted one eye, and took a look.

"Is anyone inside?" I asked nervously, scanning the street for any sign of Tripp. I couldn't have looked more suspicious.

"Looks empty," Jake said. He pulled back from the window.

"What now?"

"Now I have to figure out how to get in," Jake answered.

"How good are you at breaking and entering?" I asked.

"Not so good. Once I locked myself out of my food truck and had to call a locksmith to get in. Now I keep a spare key."

I laughed at the thought of Jake standing outside his truck, waiting for assistance. "We could break one of the panes," I said. The windowpanes were small—maybe five by five inches square—with frames around each one.

"Yeah, but all I'd be able to do is get my hand in. I'm going to look around the outside, see if there are any other options."

I started to follow Jake, but he held up a hand. "No. You wait here. You're the lookout, remember?"

"Why? Because I'm a girl?"

Jake grinned. "Yes," he said. "You're a girl. Got a problem with that?"

I shot him some dagger eyes but said, "No." Someone needed to keep an eye out for Tripp and it might as well be me. I pulled out my cell phone. "I'll call you if I see anything."

Jake nodded and headed for the side of the building. I watched for any sign of Tripp's truck, hoping I didn't look too obvious. Hopefully anyone who saw me would figure I was just waiting for someone.

Five minutes later—about the time I wondered if something had happened to Jake—I heard him call from around the corner. "Darcy!"

I walked over to the side of the building and spotted him signaling me from the back corner. "Come on!"

"You found a way in?" I asked when I reached the back of the warehouse. I scanned the area and didn't see any open doors or windows.

Jake pointed down toward the ground. A mesh grate the size of a laptop computer lay on the dirt, leaving a gaping hole at the bottom of the wall.

"You pulled that out of the wall?"

He nodded, grinning proudly at his destructive handiwork. He gestured toward the opening. "After you."

"Are you kidding me?" I cried. "I'm not going to go crawling around on the ground like a dog. I probably won't even fit through that hole. Besides, I thought I was the lookout!"

"Well, now I need you to be the lookout from the *inside*," Jake said patiently, "Watch for Tripp through that hole in the front window. And you'll fit through there just fine." He looked me up and down for emphasis and raised an eyebrow. "It's the only way in."

"But I'll get my clothes dirty!"

He eyed my T-shirt and pants. "We're trying to catch a murderer, Darcy. I think that's reason enough to get a little dust on your outfit."

"What if it's booby-trapped?"

"All right. I'll go first. Then you follow. Okay?"

I nodded, reluctantly.

Jake got down on his hands and knees and stuck his head inside the opening. Then he crawled, military-style, through the hole, inching his way through a little at a time. Moments later he had disappeared.

I knelt down on all fours and peered inside. "Jake?" I called.

"Yeah, I'm here. No booby trap. So far."

That was reassuring. I lay down on my stomach and began to worm-crawl through the rusty, cobwebby opening. All I could think about were bugs, spiders, and rats as I twisted and wiggled my way inside. The moment I cleared the opening, Jake helped me up. I brushed off my clothes, face, and hair, then shivered.

"Come on," Jake said. "We don't have much time. Let's see what we can find."

We immediately headed for the computer and printing equipment sitting on four tables. There were half a dozen folding chairs at the tables and at least a dozen cardboard boxes under the tables. Random papers in various sizes littered the floor, along with spent printer cartridges, rumpled sandpaper, and a bunch of fast-food wrappers.

"Where are the cards you saw when you peeked in the window?" Jake asked, glancing around at the tables.

"They were . . . right there. . . ." I pointed to an empty table and blinked.

Jake frowned and opened the lid of one of the cardboard boxes. It was empty. So were the second and the third. "Well, all that stuff is gone now. Just a bunch of scraps left behind. Looks like Tripp took away most of the paper trail. Even the computers are gone. All we've got here are some printers and paper cutters."

I sighed glumly. "Great. We're too late. Without the evidence, we've got nothing to prove what he was doing here. Looks like we're screwed."

Jake grabbed my arm. "Listen!"

I froze. "What?"

"A noise," Jake whispered. "It came from the front door. I think someone's here!"

We'd been in the warehouse only a few minutes—not even enough time for me to play lookout. And now we were about to be caught red-handed.

"Quick!" Jake slid his hand down my arm and took my hand. He pulled me toward the opening at the back of the warehouse. "We've got to get out of here! Fast!"

There was no way to hurry through the hole. I got on my stomach and began inching my way toward the outside, while Jake pushed my feet in an attempt to help. Just as I pulled my feet through, I heard the front door of the warehouse squeak open.

Oh my God—Jake! He was still inside!

I wanted to call to him but knew that was a bad idea. He was on his own—there was nothing I could do to help him. I just hoped he was able to hide from Tripp behind one of those boxes under the table.

Suddenly I heard voices.

A woman's voice said something I couldn't make out.

Then a man's voice: "Of course I checked everything. Took the laptops, wiped down all the fingerprints, packed up all the IDs and stuff. If that nosy chick calls the cops, they won't find anything linking us to the operation." Tripp!

The woman spoke again, softly.

"I know that!" Tripp said angrily. "Now, see if you can find it, or we could be in real trouble!"

Uh-oh. Tripp and his partner were about to do a thorough search of the warehouse. It was only a matter of time before they found Jake.

What were they looking for?

And what would they do with him if they found Jake?

Chapter 23

The only thing I could think to do was cause a distraction. Maybe that would give Jake the chance to get out of there before being caught by Tripp.

But what?

Yell "Fire!" and hope those two came running out of the building?

No, I had a better idea. Remembering that Jake had changed my ringtone, I pulled out my cell phone. With a shaking finger, I clicked on the ringtone test, turned up the volume, then knelt down and held the phone up to the escape hole. The sound of police sirens reverberated in the mostly empty warehouse and echoed against the bare walls. I just hoped Tripp couldn't tell exactly where the sound came from.

The female said something I couldn't hear.

"The police!" Tripp shouted. "It sounds like they're right outside!"

The woman said something else.

"Shut up!" Tripp yelled back. "There's nothing here to incriminate us."

"I don't care!" the woman shouted above the siren noise. "I'm getting out of here. They could get us for illegal trespass or even stolen goods. That stuff didn't exactly come from Amazon.com."

I couldn't see what was happening, but moments later I heard a window break at the side of the building. I peered around and watched a muscular arm beat out the flimsy frame that had held the glass. Moments later, two figures climbed through the opening, jumped to the ground, and took off running.

I pointed the siren in their direction as they sped to Tripp's Meat Wagon, which was parked in front of the building. Tripp pulled out in a screech of tires and was gone.

I returned to the opening at the back and got down on my knees. "Jake?" I called.

No response.

Then a hand reached out from the opening. Jake!

He slithered through, military-style, barely clearing the small passageway. He stood up, and I started to brush off the dirt from his T-shirt and jeans, then caught myself. It suddenly felt a little too intimate.

"That was *you* making the police siren?" he said, looking at the cell phone still in my hand. "Pretty clever."

"Thanks to you."

"Let's get out of here before those two realize they've just been punked and come back."

Jake led me behind the warehouse next door so we wouldn't be spotted if Tripp doubled back. Then we headed toward the street, still checking for signs of the Meat Wagon truck or its driver. The coast was clear, so we ran to Jake's truck and hopped in. Jake removed the tablecloth that covered his sign and sped off down the road.

"Whoa!" I said, still trying to catch my breath. "That was close."

"Tell me about it," Jake said. "I don't know what they would have done if they'd caught me. I'm guessing a guy like Tripp always carries protection."

For a moment, I thought Jake meant a condom. I blushed. "Oh. You mean a gun or something?"

He nodded. "About all I usually have is a pastry bag. And I forgot it this time."

I laughed in spite of the fact I was still recovering from the close encounter.

"Well, sorry about the wild-goose chase," I said. "This was another dead end, just like all the others."

Jake smiled.

"What's so amusing?" I asked, staring at him.

He didn't answer.

I frowned. "Tell me! Did you find something?"

Jake held the steering wheel with his left hand and used his right hand to dig in his pocket. He withdrew a small card and handed it to me.

"What's this?" I looked it over. On the front of the stiff, laminated card was a photo of a bearded man I didn't recognize. Next to it were his stats—name, address, date of birth, sex, eye and hair color, and so on. I ran my fingers over the signature. The handwriting was raised. "Wow, this looks real. Is it one of the Tripp's fake IDs?"

Jake shrugged. "I'll call Shelton. We won't know for sure until he runs the ID through the identify fraud unit."

"What about fingerprints?" I asked.

Jake shook his head. "Too late. It's already covered with mine, and now yours."

"Well, at least we finally have some real evidence!" I said, excited by the discovery. "Tripp thought he cleaned up everything, but he must have missed this." I held up the card. "Where was it?"

"Under one of the boxes. When Tripp came in, I hid behind the boxes under the table—it was the only thing I could think to do. I'm sure they would have discovered me eventually, but thanks to your police siren, they didn't." He glanced at me and squeezed my knee. "Anyway, when I moved the box to hide, I saw something sticking out and picked it up."

"Great!" I said. "If this proves to be a fake ID, that should be enough to get Tripp arrested for fraud or whatever. And hopefully that will lead to some answers about the murders."

"That's a big leap, Darcy. Printing fake IDs and committing murder aren't really the same. Plus I can't prove where it came from."

"But it's got to be him! Boris must have told him he didn't want to be a part of the illegal business anymore. Maybe he threatened to expose Tripp and Tripp killed him. It makes sense."

"The only proof we have—and it's not confirmed yet—is the fake ID business," Jake said. "We don't have any proof of murder. And we still don't have a connection to Jameson."

"Then we have to find something, just like we did at the warehouse."

"And how are we going to do that?" Jake asked, eyeing me. "There weren't any suspicious fingerprints in Boris's truck. Shelton said they were wiped clean. It all comes down to physical evidence."

"But Tripp was there the night Boris was killed, remember? I heard them arguing."

"All circumstantial. Not enough to pin a murder on him."

I thought for a moment as we drove into the Fort Mason parking lot. "What if Cherry Washington is the key to all of this?" I suggested. "Maybe she's hiding something. Maybe she's protecting Tripp. Like you said, everyone has secrets. If I could catch her in a lie and threaten to tell the police, maybe she'd protect herself by telling me what her involvement is."

Jake parked the van and turned off the engine. He turned to me. "There's one more thing I forgot to tell you," he said.

"What?" I asked expectantly. "Did you find more evidence?"

"Not exactly. But I did get a glimpse of the woman who was with Tripp in the warehouse."

"Oh my God. Did you recognize her?"

Jake nodded. "It was Cherry Washington."

After promising to call Detective Shelton about the fake ID, Jake headed for his truck to get ready for the day's cream puff cravers. I walked over to Aunt Abby's bus and waved to my aunt through the window. I didn't see any sign of Dillon until I entered the bus. Even with him standing right there in front of me, I still didn't recognize him.

"You've got to be kidding," I said, shaking my head.

"Meet Svetlana," my aunt said, grinning, her arms elbow-deep in dough.

"This is ridiculous," I said.

"Sorry, she doesn't speak English," Aunt Abby said, "but she understands some. And she's a wonderful help to me, aren't you, Svetlana?"

"Madness," I said.

Dillon adjusted his new wig, a black bob with long thick bangs covered in a hairnet. He was dressed in one of Aunt Abby's blue athletic suits, with the too-short sleeves pushed up and the too-short pant legs hitting midcalf. His ankles were covered by white kneesocks, and he wore a pair of large athletic shoes on his feet. I guessed that Aunt Abby had done his makeup—too much foundation, too much blush, and too much eye shadow. It was enough to make you spew your comfort food.

"I think he looks quite fetching," Aunt Abby said.

Dillon didn't speak, just shot me a daggered look and continued to man—or "woman"—a pot of water boiling on the stove.

"I think he looks like an idiot," I said. "He's not going to fool anyone."

"Now, Darcy. It worked for Mrs. Doubtfire. If you don't look too closely—" Aunt Abby began to protest.

"She's right, Mom!" Dillon said. He pulled off the wig, then grabbed a paper towel and started wiping off the greasepaint. "This isn't working. If the cops come, they're going to know it's me. I gotta split. Darcy can take over."

Aunt Abby gave me a dirty look that said, *"You just ruined everything!"*

Dillon quickly stripped out of the stretchy suit, revealing his folded-up jeans and a Comic Con T-shirt underneath. He pushed the socks and cuffs down, grabbed his laptop from a back counter, and headed for the bus doors.

"You can tell her what I found out," Dillon said to his mom. "I'll call you later."

He pulled his hoodie down over his eyebrows, glanced around outside, stepped out of the bus, and disappeared.

"Now look what you've done!" Aunt Abby said, tearing up. "He's gone again."

"I'm sorry, Aunt Abby, but he really wouldn't have fooled the police in that getup. It's better that he stays away until these murders are solved and the cops aren't around so much."

"I know," Aunt Abby said, blinking back the tears. "I just wish this was all over. I miss him."

I nodded. "I wish it was over too. But don't worry. Jake and I are working on it." I gave her a hug. "Dillon said you had something to tell me? What did he find out?"

Aunt Abby sniffed and blew her nose into a tissue, then tucked the tissue into her apron pocket. "He said he was on the computer most of the night, trying to learn more about Boris and Oliver and the others on our list."

"And . . . ?"

She shrugged. "He found out Cherry Washington is an illegal alien from Jamaica, although I don't know how that might help anything."

"Huh," I said, thinking a moment. Was that southern accent put on to disguise the fact that she was from Jamaica? "I'm guessing Tripp made her a fake ID, and Boris hired her. But you're right. I'm not sure how that would lead to murder. Unless Boris threatened to expose both Tripp and Cherry to get himself out of helping distribute fake IDs."

Aunt Abby laid out the hunk of dough and began rolling it flat.

"Anything else?" I asked.

"That's it."

Hmm. Everything seemed to point to Tripp—except for a link to Oliver Jameson. I had to find a connection. But how?

"Aunt Abby, did Dillon discover anything more about Oliver?"

"No. You already knew the restaurant was up for sale, as well as in Chapter Eleven, right?"

I sat down on the stool. "Yeah, but that's what's odd. Why would Oliver steal all those recipes from everyone if he was planning to sell Bones 'n' Brew?"

"Maybe he was going to start a new restaurant," Aunt Abby offered. "Or even his own food truck. Maybe that's why he wanted our recipes."

"But how did he manage to steal all those recipes? None of the food truckers would have even let him inside their trucks, let alone shared their recipes with him. Did he somehow break in during the dead of night?"

"I doubt it," Aunt Abby said. "Word would have spread like a grease fire around here if our locks had been broken."

"So," I said, thinking aloud, "Oliver stole a bunch of secret recipes and now he's dead. Boris may have sold a bunch of fake IDs and he's also dead. The only connection I can think of is that they were both chefs and both worked in the same general area. . . ." Another thought came to me. "I wonder if Oliver had Tripp do the dirty work for him too?"

"What do you mean?"

"I mean, maybe Oliver got Tripp to steal the recipes for him. Maybe he knew Tripp was not the most honest guy in town and hired him—or maybe he blackmailed him. Maybe Tripp had his hands in lots of different pies, so to speak. Did you ever see Tripp over at Bones 'n' Brew?"

"I never really noticed."

"Well, I'm pretty sure we have a motive for Tripp killing Boris—blackmail gone wrong. All we need now is a motive for Tripp to murder Oliver—like blackmail too. Did Tripp have something he could hold over Oliver Jameson?"

"I don't know," Aunt Abby said, washing her hands in the sink, "but you'd better get your apron on. We open up soon, and we have lots to prep before the crowds arrive."

In between slicing bread for BLT sandwiches, heating Crab Potpies, and scooping mac and cheese cups for Aunt Abby's hungry customers, I had little time to think about murder. When the lunch rush slowed, my aunt granted me a much-needed coffee break. I headed straight for the Coffee Witch and ordered two Voodoo Ventis—one for me and one for Jake.

I figured if Jake had been as busy as we were at the School Bus, he'd welcome a stimulant—in trade for today's cream puff special. When he caught a glimpse of me from the window of his truck, I held up the two coffees.

"Lifesaver!" he called out the window. "Be right out." He finished with the last customer, flipped over the BE BACK IN 5 MINUTES sign, stuffed something in a small white bag, and met me at the door. We found a bench nearby and settled in.

I started to hand him his coffee, then held back. "What are the magic words?"

He held up the white bag. "Coffee-Toffee Dream Puff?"

"Nailed it," I said, and traded him a coffee for the dessert bag. I reached in, pulled out the perfect puff, and took a bite. "Wow," I said, when I could speak again. "Wow."

"Thanks for the coffee," he said, taking a sip.

After swallowing a mouthful, I asked, "Did you talk to Detective Shelton about what we found at the warehouse?"

"I left a message. He wasn't in."

I frowned. "It sure doesn't seem like he's in much of a hurry to catch Tripp."

"Well, we still don't have anything solid on the guy, other than his illegal printing business and our suspicions."

"But now we know Cherry was in on it," I added. "That's something."

"Did you get a chance to talk to Dillon? Has he learned anything more?"

I filled Jake in on the fact that Cherry was an illegal, probably from Jamaica. I also told him I suspected Tripp had stolen the recipes for Oliver and then blackmailed him.

"Any evidence to support your theory?" Jake asked.

"No, but it's not exactly easy solving a murder while you're grilling cheese sandwiches and slicing slabs of meat loaf. I did have a thought while reheating a Crab Potpie." I popped the rest of the cream puff in my mouth.

"What's that?" Jake asked.

"Mmmffiizz," I said, then swallowed and licked my lips. "Maybe I've been concentrating too much on Boris's murder and not focusing enough on a motive for Oliver's death. Something doesn't quite fit the mix, like the wrong ingredient in a recipe. I keep wondering what Oliver was planning to do with those stolen recipes if he was supposedly getting out of the restaurant business."

"Any ideas?" Jake asked, setting his coffee cup down and resting his arms on the back of the bench. If we'd been in a dark movie theater, I would have bet he was about to put his arm around me. Too bad we weren't.

"I need to talk to Cherry Washington again—if we can find her. She may be lying low now. Maybe Tripp had something on her too and made her help him out—like her illegal alien status. Between the two of them, either one could have sneaked into the food trucks when the chefs left for a break. People seem pretty casual around here about locking their doors during the day."

Jake frowned. "Come to think of it, Cherry did come by my truck one afternoon recently. She asked me a bunch of questions about running a food truck business. Like I told you, she said she wanted to open her own truck one day."

"What did you tell her?" I said, sitting up.

"All kinds of things. I was happy to help her out."

"Did you show her your recipe file?"

Jake nodded.

"Did you ever turn your back on her?"

Jake looked at me and frowned again. Of course he had.

"That must be how she got your recipes!" I said, excited about adding another piece to the puzzle. "She probably took pictures of them with a smart phone. I'll bet she did the same thing at the other trucks—used her charms and then stole recipes when no one was looking. I'll ask Aunt Abby and a few others if Cherry ever came inside their trucks and asked questions about starting a business. We may have our recipe thief."

Jake eyebrows remained wedged together. "But that doesn't necessarily mean we have our murderer."

"No, but if we keep on stirring things up, we may just end up with a recipe for murder."

Chapter 24

There was no line at Aunt Abby's School Bus, so I gave myself permission to do a little sleuthing before returning to work. My first stop was a revisit to the Coffee Witch, where I squeezed in some questions for Willow as she served her caffeine-craving clientele.

"Willow, did Cherry Washington ever ask you about running a food truck business?" I asked her as she leaned out to hand over a Witch's Brew to a young guy in a suit.

"Yeah, why?" Willow said.

"Did you let her into your truck?"

"Yeah, but only after I made sure she wasn't planning to open a coffee truck. No way was I going to help any competition."

Willow took another order, prepared the coffee drink, and accepted the payment, while I stood aside waiting for her to finish.

"Do you have recipes for all of your drinks?"

She paused. "Sure, but I've got them all memorized. I keep hard copies, but I never look at them. Why?"

"Did you happen to show them to Cherry?"

Willow frowned. "Okay . . . what's this all about?"

"My aunt and Jake both discovered some of their recipes were duplicated and found in a Dumpster behind

Bones 'n' Brew. We're thinking maybe Cherry took pictures of them when she came asking questions about the food truck business. I'm checking with a few of the owners to see if she might have visited them too."

"Wow. If you find out she did that, let me know. I'll kill her!"

A few customers raised their eyebrows at Willow's words. She smiled and said, "Just kidding," to put them at ease, but she gave me a raised eyebrow that said, *"Half kidding."*

I questioned the chefs at three more trucks. All three confirmed my suspicion: Cherry had asked them for information while gaining access to the inside of their trucks, and had seen some of their recipes.

So if Cherry stole the recipes, would that make her the murderer? And what would be her motive? Why would she kill Boris and Oliver? Because they found out she was stealing recipes? Was her plan to use them for her own food truck? It hardly seemed like much of a motive.

Or was she stealing them for Tripp because he was blackmailing her? And why would Tripp want recipes?

I headed back to Aunt Abby's bus to finish out the day and talk over what I'd learned. About an hour later we had a surprise patron at the window of the School Bus.

Detective Shelton.

"Well, hello, Detective," Aunt Abby said, flashing her eyelashes like a lovesick teenager. "What brings you by my Big Yellow School Bus? Hungry for one of my Crab Potpies?" Was it really a potpie she was offering?

"Afternoon, Ms. Warner," the detective said, nodding

his head. "I wondered if I could speak to your assistant there for a moment." He looked at me.

I wiped my hands, removed my apron, and stepped out of the bus. "I hope you're here to talk about the message Jake left you?" I asked him before he could say a word.

He motioned to the side of the bus. I assumed he wanted to speak in private.

I followed him. "So did you talk to Tripp?"

"I did."

"Well, are you going to arrest him?"

"No, ma'am."

"Why not?" I cried.

"Because I still don't have any solid evidence that he's committed a crime."

"But the ID card—"

He cut me off. "Probably won't have any fingerprints except Jake's and yours. And there's nothing else to prove he was manufacturing bogus IDs."

"But the warehouse! What more do you need? We were there. We saw the printers. We saw him there with Cherry Washington!"

"Doing what, exactly?"

That stopped me for a moment. "Uh . . . I'm not sure. I didn't exactly *see* them inside the building. But Jake did—"

"Jake said he didn't see anything either, only caught a glimpse of them and heard their voices. And according to him, they didn't admit to making fake IDs, or murdering anyone for that matter."

"But, Detective, you *know* Tripp is up to something! After all I've told you—the argument he had with Boris, the possibility he was blackmailing the chef, his connection to Cherry, the fact that he was the one who tied up my aunt and my nephew . . ."

"You don't know that, Ms. Burnett. I can't arrest him on your suppositions or possibilities. I can't arrest him because you *think* he broke into your aunt's home or because he knows Cherry Washington."

"Did you know Cherry's an illegal alien?" I said, tossing him the latest tidbit I'd learned from Dillon.

The detective scrunched up his face. "What makes you think that?"

I couldn't give away my source—that would only get Dillon in more trouble. "I thought I overheard Cherry say something about being from Jamaica and wanting to get her green card and . . ."

"You're not a very good liar, Ms. Burnett. And, like I said, if you're withholding information on Dillon Warner's whereabouts, you could be arrested for aiding and abetting a person of interest, not to mention illegal trespass in that warehouse, which is private property."

"That's ridiculous! Somebody had to go in that warehouse to snoop around because apparently you wouldn't."

"We always follow up on all leads, Ms. Burnett. My officers did, in fact, inspect the warehouse."

"Oh," I said, surprised. "Well, did they see the printers and stuff? Did they get fingerprints? Did they thoroughly search the place?"

"Yes, and they came up empty. The printers were wiped clean. And they didn't find any fake IDs like the one you say you found."

I shook my head. Great.

"What about Cherry Washington's illegal status?" I said. "Did you look into that?"

"INS is on it, but so far she looks clean. Seems to have the proper documentation."

Crap. What did it take to get someone to solve this case?

"I understand you think a thief may have stolen some recipes," the detective said.

Finally! He had to admit that was something solid to work on. "Yes! Cherry stole them from Jake, my aunt, and a bunch of other food truckers. She got them by pretending to ask about the food truck business."

"Well, if she's in possession of them, I could take her down to the station and question her. But Jake said he found the recipes in the trash at Bones 'n' Brew."

"I think she took pictures of them with her cell phone."

"Then they're probably erased," the detective said.

Great. He had an answer for everything. I had another thought—maybe Cherry hadn't stolen the recipes for herself. Maybe she'd gotten them for Oliver, and someone—Livvy—found them and threw them out. But again, why would Oliver want them if he was planning to sell the restaurant? And why would he hide his own recipes under the desk drawer in his office?

"Anything else, Ms. Burnett?" the detective asked.

"I guess not," I said reluctantly.

"Listen," Detective Shelton said. "Breaking and entering is a serious crime. Do it again and I'll take you downtown, understand?"

I shrugged. "So is murder," I said, then headed back to the School Bus.

* * *

During the next couple of hours, Aunt Abby and I prepped tomorrow's offerings. My aunt shooed me off around five thirty, but instead of heading home, I returned to Bones 'n' Brew to see if Livvy was around.

I couldn't get those stolen recipes out of my mind.

This time the back door was locked. I went around to the front, knocked, and waited for an answer. The CLOSED sign still hung in the window, and when I peered in, the front lobby was dimly lit with only the indirect sunlight as a source. With the dark-paneled walls and heavy, dated fixtures, the restaurant screamed old-school, but not in a cute, kitschy way. If Livvy planned to reopen the place, I hoped she'd change the decor as she planned, along with the menu.

I returned to the back of the restaurant and knocked on the door, on the off chance Livvy—or someone—was in or near the kitchen. Once again, no answer. I glanced around and noticed a single car—a cream-colored Mustang—parked in the lot. The license plate read BNZNBRW. Was Livvy here but just not answering the door? Why not?

Thinking of the break-in the previous day, I wondered if she might be in trouble. I peered in through the back windows, hoping I wouldn't spot a body lying on the floor, but saw no life—or death—in the kitchen area at all.

I moved around the building to Oliver's office window, where Aunt Abby had made her famed getaway. The blinds were drawn but a crack at the bottom allowed me a peek in. I felt like a Peeping Tom as I scanned the inside of the office. The room had been tidied up, drawers were back in the desk, papers were piled neatly, and overturned chairs righted. It was as if nothing had happened in that room—especially not a murder. I wondered if the police had found anything after Livvy called them regarding the break-in. At the moment, my question would have to go unanswered, but I made a mental note to check again later.

I headed back to the School Bus to check on Aunt Abby, wishing I'd bought myself a coffee and scored a cream puff instead of wasting my time at Bones 'n' Brew. Odd, I thought, when I saw the doors to the bus wide-open. Although she rarely locked the doors when she was on the premises, she didn't keep them wide-open either.

I hopped inside.

Aunt Abby was sitting on a stool, bent over the counter and holding her head.

"Aunt Abby?" I said, thinking she was just tired after the long day.

She lifted her head. Her face was as white as her fresh apron. Her pale lips actually looked green. She groaned.

I moved to her quickly. "What's wrong?" I asked, beginning to bc alarmed.

"I . . . I think I'm going to be—"

Aunt Abby leaned over the sink and threw up.

"Goodness! You poor thing!" I said to her, feeling helpless as I rubbed her back. "Do you have the flu?"

"I don't know. . . ." she mumbled and wiped the drool from her mouth with her apron. Some of the green from her lips came off on thc apron.

"Aunt Abby! Did you eat something?" I glanced around, looking for possible spoiled food.

She nodded, her head still hanging over the sink. "I

just hope I didn't make any of my customers sick. . . ." she mumbled. "My business would be ruined . . . if it got out that I poisoned anyone. . . ." She was speaking almost incoherently. I could barely make out her words.

"Aunt Abby! What did you eat?" I demanded. "Tell me!"

She shrugged. "Everything," she muttered. "I eat all day long, sampling the food. I don't know. . . ."

Spotting the hint of green color still on her upper lip, I asked, "Was it something green?"

"Uh . . . I don't remember. . . . Wait. . . . A cream puff . . ."

The hairs on my neck stood up. "Cream puff? What cream puff?" I searched the area for a telltale sign of one of Jake's sweet treats. Finally I spotted a small paper baking liner lying on the floor at Aunt Abby's feet.

It was empty.

I picked it up and sniffed it. I recognized it immediately as one of my favorite cream puff flavors—key lime. The green on her mouth and the apron matched the green of the lime sauce Jake drizzled over his key lime–filled pastry shell.

"Was this it?" I held up the paper liner for Aunt Abby to see.

She took one look at it, crossed her eyes, and threw up again.

Resting my hand on her shoulder, I gave her a moment to recover. Then I asked, "Where did you get this?"

She groaned.

"Aunt Abby, where did the cream puff come from?"

"Uh . . . let's see. . . . It was on the pickup counter when I got back from the restroom. There was a note. . . ."

"A note? Where?"

She reached into her apron pocket and pulled out a slip of paper. "I didn't want you to know. . . ." she said as she handed the rumpled note to me.

"What are you talking about?"

She moaned.

I opened the folded note and read the neatly printed message: *"Darcy, a treat for my sweet. —J."*

Jake?

"I'm calling nine-one-one," I said, thrusting the note in my pocket.

"You think it's food poisoning?" she asked, lifting her head from the sink, her eyes glazed and half-closed.

I didn't answer, but I had a knot in the pit of my stomach that told me this wasn't accidental food poisoning. When the dispatcher came on the line, I said, "I need an ambulance. I think my aunt has been poisoned." I gave the address.

I knew that cream puff wasn't meant to poison my aunt. The note confirmed it.

That poisoned puff was meant for me.

•

Chapter 25

Five long minutes passed before I heard the sound of the ambulance arriving. By then Aunt Abby had grown even more pale and drowsy. She could barely keep her head up.

"Over here!" I called to the ambulance driver as the emergency vehicle pulled up to the food trucks. I was waving and yelling like a madwoman, trying to get their attention. As soon as they saw me, three EMTs ran from the transporter to the School Bus. Two entered; the third remained outside, talking on a radio. I backed out of the way to let them through.

"Ma'am? Can you tell me what happened?" one of the EMTs asked as she began examining Aunt Abby. The woman was talking to my aunt, but I answered for her.

"I . . . I think she was poisoned!" I said.

The male EMT glanced around, looking for evidence of poisoning. "What did she take?"

I pointed to the cream puff wrapper on the counter. "That's the last thing she ate before she got sick."

He nodded. "Food poisoning?"

The female helped Aunt Abby up to a standing position and the two of them began escorting her slowly through the bus, carrying most of her light weight on their shoulders and arms.

"I don't know," I said, wringing my hands. "All I know is someone left a cream puff on the service counter with a note. It was addressed to me." I hesitated before saying more. While the note was signed *"J,"* anyone could have written that. Getting Aunt Abby to the hospital was imperative at the moment.

I followed them out and watched as they laid Aunt Abby on a gurney. A small crowd had formed, mostly food truckers.

"I'll need that wrapper," the male EMT said.

I bounded back into the bus, grabbed the wrapper, and handed it to him as soon as I returned to my aunt's side. While the female EMT tended to Aunt Abby, the male EMT took it with his gloved hand, pulled out a plastic baggie from his pocket, and tucked the wrapper inside.

I nodded. "Will she be all right?" I felt tears fill my eyes.

"We'll take her to SF General. They'll probably pump her stomach," the female EMT said. One of the EMTs entered the back of the ambulance, while the other two hoisted my aunt on board.

"Can I ride with her?"

"No, ma'am," the female EMT answered. "You can meet her at the hospital."

"Aunt Abby," I called out, letting her know I was there. "I'll see you at the hospital in a few minutes, all right? They're going to take good care of you."

I heard her moan beneath the oxygen mask. The doors closed and I watched as the ambulance pulled into the street. It sped off, lights flashing and sirens blaring.

Someone bumped my shoulder. I whirled around and

glanced at the growing crowd that had gathered. The two vegans stood next to Willow, gawking at the drama they had just witnessed. The guys from the bacon truck and the curry truck stood back, watching from afar. Even Cherry Washington had appeared—from where? I wondered—as had Livvy from Bones 'n' Brew across the street. In addition there were a number of rubberneckers who happened to be in the area, curious to see what had happened. As I skimmed the crowd of people, I wondered if Dillon might be among them in some kind of costume. If he was, he'd done a good job of disguising himself.

And Tripp?

"Darcy?" A voice came from behind me.

I turned around to see Jake standing there frowning, a puzzled look on his face. "What happened?"

I was momentarily struck dumb.

"Darcy? Are you all right?" Jake asked. He reached out for my arm.

I stared at him for a moment before saying, "Did you drop off a cream puff at Aunt Abby's bus?"

Jake's frown deepened. "A cream puff? No."

"It was a Key Lime Dream Puff. Someone left it on the counter for me with a note signed *J*."

Jake looked utterly confused. "Darcy, I don't know what you're talking about. I didn't leave you a cream puff."

I pulled the note from my pocket. "And you didn't write this?"

He read it over. "No. That's not my handwriting."

"The question is, how did your cream puff end up on my aunt's counter with the note, just waiting for me to gobble it up?"

His eyes widened with surprise. "I have no idea. Seriously."

"You made Key Lime Dream Puffs today, didn't you? You make them every day, right?"

"Yes, but—"

"Well, my aunt ate the one intended for me, and now she's on her way to SF Gen because she's been poisoned."

Jake looked dumbfounded.

"Did you notice any of your cream puffs missing?" I asked. Someone could have bought one, poisoned it, and set it on the counter for me to eat. Jake thought for a moment. "Not that I know of . . ."

"Then how did one of your cream puffs end up at Aunt Abby's bus?"

Jake shrugged. "I have no clue, but somebody is obviously trying to make it look like I poisoned your aunt. The same way he tried to make your aunt look like she murdered Oliver."

I knew he was right. "So you have no idea who might have taken one of your puffs?"

"No, I wish I did. . . ."

"Well, let me know if you remember anything. Right now I have to get to the hospital," I said. "And call the police."

I didn't have time to talk to Jake anymore. I was sure he'd hadn't try to poison me or my aunt—we'd been through too much together—but I was at a loss as to who might have done it.

I returned to the School Bus and pulled out my cell phone. Detective Shelton was unavailable, so I left an urgent message for him to contact me and explained that my aunt had been poisoned. Then I made sure all the food was put away so it didn't spoil, turned off a couple of appliances, and closed the blinds.

Suddenly I felt the bus sway. Someone had come aboard.

"Listen, Jake, I can't—"

It wasn't Jake. Instead, I was surprised to find Livvy standing in front of me.

"Need any help?" she asked. "I heard the news. So sorry about your aunt. Is there anything I can do? I'd be glad to help you clean up or drive you to the hospital."

The hospital. How was I supposed to get to the hospital without my car? I dropped down on the nearby stool and let the tears spill down my face. My dear, sweet aunt had been poisoned and was no doubt in the emergency room, having her stomach pumped. This couldn't be happening! The killer seemed to be trying to murder us all, one by one.

Livvy came over and put a hand on my back. "She'll be all right, I'm sure," she said gently. "I didn't know her well, but she seemed to be quite a character."

I sighed and wiped my eyes with a paper towel. "I just don't understand what's going on around here! Why is someone trying to kill these food truck chefs?"

"It's not just the food truck chefs," Livvy pointed out. "My brother was murdered too, you know."

"Of course," I said. "I'm sorry. I'm just not thinking right."

"It looks like you've got everything put away. Let me drive you to the hospital. You're in no condition to do anything but be there to support your aunt."

"That's really sweet of you, Livvy," I said, sliding off

the stool. "I'd like to get there as soon as possible. And my car is in the shop." I glanced around to make sure everything was put away, turned off, and cleaned up. As I picked up my purse, I noticed one of Aunt Abby's recipes clipped to a holder.

A thought came to me. "You remember those recipes you found hidden under your brother's desk?"

Livvy nodded and glanced around the bus.

"Did you ever find other recipes, recipes that might not have been Oliver's?" I was entering uncomfortable territory here. Jake had gone Dumpster diving to retrieve those stolen recipes and I didn't want to give away that he'd found them.

"Other recipes?" Livvy said. "What do you mean?"

"I mean recipes that might have belonged to some of the food truckers here."

Livvy stared at me. "I don't understand."

I took a deep breath, trying to fine-tune how I was going to phrase my next words. "Um, my aunt found one of her secret recipes in the trash—written in her handwriting. I just wondered if they turned up in your brother's office."

"Not that I know of," she answered. "The only ones I found were his."

Well, either someone else threw those recipes in the Dumpster that night—or she was lying. And why would she lie?

"Where did she find them exactly?" she asked.

I swallowed. "In the Bones 'n' Brew Dumpster.

Her eyes widened. "You think Oliver might have stolen them?"

I shrugged.

"But why?" she asked.

"Maybe to build up business again," I offered. "Maybe he thought having those recipes would bring in more customers."

"I really doubt my brother would steal recipes—or even buy them, for that matter," Livvy said, not meeting my eyes. She nervously glanced around the bus again. "I think you're really off base here, if that's what you're implying."

I suddenly realized I'd overstepped my boundaries, suggesting her murdered brother might have been a thief.

"I just thought, since the restaurant was losing business and Oliver was planning to sell it, maybe he—"

"Wait a minute!" Livvy said. "He wasn't planning to sell. I mean, sure, he talked about retiring from time to time, especially when he was feeling burned-out by the day-to-day business. But it was our family heritage. It meant too much to him."

Hmm, I thought. Maybe Livvy didn't know about Oliver's plans to sell the place after all.

"Did he ever do business with that meat delivery guy, Tripp Saunders?" I asked. Maybe Tripp and Cherry had done the dirty work for him—and he'd paid them for their services.

"Tripp Saunders? No, the name doesn't ring a bell. He drives a meat truck?"

"He drives the Meat Wagon. Delivers meat to various food trucks and restaurants. Kind of scruffy looking. Wears these fancy cowboy boots. I just wondered if Oliver knew him."

"I don't think so. We get all of our meats from Bar None Ranch."

I switched off the lights and picked up my purse. "Well, thanks for your help. I need to get over to the hospital and see how my aunt's doing."

"Let's go," Livvy said. She turned and headed for the bus steps.

"Wait a sec," I said. Realizing Dillon had probably not heard about his mother, I pulled out my cell phone and punched his number.

The theme song from the classic Pac-Man game filled the bus.

Livvy automatically reached in her pocket, then froze. She looked at me, her eyes wide.

I'd forgotten that Dillon's phone had been stolen by the person who'd attacked him and my aunt.

I felt my skin turn ice-cold.

What was Livvy Jameson doing with Dillon's cell phone?

Chapter 26

I stared at Livvy's pocket a little too long. In the moment it took me to recognize Dillon's ringtone and realize what that meant—that Livvy was the one who broke into Aunt Abby's house, bound and gagged her and Dillon, left the threatening message, and stole their phones—I knew it was too late to run.

She smiled.

She knew I knew.

And she seemed to take delight in that fact as she pulled out a long kitchen knife from a slim side pocket of her chef's whites.

She raised the knife, ready to lunge. No poison or frozen meat from Livvy. This time it was a sure thing.

With her body blocking the bus exit, I was trapped. There was nowhere to run or hide.

I did the only thing I could do—I screamed bloody murder.

Livvy reached over and switched on the blender that sat on the back countertop. The loud whirring covered my screams for help. Pulling a roll of duct tape out of another pocket, she yanked out a couple of inches and tore it off with her teeth.

It was the perfect size for gagging my scream. I had to

think fast. Stall for time. Get her talking. Distract her. It was all I had until I thought of something better to do.

Then she lunged at me.

I dodged her and backed up a foot or so in the small space, holding my hands and arms up defensively. Frantically, out of the corner of my eye, I searched for something to use as a weapon.

First I used my mouth. "You didn't come over here to help me clean up and take me to the hospital, did you, Livvy?" I yelled over the high-pitched noise. My plan: let her know I was slowly figuring things out, then make her feel smart for being such a clever killer.

"Boy, aren't you the brilliant detective," Livvy said. "You ought to go on one of those game shows. Bet you'd win a car or something, with deduction skills like that. Nothing gets by you, does it? Except maybe a murderer."

She was so enjoying this. I felt my forehead break out in beads of sweat. A trickle ran down my back.

"But why?" I asked, still scanning the area for something to use to defend myself, other than my words. "Why kill your own brother?"

"None of your business, Nancy Dweeb," Livvy snarled. "No one will ever know it was me. I'm too good at shifting the blame on everyone else *but* me. First your annoying aunt. Then her nerdy son. Then those small-time crooks, Tripp and Cherry. Next it will be sweet Jake's turn to be the killer. After all, it was his cream puff that poisoned your aunt. I just hope it did the job before she got her stomach pumped."

In an effort to stall her, I started bombarding her with questions. Maybe she wasn't as smart as she thought she was and I'd soon have some answers.

"The detective will figure it out eventually, Livvy. You made some mistakes."

"Like what?" she asked, suddenly taken aback at the challenge.

"First of all, you said you wanted to rejuvenate the restaurant, but your brother wanted to sell the place. That didn't compute."

"Yeah, that's right," she said, shrugging. "His old ways were killing our business. But he didn't like change. I told him I wanted to use the old recipes but just update them, you know, for today's customers. But he wouldn't let me touch those recipes. He had the chef memorize them, and then hid them."

I pushed ahead. "So you lied about what time you'd arrived at the restaurant the other night. You were the one who ransacked your brother's office, then made it sound like an intruder did it."

"Yeah, and you almost caught me," she said, "but it was worth it. I finally found Ollie's recipes, so those, plus the ones I got from the food trucks, were all I needed to keep the restaurant going—and give it new life."

"But why did you need his recipes? You're a chef. You must have them memorized too."

She grinned. "Actually, I barely know how to make toast. I manage the kitchen, wear the outfit. That's all."

Whoa. She had me fooled all along.

"So you *stole* recipes from the food trucks and planned to have the chef use them?" I said.

"Actually, Cherry stole them for me."

I blinked, surprised. "Why would she do that?"

"Let's just say that Cherry and Tripp sort of worked

for me. When I found out about their little fake-ID business, I asked them to help me out with a few things."

"You mean you blackmailed them, don't you?" I said.

"Whatever. Doesn't really matter now. The restaurant is mine, and I'm keeping it. I fired the old chef. I'm hiring a new one to update Ollie's old recipes, along with using some of the food-truck recipes. I'm giving the place a whole new look and taste."

"Did Tripp and Cherry help you with the murders too?" I asked.

She laughed. "Those two clowns? Give me a break."

"So you poisoned the crab bisque and fed it to your brother."

She nodded. "It wasn't hard making it look like your crazy aunt seasoned it with rat poison. And after that argument they'd had, it was perfect timing."

"Buy why did you kill Boris? He had nothing to do with your restaurant."

"That buffoon. He found out Tripp and Cherry were helping me score the food truck recipes. Meanwhile, Tripp was blackmailing Boris about his drug-dealing history. If it got out that he was dealing again—and Tripp could make it look like he was by planting fake evidence—then Boris could lose his business. Tripp needed Boris as the go-between for Tripp's fake ID business."

"But Boris wanted out, didn't he?" I suggested, remembering what Boris had said the night I'd overheard him. "And you were worried he might expose your relationship with Tripp and Cherry. So you went to Boris's truck, threw ground pepper in his face, and bludgeoned him with that big hunk of frozen meat."

A wave of nausea passed over me as I thought of Aunt Abby. Was Livvy right? Had Aunt Abby taken a lethal dose of poison with that cream puff?

"You've gone through an awful lot of trouble, Livvy, killing your brother, then Boris, and trying to make it look like someone else. Was it really worth it?"

"Shut up, you nosy pig!" she shouted over the blender noise.

With the duct tape still in one hand, she lunged the knife at me with the other. One way or another, she was determined to shut me up. In the small space between the back storage cupboards, the counter on one side and the refrigerator and sink on the other, I didn't have much room to maneuver. I took my only option—I dropped to the floor, got on my back, and started kicking. If only I could reach a frying pan or—

I felt the tip of the knife slice my left calf. I cried out in pain and grabbed my bleeding leg, curling up in a ball.

Livvy raised her hand again, ready to bring the knife down on me one final time.

I reached out and pulled open a drawer underneath the work counter. Swinging it with both hands, I knocked her legs out from under her. She fell to the floor. I tried to get up so I could escape, but she still blocked my exit.

I started grabbing everything I could get my hands on to pummel her. I threw an eggbeater down on her, followed by a toaster, a blender, a can opener, and finally a coffeemaker. She looked as if she'd been in an appliance shop during an earthquake.

I started to step over her when she grabbed my ankle.

I fell back to the floor, barely missing the corner of the counter, landing on my side and getting the wind knocked out of me. With my face pressed to the floor, all I could do was gasp for breath.

Then I saw something hidden under the stove. Something I'd forgotten about. Just as I reached underneath for it, Livvy took another swipe at me, tearing my shirt and narrowly missing my side.

I looked up and saw Livvy reared up on her knees, holding the knife.

She'd tried to stab me again!

She raised the knife once more. Adrenaline kicked in. I pulled out the small box I held in my hand, tore off the lid, and threw the grainy contents in her angry face. A cloud of fine powder circled her head a few seconds before she started coughing violently.

Rat poison.

With Livvy racked by coughs, I rose and grabbed a nearby apron to cover my mouth and nose so I wouldn't inhale the poison. Then I sat down on Livvy's back, hard, flattening her like a human pancake.

Holding my breath, I grabbed one of Livvy's hands and yanked it behind her back, then wrapped the apron string around it, grabbed the other one, and tied them together with the apron strings, trussing her up like a turkey on Thanksgiving. Ripping the duct tape off her wrist where it had stuck, I secured the strings with the tape.

Seconds later I burst through the door of the School Bus, let out my breath, and began yelling and screaming as I hobbled toward Jake's truck.

"Jake! Help! Come quick!"

Jake spotted me from the service window and called out, "Darcy?"

"Hurry! She's in Aunt Abby's bus! Call nine-one-one!" I repeated myself several times before I saw him finally bound out of the truck, his cell phone in his hand.

"Your leg is bleeding! What happened?" he said, following me as I stumbled back to the bus.

I pressed on my calf to keep the pain at bay. The adrenaline was starting to wane. In spite of the wound, I wanted to make sure Livvy didn't get away.

"Darcy, you need a doctor!" Jake said as we reached the bus.

"I'm okay," I said. "It's just a superficial cut. Hurry. Make sure she's still tied up!"

"Who?" Jake asked.

"Livvy! She did it! She killed them both! And she poisoned Aunt Abby! I have to make sure she's not going to get away!"

I knew I wasn't making complete sense, but there would be time for that after the police came and took Livvy into custody. What mattered now was making sure she was still tied up in the bus. I started up the stairs.

A forceful shove knocked me back down to the ground. Livvy, her face still white with powdery residue, her hands still bound behind her back, jumped down the steps.

And right into Jake's massive arms.

"Hold on!" he yelled as he caught her and gripped her tightly. He spun her around and grabbed her by her bound wrists.

"Let go of me!" Livvy screamed as she squirmed. She tried kicking Jake, but he held her in a death grip, giving her little room to move. By now a few of the chefs had stepped out of their trucks to see what all the commotion was about.

"Someone call the police!" I shouted.

"Anyone got any duct tape?" Jake called out to the crowd while he held Livvy firmly.

There was the roll Livvy had pulled out inside the bus, but before I could say anything, Willow called out, "I do!" She ran back to her coffee truck and returned moments later with a roll of silver tape. "This stuff is great! It fixes everything!"

Sierra and Vandy stepped forward. "Vandy, wrap her legs while I hold them," Sierra said. She took the tape from Willow's hand and gave it to her partner. Those years of working out and buffing up paid off as Sierra forcefully grabbed and held Livvy's legs in a bear hug, giving Vandy the chance to wrap her up.

Moments later Livvy resembled a silver mummy, wrapped up in shiny tape from her ankles to her legs to her arms and torso. Before she toppled over, Jake laid her on the ground. When she wouldn't stop screaming, mostly obscenitics, Sierra tore off a piece of tape and slapped it on Livvy's mouth. The onlookers cheered.

I grinned. *What goes around, comes around,* I thought, remembering the moment I found my aunt had been similarly silenced by duct tape.

"Did anyone call nine-one-one?" Jake asked, glancing around.

"I did," said a tourist wearing sunglasses, a straw hat, a Hawaiian shirt, cargo shorts, and a camera around his neck. "They're on their way."

I shook my head.

Dillon.

Chapter 27

Dillon split moments after I told him about his mom. I assumed he was headed for the hospital—and avoiding the cops. Good thing. The police arrived five minutes later. While Jake talked to Detective Shelton, Willow cleaned my leg wound with water and antiseptic and covered it with coffee filters, which she said were better than gauze. How she knew this was a mystery to me. She taped the filters on my body with good old duct tape.

After she fixed me up and told me I was going to live, I explained to the curious food truckers and straggling onlookers what had happened inside the School Bus—that Livvy had attacked me with a knife, that I'd fought back by throwing everything but the kitchen sink at her—including rat poison—and that she'd admitted to killing her own brother as well as Boris.

Jake drove me to the hospital and waited in the cafeteria while the doctor treated my leg wound. It was just superficial, and I was out of the ER in thirty minutes. I joined Jake in the cafeteria and we spent the next forty minutes drinking bad coffee that tasted like hospital antiseptic while we waited to see Aunt Abby when she got out of recovery.

While Jake got us some water, I glanced at my cell

phone, willing it to ring. The nurse had promised to call, and I was dying to hear how my aunt was doing. More than that, I wanted to see for myself that she was all right.

"So how did you figure it was Livvy?" Jake asked.

I took a sip of water. "It was Dillon's ringtone that clued me in when Livvy was in the bus. I called his number and it rang in her pocket. That's when I realized she was the one who had attacked Aunt Abby and Dillon and took their cell phones to call me."

Jake reached out and patted my hand. The warmth of his touch gave me a tingle that distracted me from the pain in my side.

"So," I said, trying to wrap up the details swimming around in my head. "Livvy attacked my aunt and cousin to scare me off, then stole their phones and called me with Aunt Abby's phone, pretending to be my aunt so I'd go to her house and discover that she'd been attacked."

"Pretty much. She probably did it to get you out of the restaurant before you discovered any evidence, and meant it as a warning."

"Did the police say anything about her motive?"

"Yeah, Shelton said she confirmed what she told you—that she killed her brother because he wanted to sell the restaurant and she wanted to keep it."

"Greed?"

"More like control, I think," Jake said. "Maybe recognition. You said she said she did most of the work, yet their father gave the majority of the business to Oliver. She probably always felt she deserved it. Turns out she isn't a chef, only the kitchen manager. But she'd planned to hire a new chef and needed those original recipes, plus the food truck recipes, to update the menu. I guess she'd made photocopies of the stolen recipes, then tossed out the originals into the Dumpster to cover her tracks. Only, I'd happened to see her with the bags of trash."

"But why did she pick on us—first my aunt Abby, then Dillon, then me?"

Jake shrugged. "Maybe you wrote a bad review of the restaurant in the past, and she never forgot it."

"Very funny," I said. But Jake was right. I *had* written a poor review after hearing from several people that the place wasn't good anymore. I'd wanted to see for myself, and it was true. The place had gone downhill.

"Well, I'm glad Willow or the vegans weren't the murderers. If they can't kill animals, surely they can't kill human beings. And just because Vandy ate a hamburger doesn't mean she's a murderer. But I kept them on my list because they didn't get along with Boris."

"Like you kept me on your list," Jake said, looking at me with those dark eyes.

I smiled weakly. "Sorry about that, but I never really suspected you."

Jake shook his head. I wondered if he'd ever forgive me.

My cell phone ring broke the awkward silence. I picked it up and said, "I'll be right there!" After I hung up, I said to Jake, "Aunt Abby is out of ICU. I need to see her. You want to come?"

"Sure," Jake said, rising from the table.

We tossed our drink containers into the recycle bin and headed for the elevator. Getting off on the third floor, we made our way through the labyrinth of hallways to Aunt Abby's room, where she was still recovering from having her stomach pumped. She was sound asleep when we entered. To my surprise, Dillon was sitting in a chair by her bed. He was working on his laptop—not a surprise.

"Dillon!" I said, actually glad to see him. I was even more delighted to see him dressed in his own clothes and not like a tourist, in spite of the fact that his faded jeans were holey and his threadbare shirt sported a picture of Sheldon Cooper from *The Big Bang Theory*.

"What? No nurse costume?" Jake teased.

"Very funny," Dillon said.

I shushed both of them. "She's sleeping!" I turned to Dillon and whispered, "Seriously, what are you doing here without a disguise? Aren't you worried about being arrested?"

Dillon looked at Jake.

"They dropped the charges," Jake answered for him.

"What?" I said.

Dillon nodded. "Jake talked to the detective. Told him I'd practically solved the case with my computer. Shelton let me off, since obviously I didn't kill anyone."

"What about the feds?" I asked. "All that computer hacking?"

He shrugged. "I still have to deal with them. But I think I'm pretty safe here. For now."

I sighed. "Well, at least Aunt Abby is okay." I looked down at her and gently held the hand without the IV. "Has she been asleep the whole time?"

"Pretty much," Dillon said. "She opened her eyes and smiled when she saw me, then faded. Doc said she'll be fine. But I think she's off cream puffs for a while." Dillon actually cracked a smile at his own attempt at humor. I hadn't known he had it in him to make a joke.

"Well, let's let her sleep. I'll come by later and see her. I've got a crime scene cleaner coming to clear out the poison I threw all over the inside of the bus, so I wouldn't recommend you crash there tonight, Dillon."

"I'll be fine here for now," he said. "I'll go home later, maybe."

I bent down and gave my cousin an awkward hug; then Jake and I stepped out of the room.

We ran into Detective Shelton just outside the door.

"What are you doing here?" I asked him, surprised at the visit.

"Just wanted to see how your aunt was doing," the detective said, his hands clasping a bouquet of flowers. "She's been through a lot."

"That's so sweet of you," I said, grinning. "But she's asleep right now."

He nodded. "I'll just leave these and let her sleep," he said. Was that a blush beneath his mocha complexion?

I moved aside to allow him in. He took a few awkward steps and entered the room.

Hesitating, I heard a flirty but raspy voice say, "Why, hello, Detective Shelton. . . ."

I turned to Jake. "That little faker!" I started to go back in, but Jake caught my arm and stopped me.

"Come on. Let's give them some privacy."

"But Dillon's in there!" I argued.

Seconds later, Dillon appeared in the hall, a sheepish grin on his face. "Guess I'll head home after all," he said. "Mom seems to be in good hands at the moment."

I smiled at Dillon and took his arm.

"How about we head home together?" I suggested as we walked to the elevators.

"You two want to come over to my place for some cream puffs?" Jake offered. "I've got a loft in the marina with a great view of the bay."

I shook my head. "Sounds lovely, but I'm exhausted. I have to go home and feed Basil. And explain to my ex-boss why I never got that review of the festival or that article on the contest written for the newspaper. And start writing my cookbook. Besides," I added, patting my stomach, "I really need to lay off the puffs for a while."

"I hear you," Jake said, smiling, although he looked a little disappointed. "Need a ride?"

"I've got mom's car," Dillon said.

Jake nodded and walked us to Aunt Abby's car in the hospital parking lot in silence. But as soon as Dillon was behind the wheel, Jake pulled me close.

"Rain check," he whispered, gazing into my eyes.

And then he kissed me.

Food Truck Recipes

Aunt Abby's Crab Potpies

½ cup plus 2 tablespoons butter
3 cups chopped onion
1 cup chopped celery
1 cup chopped carrots
1 cup frozen peas
¼ cup flour
2 cups peeled and diced potatoes
2 cups clam juice
2 teaspoons lemon zest
1½ teaspoons seafood seasoning
½ teaspoon salt
1 pound crabmeat
1 (14-ounce) package refrigerated piecrusts
1 egg, beaten
1 tablespoon water
tartar sauce (secret ingredient)

Preheat the oven to 375°F.

Melt 2 tablespoons of the butter in large pan over medium heat.

Add the onion, celery, carrots, and peas, and cook for 5 minutes.

Stir in the flour and cook for 1 minute.

Add the potatoes, clam juice, lemon zest, seafood seasoning, and salt; bring to boil.

Cover, reduce the heat to low, and simmer for 15 minutes, until the potatoes are tender.

Remove from the heat.

Melt the remaining ½ cup butter in a frying pan over low heat; cook and stir for 3 minutes until golden brown.

Combine the butter and crabmeat, add to the vegetable mixture, and stir.

Unroll the piecrusts, place 6 ramekins on the crusts and cut out circles of piecrust the same diameter as the ramekins to cover the pies.

Spoon the crab mixture into the ramekins.

Whisk the egg with the water and brush the cutout piecrusts with the egg wash.

Place a crust circle, egg wash side down, over each ramekin of crab mixture and seal the edges of the crust to the edges of the ramekin.

Pierce the crusts a few times with a knife or fork to create vent holes.

Place the ramekins on a foil-lined baking sheet.

Bake for 25 to 30 minutes, until golden brown.

Top with tartar sauce.

SERVES 6

Jake's Tiramisu Dream Puffs

½ cup water
4 tablespoons butter
pinch of sugar
pinch of salt
½ cup flour
2 eggs, beaten
1 teaspoon instant coffee
⅓ cup heavy cream
2 tablespoons powdered sugar
3 tablespoons mascarpone cheese, at room temperature
⅛ teaspoon vanilla extract
1 teaspoon grated semisweet chocolate
powdered sugar or chocolate syrup

Preheat the oven to 350°F.

Combine the water, butter, sugar, and salt in medium pan and bring to a boil.

Remove from the heat and add the flour.

Place back on medium heat and stir well with wooden spoon for 30 seconds.

Remove from the heat and pour into a heatproof bowl; stir for 1 minute.

Combine the eggs with the flour mixture in four additions, stirring constantly until the batter is smooth.

Add the instant coffee and stir until well mixed.

Line a baking sheet with parchment paper.

Scoop the mixture into balls and place on the prepared baking sheet, leaving 2 inches between puffs.

Bake for 30 minutes, until golden brown, light, and crisp; cool on a rack.

Beat the cream and powdered sugar until firm peaks form.

Add the mascarpone cheese, vanilla, and chocolate to the whipped cream and fold in gently.

Cut off the top half of each puff, fill the base with 1 teaspoon of the cream mixture (or more, as needed), and replace the top.

Sprinkle with powdered sugar or drizzle with chocolate syrup.

MAKES 8 TO 12, DEPENDING ON THE SIZE OF THE PUFF

Willow the Coffee Witch's Cara-Magical-Cino

2 shots espresso
3 tablespoons sugar
1 cup low-fat milk
2 cups ice
3 tablespoons chocolate syrup
3 tablespoons caramel sauce
pinch of cinnamon
whipped cream

Combine the espresso, sugar, milk, ice, chocolate sauce, caramel sauce, and cinnamon in a blender.

Blend on high until the ice is crushed and the drink is smooth, 30 to 45 seconds.

Pour into two glasses and top with whipped cream.

Drizzle extra caramel and chocolate over the whipped cream, if desired, and serve with straws.

SERVES 2.

Turn the page for a sneak peek
at the next Food Festival Mystery,

Death of a Chocolate Cheater

Coming from Obsidian in summer 2015.

"Darcy, did you know chocolate is a valuable energy source?" my aunt Abby asked as she handed me one of her "homemade" lattes. By homemade, I mean she'd used her instant one-cup machine, pressed a button, and voilà. "I just read that one chocolate chip can give you enough energy to walk a hundred and fifty feet."

"Great." I took a sip of the freshly made hot drink and washed down a bite of a day-old brownie I'd found in the refrigerator. "I'm gonna need about seven billion of them to get going this morning."

Aunt Abby settled onto the empty barstool at her kitchen counter with her special "Lunch Lady" mug and continued reading from the San Francisco Chocolate Festival brochure. It was a good thing I'd found the brownie, or I would have run out and bought a bag of chocolate chips. Just the word "chocolate" made my mouth water.

"And it says here that chocolate has great health benefits," Aunt Abby said as she continued reading. "It helps alleviate depression, lower your blood pressure, reduce tumors, relieve PMS. . . ." She glanced at me.

I eyed her. "Are you hinting that I've been crabby the past few days?"

She raised a perfectly drawn brow at me. "I'm just saying chocolate supposedly increases serotonin and endorphin levels, in case they happen to be low."

I knew she was referring to my recent dark mood. Ever since I had been let go from the *San Francisco Chronicle* three months before, I'd been helping my sixtysomething aunt serve comfort food from her Big Yellow School Bus food truck. Her "busterant," as she called it, was parked at Fort Mason, not far from her Russian Hill home. I was working there to make ends meet now that I wasn't collecting income from my reporter's job—and it was likely to stay that way until I sold my future bestselling cookbook featuring recipes from food trucks, the culinary phenomenon that had recently swept the country. Then I would move out of my aunt's RV, which was parked in her side yard . . . if I ever planned to get on with my life-after-Trevor, my cheating ex-boyfriend.

Unfortunately, life wasn't progressing the way I'd hoped. I was beginning to think I'd be serving Principal's Pot Pies and Custodian's Crab Mac 'n' Cheese for the rest of my days. The only respite from the daily food truck workout was my budding relationship with Jake Miller, the dreamboat from the Dream Puff Truck. The only trouble was, I'd been sampling so many of his creamy concoctions that the result was beginning to show around my waist.

Until recently, that was. I hadn't had a cream puff in a couple of weeks. Jake had been acting oddly, and I hadn't seen him much lately.

I yawned, trying to wake up, and took another sip of the latte. "Are you sure this isn't decaf?"

Aunt Abby shook her head, her face buried in the brochure. Her Clairol-colored fire-engine red curls swung back and forth. "Chocolate contains caffeine, you know. Maybe you should pour some chocolate syrup in that cup."

"I'd have to add the whole jar to get the same amount of caffeine that's in a cup of coffee. Maybe I'll just have another brownie."

"True," Aunt Abby said. "There are even more benefits to chocolate. Did you know it contains iron, helps prevent tooth decay, and has antioxidants that help minimize aging?" She patted her porcelain skin. The only giveaways to her age were the tiny laugh lines around her eyes. I wondered how much chocolate she'd consumed over the years.

"Stop!" I finally said, holding up a hand. "I've gained five pounds from eating all of Jake's chocolate cream puff samples, especially those Mocha Madness ones. No more talk about chocolate! Just hearing about it is making me fat." I put down the brownie and sipped my coffee.

"Well, you'd better get used to it," Aunt Abby said, "because I have a surprise."

"Oh?" I asked warily, peering over my coffee mug. It was too early in the morning for one of Aunt Abby's surprises.

"I just signed us up for the Chocolate Festival Competition!"

I set my mug down with a clink. Coffee sloshed inside it like a mini tsunami. "But your specialty is comfort foods, not chocolate."

Aunt Abby frowned at me. "*Hmph*. Are you forgetting

my Chocolate-Covered Potato Chips? My Chocolate–Peanut Butter Sandwiches? My Chocolate Pasta? My Chocolate Pizza? I've seen you sneak plenty of those chocolate leftovers at the end of the day." She eyed the half-eaten brownie.

She was right. Aside from her usual fare of American comfort foods with school-themed names such as Cheerleader's Chili, Coach's Cole Slaw, and Bus Driver's BLTs, my aunt Abby had put her own chocolate twist on classic cuisine. Her chocolate-dipped, raspberry-iced Twinkies were to die for.

I loved just about everything on my aunt's School Bus menu, but I wondered whether her chocolate offerings were good enough for the prestigious San Francisco Chocolate Festival. The annual event featured renowned chefs from around the world competing for some hefty prizes. It seemed out of my aunt's league.

"Don't you think my chocolate goodies are worthy of awards?" Aunt Abby asked.

I cleared my throat and backtracked, worried I'd hurt her feelings. "Oh, sure they are . . . but it's a tough competition. Remember last year's winner, George Brown? He owned his own gourmet chocolate shop and took home the grand prize with his chocolate-covered bacon. Which, by the way, wasn't bad."

"Yes, I remember. This year he's one of the judges. But nothing beats the creation I've come up with this year." She smiled mysteriously. "Not even chocolate bacon."

"Really? You've got something new planned? What is it?"

"Top secret. If I tell you, I'll have to—"

"I know, I know—kill me. Just give me a hint, then. Chocolate-covered snickerdoodles? Chocolate-dipped Danish? Chocolate-frosted cinnamon buns?"

She harrumphed. "Very funny. Now you'll just have to wait and see."

I shrugged in response to her secretiveness. "It's going to be a lot of extra work, you know. Are you up to it, in addition to running your busterant?"

For that matter, was I, as one of the A-team assistants? I didn't have time for a lot of extra work. I had a book to write, a career to develop, a life to begin.

"What extra work?" came a low voice from behind me.

Dillon, Aunt Abby's twenty-five-year-old son, sauntered barefoot into the kitchen. Tall and slim like his deceased father, he wore a thin, shaggy robe over his bare chest and Superman boxer shorts. His curly brown hair looked as if it hadn't seen scissors, gel, or even shampoo in days, nor had his face seen a razor.

He went directly to the pantry, opened the door, and stared at the loaded shelves. "Mom, you're out of cereal."

"Yes, dear," Aunt Abby said to her boomerang son. Dillon had been "asked" to leave his university because of some suspected hacking activity and had moved home to "reconfigure" his life goals. In other words, to sponge off his mom and play computer games.

"Got any more of those chocolate whoopie pies you made last night?"

"Dillon! Those were supposed to be top secret." Aunt Abby shot a look at me. "Well, Darcy, now you know my secret weapon for the chocolate competition—my newest creation: Killer Chocolate Whoopie Pies. But both of you need to keep quiet about this. I don't want anyone to find out and steal my idea before the contest begins."

"Killer Chocolate Whoopie Pies?" I asked, stunned at her entry choice. I wasn't even sure what a whoopie pie was.

"It's my own recipe," Aunt Abby said, as if she'd read my mind. "Instead of using cakey chocolate cookies, I use brownie cookies. And instead of vanilla filling, I use chocolate buttercream frosting. And then I dip the whole thing in melted chocolate and add sprinkles."

It sounded like overkill, but when it came to chocolate, maybe there was no such thing.

"So where are they?" Dillon said, opening the refrigerator door.

"I hid them in the crisper section," Aunt Abby said. Dillon opened the refrigerator drawer, hauled out a plastic container, and set it on the counter. After withdrawing an Oreo-sized "pie," he popped it in his mouth.

"Want to try one, Darcy?" Aunt Abby asked. She picked up the container and brought it over to the kitchen island where I sat. Dillon followed her like a hungry puppy and plopped down on the barstool next to me, licking the chocolate off his lips.

I reached in and took one of the chocolaty spheres. Taking a tentative bite, I let the sweet morsel dissolve in my mouth. The flavor flooded my tongue.

Wow. Chocolate heaven.

"This is incredible!" I said when I could talk again.

"Awesome," Dillon agreed, then popped another one into his mouth. He smiled, revealing chocolaty teeth.

"You may actually have a shot at winning this thing," I said. "What's the prize?"

"Den fouszen dollars," Dillon said with his mouth full.

"Ten thousand dollars?" I repeated. I was used to Dillon's food-obstructed speech.

"And a chance to appear on that Food Network show *Chocolate Wars*," Aunt Abby added, batting her mascaraed eyelashes in excitement.

"Wow," I said again. "That's a lot of money." I knew Aunt Abby's dream was to appear on one of the many cooking shows on TV, but the money would certainly come in handy as well. "When's the festival?"

"In two weeks," Aunt Abby said.

I gulped. "Well, we'd better get to work!"

Half an hour later, I was on my way to Fort Mason to help Aunt Abby in her Big Yellow School Bus and begin the day of serving comfort food to hungry patrons. I hoped to see Jake, since he'd seemed too busy the past few days to stop by or meet after work. I wanted to tell him about Aunt Abby entering the Chocolate Festival competition.

As I drove down Bay Street to the marina, I thought about the annual festival and competition. Although I'd covered the event for the newspaper, this would be the first time I'd get to see it from a contestant's point of view. The festival was held near Ghirardelli Square, home to one of the original chocolatiers of San Francisco. Last year, fifty thousand people had paid the entry fee to taste the mouthwatering wares of two dozen entrants. I'd learned from Aunt Abby that any legitimate vendor could participate, as long as he or she offered something chocolaty—and could make enough for fifty thousand people! Each entry in the competition would be judged by a select panel of experts in the chocolate industry. And while the thought of tasting all that chocolate had my heart beating faster, it was the winner's ten-thousand-dollar check that really excited me. Aunt Abby had promised Dillon and me each a third if we won.

I pulled up to the permit-only parking lot at Fort Mason in my VW Bug and headed for the circle of food trucks parked in an adjacent lot. The area was home to a dozen permanent vendors, including my aunt, but other trucks came and went, depending on how popular they were. There was always a long list of new trucks vying for the few nonpermanent spots. My aunt had been fortunate—her comfort food menu was a hit with people who longed for "mom's home cooking."

I spotted Jake outside his Dream Puff Truck, and I swung by to say good morning, tell him about Aunt Abby, and see whether I could snag one of his Dream Puffs of the Day. The hand-printed blackboard sign read TODAY'S SPECIAL: CHOCOLATE RASPBERRY MOCHA MOUSSE.

OMG. It was all I could do to keep from drooling down the front of my "Big Yellow School Bus" T-shirt.

He was filling bowls with toppings for his dreamy delights.

"Do you have anything with no calories?" I asked, coming up behind him.

He whirled around and gave me that adorable, toothy grin. "Darcy!"

"Morning, Jake," I said, unable to stifle my own smile.

"It's been awhile," he said, looking me over. "You look . . . really nice."

I ran my fingers self-consciously through my shoulder-length auburn hair. "You've been busy," I said.

I'd told myself that Jake had been too busy with his food truck to do much socializing, but in truth, I was beginning to wonder if his interest in me was starting to wane.

"Yeah, sorry about that, Darcy. Things have been unusually hectic," he said as he arranged the condiments on the outside shelf. He looked incredible in his white "Dream Puff" T-shirt and faded jeans.

"Oh, I know how it is. Me too. You know—lots of stuff going on. . . ."

Yeah, right.

"Actually, I've been dealing with something the past couple of weeks," he said, brushing his sun-lightened brown hair off his forehead, "but, hey, if you're free later tonight, how about we get a drink and catch up?"

"Sounds great," I said. "I've got some news to share."

"Really? What's up?"

"I'll tell you tonight," I said mysteriously. I just hoped Aunt Abby hadn't already blabbed her news about entering the Chocolate Festival competition. She had a habit of sharing everything—including details of my personal life—with anyone who would listen.

"I'll look forward to it," Jake said. He reached in through the open truck window and pulled out a two-bite cream puff nestled in a paper doily. The delicate puff was filled with a pinkish mocha-colored cream, drizzled with dark chocolate, and topped with a red raspberry. "Want to try my latest?"

I smacked my lips. "Love to! Is it today's special?"

He nodded. "Let me know what you think."

I took a bite. The creamy mixture spread over my tongue and melted away in seconds, leaving me the crunchy shell to savor.

Jake reached over and with his fingertip wiped away the raspberry mocha mustache I apparently wore. Then he licked the tip of his finger.

Whoa. I suddenly felt dizzy. I didn't know which had my heart racing so fast—Jake's dreamy cream puff or the mustache removal I'd just experienced.

I held up the remainder of the cream puff. "This is to die for," I managed to say.

"You like it?"

"You've outdone yourself."

"Great," he said, grinning again. "Because I just signed up for the Chocolate Festival competition, and that's what I'm entering."

I felt my smile droop. Oh no! Jake was entering the competition? With that killer cream puff? Suddenly my news about Aunt Abby's entry didn't sound so exciting.

"Are you okay?" Jake said, obviously noticing my reaction to his announcement.

"Oh, yes . . . of course!" I said, mustering up some enthusiasm. "That's . . . great! I'm sure you'll do well. . . ."

"Hope so. I don't care about being on the TV program, but I can always use the money."

"No—yes—sure! It's definitely a winner." I pointed to Aunt Abby's bus. "Uh, I . . . gotta go. I'm going to be late. You know what a tyrant my aunt can be. See you tonight?"

He smiled.

I turned and hustled on toward my aunt's school bus before I blurted the news. It wasn't that I didn't want

Jake to win. I just wanted us to win more. Now how was I going to tell him about Aunt Abby?

As I reached the bus, something else Jake had said bothered me. It wasn't the contest or the fact that we hadn't seen each other much lately. He'd mentioned the reason he'd been busy was that he'd been dealing with something.

Something important enough to keep him from spending time with me?

Or some*one*?

Before I started plotting his imaginary girlfriend's demise, I stepped into the bus, wondering how I would break the news to Aunt Abby about Jake's entry into the competition. Not only would she be competing against some of the best chocolate chefs in the world, but now she'd be going up against her friend Jake Miller.

But instead of busily preparing today's menu selection, my aunt was on her cell phone. She was blinking rapidly and had her hand on her chest as if she might be having a heart attack.

"Aunt Abby!" I rushed over to give her some support. "Are you all right? You look like you're about to collapse."

Lowering the hand that held her phone, Aunt Abby did collapse—onto a nearby stool. She set down the phone and stared blankly at it.

"What is it, Aunt Abby? Are you ill? Do you want me to call a doctor?"

She shook her head. "I'm fine," she said breathlessly.

"Did something happen?"

Still staring at the phone, she said, "That was Reina Patel. . . ."

I shrugged, not recognizing the name.

"She's the Chocolate Festival coordinator. The one who decides who's eligible to compete, the one who selects the judges, the one who's in charge of the whole event."

"Did something happen? Are you disqualified from competing for some reason? Because if she says you can't participate, well, I'll just go down there and—"

"No, no," Aunt Abby said, cutting me off. "I'm still in the competition—"

"Good," I said, cutting *her* off, "because I've got some news—"

She held up her hand to stop me. "Reina called to tell me they've had a little glitch in the competition. That's what she called it—a little *glitch*."

"What kind of glitch?"

Aunt Abby sighed. Her shoulders sank. "Apparently they're looking for a new judge to replace George Brown."

"Why? Did he quit?" I asked, still anxious about telling her that Jake had joined the competition.

"No," she said. "George Brown is dead."